J. A. JANCE

TAKING THE FIFTH

A J. P. BEAUMONT NOVEL

wm

WILLIAM MORROW

An Imprint of HarperCollinsPublishers

Excerpt from *Sins of the Fathers* copyright © 2019 by J. A. Jance

TAKING THE FIFTH. Copyright © 1987 by J. A. Jance. All rights reserved. Printed in the United States of America. No part of this book may be used or reproduced in any manner whatsoever without written permission except in the case of brief quotations embodied in critical articles and reviews. For information, address HarperCollins Publishers, 195 Broadway, New York, NY 10007.

First William Morrow premium printing: October 2004
First Harper premium printing: January 2010
First Avon Books mass market printing: June 1987

Print Edition ISBN: 978-0-06-195854-0
Digital Edition ISBN: 978-0-06-176089-1

Cover design by Amy Halperin
Cover photograph © 400tmax/iStock/Getty Images

William Morrow and HarperCollins are registered trademarks of HarperCollins Publishers in the United States of America and other countries.

22 23 BVGM 10 9 8

for D.A.L.
If all the world's a stage,
then God must be the head carpenter.

TAKING THE FIFTH

CHAPTER 1

THE AID CAR WAS THERE, SITTING NEXT TO THE RAIL-road track with its red light flashing. But for the guy on the ground, the guy lying on his stomach with his face in the cinders and dirt beside the iron rails, it was far too late for an aid car. He didn't need a medic.

What he needed was a medical examiner. And a homicide detective.

That's where I came in, Homicide Detective J. P. Beaumont, of Seattle P.D. I was there along with my pinch-hitting partner, Detective Allen (Big Al) Lindstrom. After working until midnight on our regular shift, we had been called back when the body was found. Now we were standing by, waiting for Dr. Howard Baker, King County's medical examiner, to arrive on the scene.

Doc Baker isn't a morning person, and this was very early morning. It was ten to five on a cool summer day, just after the longest day of the year.

Although the horizon was hidden from view by the Alaskan Way Viaduct directly above us, a predawn glow was breaking up the darkness around us, and the waterfront odor, heavy with wet creosote, filled my nostrils.

We waited in a small, hushed group until Doc Baker's dark sedan came tearing through the parking lot and jerked to a stop less than two feet from where we stood. Nobody bothered to move out of the way.

"All right, all right," Baker grumbled, easing his more-than-ample frame out of the car and taking charge. "What have we got?"

"I'm betting on a drunk," Big Al told him. "Some wino from up by the market who got himself clobbered by a passing freight train."

Al was referring to the Pike Place Market, which sat on the bluff directly behind us, a hundred or so steep stair steps above our heads.

The market is a popular Seattle tourist attraction during the day. At night, parts of it still maintain an upscale, touristy atmosphere. But there are other parts of it, dark underbelly parts, that do a Jekyll-and-Hyde routine as soon as the sun goes down. For instance, almost every night the blackberry-bordered parking lot beneath the market itself becomes a savage no-man's-land, a brutal setting for beatings, rapes, and muggings that is all too familiar to officers assigned to the David sector of Seattle P.D.

Doc Baker glowered at Al for a moment. The medical examiner's shock of white hair was uncombed and standing belligerently on end. "We'll see about that," he said, grunting, and rumbled away, dragging a train of technicians as well as a nervous young police photographer in his wake.

A squad car stopped nearby. Two uniformed officers got out and walked over to us. "Any luck finding out who reported it?" I asked.

They shook their heads in unison. "Not so far," one answered. "The call came in to 911 from a pay phone down by the ferry terminal about three-fifteen. Near as I can tell, that's the closest public phone at that hour of the night. The caller was a woman, but she didn't leave a name."

I nodded. "That figures."

Turning away, I looked back toward Doc Baker and his group of assistants. They were gathered in a small, closely-knit clump around the body, which was sprawled within inches of the track itself. To one side yawned the entrance to the Burlington Northern Tunnel, a railroad tunnel that cuts through a rocky bluff and then burrows south and east under downtown Seattle, from Alaskan Way and Virginia to the King Street Station a mile away.

I felt the rumble of a train long before its warning whistle sounded or its bright headlight flashed from deep inside the tunnel. Doc Baker and his cohorts scurried out of the way.

The freight train emerged from the black tunnel like a slow-moving demon escaping the jaws of hell, with a heavy, evil-smelling cloud of smoke, laden with diesel fuel, boiling around it. Minutes after the caboose had disappeared from sight, the dense smoke still eddied around us like a thick, gritty fog.

As the haze began to clear, Doc Baker charged back toward the body. The photographer, a young woman in her mid- to late-twenties, seemed to hang back, but Baker ordered her forward with an imperious wave of his hand.

Al Lindstrom favored the photographer with a bemused grin. "She's a looker, all right," he commented, "but I bet this is the first time she's taken pictures of a real body. Understand she's a journalism major who just graduated from Evergreen."

Evergreen College is an exceedingly liberal liberal arts school in Olympia. "A journalism major!" I croaked. "What's she doing working for us?"

I'm of the common law-enforcement opinion that anyone remotely connected with journalism can't be trusted. Even the good-looking ones. Especially the good-looking ones.

"Jobs must be pretty scarce in the newspaper racket these days," I added.

By then the young woman in question was squatted next to the body, pants pulled taut across the gentle curve of her backside, a detail that didn't escape any of her appreciative audience, except maybe Doc Baker. Attempting to follow the M.E.'s barked orders on angle and focus, she lost her balance and tipped to one side, scrambling to right herself in the railroad-track dirt and debris.

I didn't envy her. It's not so bad working *with* Dr. Howard Baker. He accords detectives a certain amount of grudging respect. But I think it would be hell on wheels working *for* him, especially as a lowly peon.

At last Baker got up off his hands and knees and strode over to us. By now our little group consisted of Al Lindstrom; the two uniformed officers; a pair of criminalists from the Washington State Patrol Crime Laboratory; Sergeant Lowell James, Seattle P.D.'s night-shift Homicide squad leader; and myself.

"How's it going, Dr. Baker?" Sergeant James asked.

James is a soft-spoken black man whose careful observance of protocol and keen instinct for detail has moved him steadily and deservedly forward in the department while his less able counterparts are still squawking about racial discrimination and quotas.

"Have anything for us yet?"

Baker shrugged. "The officers found a wallet, probably his, on the ground next to the body. No money, but they tell me there's an uncashed payroll check. He has a pearl earring in his right ear."

"Doesn't sound like robbery, then," Big Al put in.

Baker nodded. "You've got a driver's license for a change. Picture looks about right, although it's hard to tell for sure. His face is pretty badly messed up. The name on the license and the paycheck is the same, Richard Dathan Morris. Address is 1120 Bellevue Avenue East."

I took out my notebook and jotted down the

name and address. "You handling this case, Beau?" Baker asked.

"Looks that way. Big Al and I wound up pulling call duty after we finished our regular shift at midnight."

The medical examiner nodded. "All right. The paycheck is written on the account of some outfit called Westcoast Starlight Productions. We also found a union card from IATSE Local 15."

"Wait a minute. Hold up. What's the name of the union?"

"IATSE. International Alliance for Theater and Stage Employees."

"And the other thing. What was that?"

"Westcoast Starlight Productions."

"What the hell's that?"

"Beats me," Baker replied. "You're the detective."

"Anything else?"

"A matchbook from the Edgewater Inn. It was under the body. I can't tell yet if it was something that belonged to the victim or if he just happened to land on it."

"Any ideas about the cause of death?" Al asked.

"No sign of booze. At least, no noticeable sign of booze or drugs, either one. He has some puncture wounds."

"Knife?" I asked.

Baker frowned and shook his head. "Definitely not a knife. But I'm not sure what. I've never seen anything quite like it."

"Is that what killed him, you think?"

"The punctures? I doubt it. None of those injuries look that serious."

"So we wait for the autopsy?" Al added.

Baker smiled a cantankerous, superior smile. "You got it," he answered lightly.

"And when will you schedule that?" Sergeant James asked.

"ASAP. The minute we get him into the office. It's too late to go back home to bed. If we finish up soon enough, maybe I can take off early this afternoon."

The photographer had completed her picture-taking and had moved quietly to the outskirts of the group. There she waited patiently for a break in the conversation.

I confess to some slightly lecherous mind-wandering when I looked at her closely. She was a small-boned girl, slightly built, but the curves were in all the right places and proportions. She wore beige cords, cinched tight around a delicate waist. At first glance my thought was that a strong wind would blow her away. She had large, luminous gray eyes and a somewhat waiflike appearance. A beguiling smudge of dirt from the railroad bed darkened one cheek, and a meandering wisp of hair had broken loose from a supposedly businesslike knot at the back of her neck.

"I'm finished now," she said.

Doctor Baker wheeled on her. "Well, it's about time." He grunted as if the delay was somehow all her fault. I couldn't help feeling sorry for her.

"Let's load him up and move him out," Baker

continued, calling to his waiting technicians. "No sense wasting any more time."

He turned and started toward the body, then stopped and looked back over his shoulder. "You two will notify the next of kin?" Baker asked, addressing the question to Al and me.

"We'll handle it," I told him.

With Baker's departure, the group disintegrated as the crime-scene team set about their business and the David-sector patrol officers returned to their squad car. Within seconds I found myself standing alone beside the photographer, who was busily stowing her equipment in a shoulder-strapped camera bag.

She looked young and vulnerable. I felt an awkward, middle-aged urge to smooth over the medical examiner's brusque behavior.

"I'm sure Doc Baker's bark is worse than his bite," I murmured. It was small comfort, tentatively offered.

Zipping the camera bag shut with a decisive tug, she glanced up at me, still with the dark smudge on her face but with a smile tickling the corners of her mouth. "Don't worry about me, Detective Beaumont. Doc Baker doesn't scare me. I've had my shots."

She turned on her heel and walked away, leaving me wondering how she had known my name when I didn't know hers. So much for being blown away by a strong wind.

So much for first impressions.

I tagged along after Sergeant James and Big Al,

who were bird-dogging the crime-scene investigators. They were carefully surveying the area from which the body had been removed. By now the sun was well up, and it was easy to see that the entire length of railroad track was littered with loose garbage blowing this way and that in the early-morning freshening breeze off Puget Sound.

There were empty pizza boxes and paper cups still with plastic tops and straws attached. There were paper towels and napkins and more than a few used disposable diapers. Included was the usual assortment of beer cans and wine bottles, some shattered and some not.

Nobody who ever worked crime-scene investigation thinks of it as glamorous. It's tough, painstaking, stinking, dirty work.

It requires persistence, skill, attention to detail, and a certain amount of luck. And judgment. It's always a judgment call to determine whether the jagged shards of a smashed cheap wine bottle should be picked up or ignored, to tell if one piece of junk is in its natural habitat, if it is somehow out of place, or even if it's important.

It's human judgment, too, that sets up the limits of the crime-scene area, that decides how big an area should be searched.

Al and I were almost ready to leave to follow up on the Bellevue Avenue address when one of the Washington State Patrol criminalists gave an excited whistle. He was nearly a block away, standing next to a blackberry bramble that virtually covers that side of the bluff. He motioned us toward him.

"What do you think of that?" he demanded, pointing toward something on the ground.

I looked where he pointed. There, partially hidden in the foliage, was a shoe, a cobalt blue leather shoe with a five-inch stiletto heel.

"That look like blood to you?" he asked.

Dark splotches covered the heel and had wicked up onto the body of the shoe itself. It did indeed look like blood.

The second criminalist reached us and dropped down on all fours to examine the shoe more closely. Finally he straightened up, leaving the shoe where it was.

"We have a bingo," he said quietly. "That sure as hell looks like blood to me. And I think that's a human hair where the rubber tip should be."

Big Al Lindstrom caught my eye and shook his head. "He musta done something that pissed her off real good," he said thoughtfully.

"And she must be one hell of a handful," I added.

CHAPTER 2

BELLEVUE AVENUE EAST RUNS NORTH AND SOUTH along the western flank of Seattle's Capitol Hill. It consists mainly of small- to medium-sized brick apartment buildings, four or five stories high, most of them carefully landscaped and well maintained. I was surprised, then, when we pulled up in front of 1120 which turned out to be a single-family residence.

Actually, the house was little more than a cottage. There was an air of benign neglect about it. No one had deliberately destroyed anything, but the outside shingles were cracked and peeling, the grass had gone to seed, the low hedge surrounding the place was badly in need of trimming, and weeds had invaded what had evidently once been a prized rose garden.

From the looks of it, I would have guessed it was a house in search of gentrification, a forlorn relic someone was hanging onto, all the while hoping a developer would show up to buy it, preferably someone with a bottomless checkbook stashed in his hip pocket. There are lots of places like that around cities these days, areas where existing buildings fall into disrepair while greedy owners wait for the pot of gold at the end of some fast-talking developer's rainbow.

The porch may have been sagging and peeling, but on that unusually summery June morning it was also warm and sunny. A well-fed, blue-eyed Siamese cat occupied a place of honor directly in front of the door. Ignoring us completely, he concentrated on washing one luxuriously outstretched hind leg. Only when I knocked on the door behind him did the cat give his head a disdainful shake, stand up, arch his back, and stalk off the porch. In the cat's book, we were unwelcome interlopers who had invaded his private patch of sunlight.

The door was an old-fashioned one with horizontal wooden panels across the bottom and a frosted woodland scene etched into the glass window near the top. After knocking, we waited several long minutes, but there was no answer. I knocked again, louder this time, but still no one came to the door. Disregarding years of my mother's patient training, I pressed my face against the window in the door and peered inside.

Curtains covered most of the window, but toward the bottom, below the intricate frosted design, the curtains parted slightly. Through the narrow opening I could see the disorderly shambles inside. Clothes were strewn everywhere. Trash littered the floor next to an overturned garbage can. A wicker chair lay on its side near the door.

"Ransacked, you think?" Al asked when I stepped back from the window and told him what I had seen.

"Can't tell. Maybe, or maybe Richard Dathan Morris was just a first-class slob."

We had no search warrant and no reason to disregard proper channels for obtaining one. Besides, searching the house was premature until we had at least verified Doc Baker's preliminary identification. We decided to canvass the neighborhood in hopes of gleaning some useful bit of information about Richard Dathan Morris.

We worked our way through a series of nearby apartment buildings one by one, including those on either side of Morris's house as well as the one directly across the street. No luck. Nobody knew anything, or if they did, they weren't talking. We unearthed no connections between the surrounding apartment dwellers and their deceased neighbor in the derelict little house.

Shoe-leather work takes time. Walking and talking and fishing for information isn't an instantaneous process. An hour and a half or so later, we emerged from the semidarkness of the last apartment-building foyer and blinked our way into blinding morning sunlight. Walking side by side and squinting into the unaccustomed sunlight, we headed for the car, only to dodge out of the way of a speeding minivan. It almost took a chunk out of Al's kneecap as it skidded to a stop in front of our vehicle.

"Hey, watch it," Al cautioned the driver, who bounced out of the van and hurried around to the back of the vehicle, where he pulled open a cargo door.

"Sorry about that," he said.

We got into our car. Al was driving. He started the motor and looked out the back window to check oncoming traffic. Meanwhile, I watched as the driver of the van and his helper removed a stretcher from the van and started purposefully toward the small house, carrying the stretcher between them.

"Al, take a look at that."

They carried the stretcher onto the porch, knocked, and then stood waiting. Moments later the front door swung open and the cat sauntered outside. In our absence, someone had come home and let the cat in. The door opened wider, revealing a young man wearing a white uniform of some kind. There was a short conversation; then he motioned the two men to bring their stretcher into the house.

"We'd better check this out," I said.

Al nodded and shut off the engine. We scrambled out of the car and were on the porch almost before the door finished slamming shut behind the men with the stretcher. When I knocked, the man in the white uniform returned to open the door.

He was maybe five ten or so, with short, clean-cut hair that reminded me of a fifties flattop. His narrow, handsome face had a gaunt look to it. Dark shadows under his eyes said he wasn't getting enough food or sleep or both. A name tag on the breast pocket of his white uniform told us he was Tom Riley, R.N.

"Detective J. P. Beaumont, Seattle P.D.," I said, holding out my ID.

"Nobody called for any cops," Riley said abruptly. He turned away and slammed the door behind him.

"Guess he doesn't care much for police officers," Al muttered.

"Did you see that?" I asked.

"See what?"

"The mess. Inside. Somebody cleaned it up."

"Maybe we'd better try again," Big Al said. This time he knocked.

When the door opened the second time, I positioned myself so I could peer into the room over the shoulder of Tom Riley, R.N. Behind him I caught a glimpse of the driver and his helper busily dressing for what looked like a field trip into an operating room. Both had put on surgical masks and germ-free booties and were in the process of donning rubber gloves.

"I'm Detective Al Lindstrom with Seattle P.D.'s Homicide squad—" Al began.

The nurse cut him off. "I already told you. We don't need any cops."

"We're here concerning a homicide—"

"This isn't a homicide, for God's sake," Riley

interrupted. "Don't you understand plain English?" He tried to shut the door again, but my foot got in the way. Thank you, Fuller Brush. I worked my way through college selling brushes door to door, and some of the training still proves useful.

"Excuse me," the driver said, clearing his throat. "We're a little pressed for time. If you could just show us where the deceased is, we'll get started."

For a moment, I thought maybe I was losing my mind. What deceased? Whose body? I was under the impression we had just bundled up Richard Dathan Morris's body and sent him off to the medical examiner's office for an autopsy. How could he be dead in two places at once?

As though forgetting us entirely, Riley swung away from the door without closing it. He nodded slowly, making a visible effort to control himself. "Right," he managed. "This way."

He walked across the room and disappeared down a darkened hallway, followed by the two men and their stretcher. For a brief moment, Al and I paused on the front porch, exchanging questioning glances. We hadn't exactly been invited into the house, but we hadn't exactly been ordered to stay out either.

Al shrugged his shoulders. "Why not?" he said.

We hurried through the front door and followed the stretcher down the hallway. At the far end of the hall a bedroom door stood open.

That's where we all ended up, inside that darkened bedroom. The room was incredibly hot and stuffy. The windows were shut and heavily curtained, and the stifling atmosphere was thick with the medicinal odors of long illness. Riley went to the window, raised the curtain, and opened the window itself, allowing a hint of fresh air into the room.

"The sunlight hurt his eyes," he explained. "And he was always cold."

A hospital bed stood in the middle of the room, occupying most of the space. On it lay the blanket-covered figure of a man. The patient lay on his side with his face turned away from us. Seen from the doorway, he appeared to be asleep. It was only when I stepped to the foot of the bed so I could glimpse his face that I encountered the unnatural pallor, the open-eyed, slack-jawed, frozen mask that indelibly separates the living from the dead.

One thing was certain the moment I saw him: this dead man wasn't *our* dead man. Richard Dathan Morris was still safely in the hands of the medical examiner. That made me feel better. At least I wasn't slipping.

The driver looked at Riley. "If you'd like to go back out to the other room and wait . . ." he offered.

"No. I'm all right," Riley answered. "Go ahead."

Totally focused, Tom Riley, R.N., stared at the corpse. A series of expressions played over the nurse's face, a combination of sorrow, revulsion, and something else, some other ingredient I couldn't quite identify.

The driver turned to me, ready to ask Al and me if we were going or staying. Silently, I shook my head. We weren't budging, but I didn't want him calling Riley's attention to us either. I don't think it had dawned on him yet that we were in the bedroom too.

Deliberately, cautiously, the two men placed the stretcher beside the bed. They approached the corpse warily, like little kids afraid of a bogeyman. It was almost as though they expected the dead man to jerk awake, sit up, and grab them.

I've seen more than my share of mortuary types in my time. They're usually in and out in a jiffy; wham, bam, thank you ma'am, the less time spent the better. These two were taking their time, taking care, making sure each movement was slow and meticulous. Something was definitely out of whack, but I couldn't tell what it was.

"Can we wrap him in these sheets?" the driver asked, directing his query to Riley.

The nurse nodded. "Sure. Go ahead."

Reaching down, the driver gently moved a pillow out from under the dead man's head, shoving it to the far side of the bed. It tottered there briefly, then fell to the floor.

My vast experience with pillows tells me that they usually fall silently. This one didn't. It landed on the room's hardwood flooring with a resounding thump.

I was standing at the foot of the bed. I took one more step to the side so I could see the pillow. A plastic package of some kind had slipped halfway out of the pillowcase onto the floor beneath the bed, right beside Tom Riley's foot.

Instinctively, I moved toward the package. Cops are trained that way. If something doesn't make sense, check it out. Ask questions. Get answers. I was quick, but Tom Riley was quicker.

Enraged, he lunged at me, bellowing with anger. "What are you doing here? I told you to get out!"

That must have been the first moment he realized we were in the room. I saw him charge toward me, but it was too late to make any evasive maneuver. We collided in midair with such force that it knocked the wind out of us both. We fell to the floor in a tangled heap. Riley made one futile grab for my neck, but he came up empty-handed when Al Lindstrom lifted him bodily into the air.

Al shoved Riley against a wall and held him there with his feet dangling several inches off the ground. We don't call Al "Big Al" for nothing. His arms are thick as tree limbs, and he's as strong as the proverbial ox. He was evidently one hell of a wrestler in his youth. Even now he's no slouch.

As soon as I was sure Riley was permanently out of commission, I reached under the bed far enough to lift the pillowcase and uncover the package. It was about the size of an ordinary brick, wrapped in clear plastic, and carefully taped shut.

I've never worked Narcotics, but I've seen enough

stuff to recognize drugs when I see them. It looked like cocaine, deadly, compact, powdery cocaine. It could have been powdered sugar, but people don't generally hide powdered sugar in their pillows. And they don't generally die over it either.

Riley found his voice again, sputtering over Al's restraining arm. "Don't you touch anything, you bastard. You've got no right to be here. Get out, goddamn it! Out!"

Studying the package, I ignored Riley's outburst. "Looks like coke to me," I said to Al.

The guys from the mortuary stood watching us stupidly, as if we were a traveling vaudeville show there for no other reason than their personal entertainment and benefit.

"Hey, Roger," one whined to the other. "Are we moving this guy or not?"

"Not!" I barked. "You don't touch him or anything in this room until I talk to the medical examiner's office."

At that Tom Riley renewed his struggle, kicking and fighting to get free of Al Lindstrom's vise-like grip. "You do as you were told," he roared at the driver. "The medical examiner already knows about it."

I walked over to where Al held Riley with his back to the wall, chinning him effortlessly on one solid forearm.

"Doc Baker? How does he know about it?" I demanded.

"I called him. Almost an hour ago. As soon as I found the body."

"Why isn't he here, then?" It was hard to believe the medical examiner's office was backed up that far. Surely they could have dispatched someone in less than an hour.

"Because he doesn't have to be." Riley sounded calmer now, almost rational.

"Since when is Doc Baker too good to check out an OD?"

Riley stared at me incredulously. "You think that's what it is? An overdose?"

I answered his question with one of my own. "Don't you? When we find a dead man with half a pound of cocaine hidden in his pillowcase, we can usually draw some pretty logical conclusions."

Something strange happened to Tom Riley's face then. It contorted suddenly. At first I thought he was going to burst into tears.

I was wrong. Instead he began laughing, a strangled, air-gulping, rib-breaking, all-consuming laugh.

As I stood in that stuffy, confining bedroom with a man dead on the bed behind me, Tom Riley's eerie, unnatural laughter made the hairs stand up on the back of my neck.

At last he grew quieter and regained enough composure so he could talk. "Jon didn't OD," he declared firmly.

"He didn't? What did he die of, then?" I demanded.

"AIDS."

Tom Riley's single-word answer crackled through the silent room like heat lightning in a tinder-dry forest. Al Lindstrom's stranglehold collapsed and Tom Riley, a limp, boneless rag doll, slipped silently to the floor.

"AIDS! Holy shit!" Big Al muttered, a stricken expression on his face.

Tom Riley took one look at Big Al's face and began to laugh again.

Al Lindstrom didn't think it was funny.

I didn't either.

CHAPTER 3

Doc Baker's mood hadn't improved any by the time I got him on the phone. Over his secretary's strenuous protests, I had insisted that he be called away from an autopsy-in-progress.

"Beaumont, you jerk, what did you say the name was?"

"Thomas. Jonathan Thomas."

"Sure. His nurse called in earlier this morning. I already had the notice from the attending physician. My people told Riley to go ahead and have them move the body."

"Just like that? Without bothering to send somebody over? Without checking?"

"You been living under a rock or something, Beau? Jonathan Thomas died of AIDS. AIDS! His doctor notified my office over a week ago that death was imminent."

"What does that have to do with whether or not you send somebody out?"

"Look, when an attending physician tells us his patient is dying of AIDS, we believe him. We take his word for it. He gives us a written notification that he's willing to sign the death certificate to that effect, and we let it go at that. We're out of it, understand?"

"But we found drugs hidden in his bed. It might have been an overdose. Or what if he was murdered?"

"What if? He was dying."

"Doc, we need an autopsy here."

"You don't need an autopsy, you want one. There's a big difference. And who the hell do you think is going to do it? My people don't want to, I can tell you that much, and I don't blame them a bit."

"But, Doc."

"Don't you 'But, Doc' me. My office has a written procedure for cases like this, and we're following it to the letter. If you want an autopsy, get the attending physician to do it. Now, if you don't mind, I'm going back to the autopsy I was doing before I was so rudely interrupted."

He slammed the receiver down in my ear. I turned to face the people in Jonathan Thomas's living room who were waiting to hear Doc Baker's answer.

Riley stood with his arms across his chest, glaring at me. "Well?" he demanded.

I nodded to the driver from the mortuary. "Go ahead and take him away," I said. "But no embalming, and no other preparations until after I check with his doctor, is that clear?"

He nodded. "You won't get no argument from me."

I handed him my card. "My name's Beaumont, Detective J. P. Beaumont. Now, where are you taking him?"

The driver glanced at my card and pocketed it. "Ramsey and Son Funeral Home over on East Pine."

With that, he and his partner disappeared down the hallway. Al Lindstrom, Tom Riley, and I waited in the living room without exchanging a word until the two men returned, carefully carrying the body-laden stretcher between them.

Riley went to the door and held it open for them while they gingerly maneuvered the stretcher through the doorway and down the front steps. Only after the body had been loaded into the van and the vehicle had disappeared around the corner did Riley come back inside.

He glanced at Al and me in undisguised disgust. "Why are you still here?"

"We want to talk to you about Richard Morris," I said.

Riley shrugged. "That worthless asshole? What about him? He should be home any minute. You can talk to him yourselves."

"I take it he's not a friend of yours?"

Riley's narrow lower lip curled downward in a

sneer of absolute contempt. "Hardly. Jon should have thrown that creep out months ago."

"Why?"

I didn't volunteer the information that Richard Morris would never be coming home again. That's not my style. Asking questions is a Homicide detective's prime directive. Ask first; tell later. Take first; give later. Ask any detective's wife. More likely, ask his ex-wife.

Tom Riley hit us with an indictment of Richard Dathan Morris that bore a close resemblance to an ex-wife's ravings. "Because Rick's still out running the streets, for one thing, damn him. And because he doesn't give a shit about anybody but himself. And because he wasn't here last night when Jon needed him."

"Did you see him at all last night?" Al interjected.

"He was here when I left. At eleven. Said he'd be home all night, the lying son of a bitch. I can't believe he took off and left Jon here alone. So help me, when I find him . . ." Riley let the remainder of his threat trail off unspoken.

Suddenly Riley gave me a sharp look, as though he had finally realized the focus and direction of our questions. We hadn't come about Jonathan Thomas after all.

"Has Rick done something wrong?" he asked suddenly.

Riley's abrupt shift in demeanor didn't escape me. He had been rude and short with me to the point of physical violence when I had attempted to interfere with the removal of Jonathan Thomas's body. But now, once he understood my questions were really about Richard Morris, now that I had held out the possibility that Morris was in some kind of trouble with the law, Riley switched to being downright cooperative.

Bearing this in mind, I, too, slipped into a different approach, addressing Tom Riley with far more deference and respect than I had used before. Respect is a useful tool, and when applied in reasonable proportions it inflates egos at the same time it loosens tongues.

"We don't know, Mr. Riley. That's what we're trying to find out, why we came here in the first place. If you could just tell us whatever you can remember about last night, it would be a big help."

Tom Riley walked over to the couch and sat down, rubbing his eyes wearily. "He worked yesterday," he said.

"Morris did? Where?"

"At the Fifth Avenue, from eight in the morning until ten last night. At least, that's what he said."

"At the Fifth Avenue. The theater?"

Riley nodded. "That's right. He was doing a load-in."

"Load-in?" It wasn't a term I recognized.

"A setup for a bus-and-truck show. He's a stagehand."

"For a what?" It seemed like Riley was speaking a foreign language.

"You know, one of those traveling road shows."

"Do you know which one?"

"No idea. Some singer, I guess. I didn't pay any attention. Rick's such a blowhard that I don't listen to half of what he says."

"What time did he come home?"

"Around ten. I was just finishing putting Jon down. You know, giving him his medications, that sort of thing."

Somehow, in the constant opening and closing of the front door, the cat had wandered back into the house. It chose that moment to insinuate itself into Tom Riley's lap, where it curled up comfortably. For several long moments Riley sat there, absently stroking it, as if drawing some comfort from the cat's silent presence.

The man sitting quietly with the contented cat in his lap was far different from the one who had taken a murderous lunge at me in the bedroom a short time before. Over the years, I've learned to pay attention to animals and how they react to people. They seem to have a phenomenal way of sorting the good from the bad, of attaching themselves to kind, compassionate people and avoiding the ones who are mean and aggressive. That fat, sleek cat was giving Tom Riley a hell of a good character reference.

"May I ask you a professional question, Mr. Riley?"

He started quickly, the way a person does when he's fallen asleep in church or when his mind has wandered during the course of a conversation. "Pardon me?"

"I'd like to ask you a professional question."

"All right."

"Did anything about Jonathan Thomas's condition last night lead you to believe that he would die before morning?"

He shook his head. "Not really. He was weaker than he had been. That was to be expected, but I didn't think it was that bad. It's been bothering me all day. I should have paid closer attention. I should have known the end was that close."

"What about his breathing—had it changed at all?"

"No."

"If you had known the end was near, would you have left or would you have stayed all night?"

My question cut right to the bone. Tom Riley's gaze met mine, but his lower lip trembled. "I would have stayed," he murmured.

"How long were you Jonathan's nurse?"

"Five months."

"That's a long time," I said gently. "Obviously you cared deeply about your patient. But why are you so opposed to an autopsy?"

"He didn't want it. Gave specific orders. Besides, hadn't he suffered enough indignity?" Riley asked.

"What if he was murdered?"

"Why would anyone bother to murder someone with only a week or so to live? That was all he had, at the most."

"What if they didn't want him to suffer?"

"You mean a mercy killing? Euthanasia?"

"It's not unheard of. Would Rick Morris have been capable of something like that?"

"Are you kidding? He's the most selfish person I ever met."

"What about Jonathan's parents?"

Riley shook his head. "I never met them. Jon told me they disowned him a year or so ago."

"What about you?"

The last question, out of the blue, was calculated to blindside Tom Riley, to shock him into some kind of admission, if possible, or to reveal a reaction that would tell us he was hiding something. It didn't work.

"I wouldn't have left him to die alone," he said quietly.

It was an odd reaction. Innocent people yell like mad when you accuse them of something they didn't do. Guilty ones hide out in side issues. I had expected a hot denial to my blunt accusation. Instead, Riley had merely deflected my question.

I was silently mulling over Riley's oblique response when Al stepped into the conversation. "You said you didn't know his parents, that they had disowned him. Do you know where they are, what their names are?"

Riley got up and left the room. He returned, carrying a manila file folder. He opened it, shuffled through several pages, then picked out one and read from it. "Their names are Dorothy and William B. Thomas. They live over in Bellevue." He handed the paper to Al, who scanned it and made a few brief notes in his notebook.

"Jon kept the folder by his bed," Riley continued. "He made notes in it about what he wanted done, what mortuary, what kind of service, who was to be notified—that kind of thing. Including no autopsy," he added, glancing meaningfully at me.

Al finished making his notes; then he gingerly handed the paper back to Riley like it was a loaded hand grenade. Unconsciously, he rubbed his hand on his pants. It was clear the very idea of AIDS scared the living crap out of Big Al Lindstrom.

"Was he still lucid at the end?" I asked.

"Sometimes."

"The boys from Narcotics will be here in a few minutes to pick up the package. Is it possible that Jonathan was masterminding a drug ring of some kind from his sickbed?"

"Jon? Are you kidding? He wouldn't have done something like that. Never. I knew him."

"What about Rick?"

Riley shrugged. "He's another story," he said.

"You mean he could have been into selling drugs?"

"I don't trust him any farther than I can throw him. He could be into anything."

"Including dealing drugs?"

Riley nodded.

"What time did you get here this morning?"

"Seven-thirty or so."

"And what was the place like when you got here?"

"It was a mess, a pigsty."

I looked around the somewhat shabby living room. It wasn't nearly the mess it had been when

I had first seen it through the parted curtains. "Who straightened it up?" I asked.

"I did," Riley answered. "Sometimes Jon would want me to wheel him out here. He complained that the bedroom was boring. I didn't want him to see the place like that. It would have upset him. Besides, I looked in on him and thought he was asleep. I cleaned up while I was waiting for him to wake up."

"It wasn't a mess when you left here last night?"

He shook his head. "I figured Rick had invited people over during the night. He's never learned to pick up after himself."

"And he never will," I added quietly.

Riley frowned and gave me a searching look. "What do you mean, he never will?"

"We believe that Richard Darthan Morris was the victim of a homicide late last night, down near the Pike Place Market."

I watched carefully to see what kind of shock value my words might have on Tom Riley, R.N. If I expected an overreaction, I was in for a real disappointment.

"Good riddance," he said quietly.

And that was all.

CHAPTER 4

Two detectives from Narcotics stopped by a short time later and took charge of the package we'd found in Jonathan Thomas's bedroom. By then, Tom Riley had decided to be more cooperative. He allowed us to go through the place pretty thoroughly. I guess we all expected to find a collection of drug paraphernalia somewhere on the premises. No such luck. The only drug-related equipment was that found with the sickroom supplies in a cabinet to which Riley claimed to have the solitary key.

When our search was completed, we took Tom Riley over to the medical examiner's office. His positive identification of Richard Dathan Morris was pretty much routine. When it was over, we returned to the house with Riley, where he gave us the name and address of Morris's widowed mother, a Mrs. Grace Simms Morris, who lived ninety miles or so north of Seattle in Bellingham.

Riley left the house when we did, taking with him the newly orphaned cat. We assured him that after conferring with Jonathan Thomas's doctor we would notify his parents of the death. The nurse seemed grateful to be relieved of that particular duty.

Doc Baker had been involved in a conference call when we stopped by to make the identification, but he had left word that he wanted to see us, both Al and me, ASAP. So back we went to the medical examiner's office in the basement of Harborview Hospital on First Hill.

"It was a fall that killed him," Baker began, regarding us inscrutably as we seated ourselves in his office.

"A fall? What fall?" I demanded.

Doc Baker shoved Richard Dathan Morris's file folder in my direction, reached into his desk, and pulled out some paper clips, which he began to pitch toward the chipped blue vase that always sat in his windowsill. Tossing the clips offhandedly as he spoke, he nonetheless hit the lip of the vase with almost total accuracy.

"Not the fall, actually. Hitting the ground was what killed him." The medical examiner smiled, amused by his own black wit.

"The holes in his head and chest had nothing to do with it?"

"Nope. Superficial damage only. Nothing fatal."

"Could you tell what made them?" Al asked.

"A little bird told me the crime-scene investigators found what appears to be a bloodstained high-heeled shoe in the area. That would certainly be consistent with the kinds of injuries we found. We found a piece of rubber in one of the wounds that may very well be the tip of the heel. We gathered some other trace evidence as well, bits of foreign materials, from those puncture wounds. We'll have to see if any of them matches up with what the crime lab finds on the shoe."

Baker paused and shook his head wonderingly. "She must be some kind of broad."

"What do you mean?"

"The holes weren't fatal, but still, it takes a hell of a lot of strength to push the tip of a heel into someone's body far enough to make a hole, especially if that person is fighting back."

"Was he?" I asked.

"I'd say so," Baker answered.

"Scratches? Tooth marks?"

The medical examiner shook his head, his mane of white hair fluttering in the resultant breeze. "No bite marks, but we found scratches, lots of them. Most of them appear to have been inflicted by the victim rolling around in a blackberry bramble. None that we could definitely attribute to fingernails."

"Drugs?" Al asked.

Baker had exhausted his supply of paper clips. Now he paused and rummaged in his desk for more ammunition. "Preliminary findings say no. We're running some additional tests though. Those take time. That's all we've got so far."

Baker waited impatiently until I finished a brief scan of the contents of the folder. When I looked up, he was holding out his hand for me to give the folder back. His message was clear: Here's your hat. What's your hurry?

Big Al and I took the hint and got up to leave.

"By the way," I added casually, pausing with my hand on the doorknob. "I still need the name and telephone number of Jonathan Thomas's attending physician."

"The hell you do! What kind of wild hair's up your butt, Beau? Why are you so goddamned interested in that guy? Get his number from my secretary on your way out."

"Did you find any AIDS antibodies in Richard Dathan Morris?" I asked innocently.

Baker's face clouded. "We didn't look. Why?"

"Maybe you should. He was Jonathan Thomas's roommate."

With that, I closed the door to Doc Baker's office. Behind us a paper clip pinged off the vase and ricocheted into the windowpane, followed by a rumbled oath.

"You screwed up his concentration," Al said with a half-assed grin.

We stopped by the secretary's desk long enough to pick up the name of Jonathan Thomas's personal physician, a Dr. Wendell Johnson of the Capitol Hill Medical Group on Broadway.

Stepping outside into the still-brilliant sunlight, Big Al looked up at the blue sky overhead. He stretched and yawned. I read him loud and clear. It was time to go home. Past time to go home.

"Maybe she killed him in self-defense," he suggested wearily, moving toward the car. "He attacked her, and she hauled off her shoe and beat the living crap out of him. How does that grab you?"

"It won't hold water," I countered. "If Morris was gay, why attack a woman?"

Al shrugged. "Beats me."

Big Al Lindstrom is known around the department for his ultraconservative, middle-American, motherhood-and-apple-pie, Eagle Scout mind-set. I couldn't resist taking a poke at him, just to see how he'd react.

"Maybe Morris was AC/DC," I added. "What if he was a switch-hitter and he and the woman were after the same guy?"

Big Al made a face. "Just talking about it makes me want to puke. Let's call it a day. We can tackle this mess again later. We'll handle the notification of next of kin as soon as we come back on duty this afternoon."

As Al walked away, I stopped and glanced up at the looming presence of Harborview Hospital behind us. My regular partner, Detective Ron Peters, was in Harborview, had been there for more than two months, recuperating from an accident. He was up on the fourth floor, the one they call the rehabilitation floor, where doctors and nurses were trying to glue his broken neck and his shattered life back together.

It wasn't visiting hours, but over the weeks the nurses had come to know me well enough to let me come and go pretty much as I pleased.

"I'm going to stop by and see Peters," I told Al. "How about if you take the car back to the department? I'll hoof it down the hill when I'm ready."

"Okay. Say hello to ol' Ron for me, would you?"

I nodded, but I doubted a cheery greeting from Big Al Lindstrom would do much to lift the thick pall of depression that surrounded Ron Peters.

After the accident, the initial diagnosis of Peters's condition had labeled him a C-6 Quadriplegic Incomplete, which meant, among other things, that although his neck was broken, the spinal cord itself hadn't been severely damaged and there was reason to hope that he would eventually recover some, if not all, of his bodily functions.

But that thread of hope had also meant that for almost two months, Peters had been stuck in rigorous traction with steel bolts drilled into his skull supporting sixty pounds of weight. His neck injury meant he could choose to lie on one side or the other, but never on his back or his stomach. He was beginning to get some movement in his arms, but that was about it. Eventually was proving to be just that—eventually.

During his first month in the hospital they had kept Peters so doped up that I don't think he cared what was going on around him. But now, as the long weeks of physical confinement continued, as he remained totally dependent on other people for his most basic needs, Peters had fallen into a bleak chasm of hopelessness.

The nurses told me that wasn't at all unusual for someone in his condition, that he had to be shown there was a reason for him to go on living. I came by to visit regularly, but he rarely spoke in anything other than monosyllabic grunts.

Attempting to cheer him up, one day I brought along his daughters, six-year-old Heather and seven-year-old Tracie. I thought seeing his kids might give him the needed motivation to fight back, to try to get better. No such luck. Within minutes of their arrival, he asked them to turn on the television set and then proceeded to ignore them completely in favor of the nightly news. I had taken two heartbroken girls back to their temporary quarters in my downtown condominium.

Maxine Edwards, the girls' regular baby-sitter, had comforted them as well as she could, soothing them and drying their faces. When subsequent visits weren't any better, I finally took the bull by the horns and packed the three of them off to southern California for a two-week vacation.

It's times like that when it's nice to have money. I put in a call to Kelly, my teenage daughter, who lives in Cucamonga with her mother and stepfather. Since I was footing the bill, Kelly readily agreed to serve as tour guide for the duration of their visit.

I had received several delighted phone calls from the girls. They were having a ball. Disneyland, Universal City, and Knott's Berry Farm would never be the same. But Peters had not been happy when he heard about the trip. In fact, he had been pissed as hell. We had exchanged ugly words over it. He said they shouldn't have gone, since it wasn't something he could afford to pay for himself. I told him he had placed the girls in my custody for as long as he needed them there, and I was more than prepared to handle all the accompanying expenses.

The girls had sent home a collection of gaudy postcards addressed to their father, all of them bearing clumsily scrawled notes telling him to get well soon. As a matter of fact, I was packing the whole batch of cards in my jacket pocket, had been for several days, while I put off going to the hospital and having what I expected to be a nose-to-nose confrontation with their father. I wasn't looking forward to his reaction once he saw the cards.

It was time to go though. However tough it might be to face him, I couldn't, in good conscience, put it off any longer.

I rode an elevator up to the fourth floor. Peters's roommate, a diving-accident victim, was gradually making the transition out of bed and into a wheelchair. He was out of the room when I got there. Peters was lying on his side, an open newspaper propped clumsily on the bed beside him.

"How's it going?" I asked, doing my best to sound jaunty and cheerful.

"About the same," he said, not looking up.

"Any word about when you'll get out of this ungodly contraption?" I patted the overhead traction frame.

"When they're damned good and ready," he replied morosely.

As usual, Peters wasn't in a particularly conversational mood. I struggled to carry on my one-sided monologue.

"Big Al and I started a new case today," I said, hoping to strike some small spark of interest. "Some gay creep got himself plugged full of holes from a high-heeled shoe and then got thrown down beside the railroad track. You know where the Burlington Northern Tunnel entrance is? There behind the Pike Place Market?"

I paused to give Peters an opportunity for comment. None was forthcoming. I plunged on.

"Eventually, we found this character was some kind of theater stagehand who had worked at the Fifth Avenue the day before. Anyway, we went to his house and discovered that his roommate died last night too, right there in the house. Doc Baker insists it's just a coincidence, that the roommate died of AIDS. Since Baker says his death was expected, the medical examiner's office refused to do an autopsy."

"Why do you want one?"

Peters's question startled me. Over the weeks,

I had gotten used to carrying on totally one-sided conversations. Now, unexpectedly, he was showing a smidgeon of interest, a sign that he was emerging from his self-imposed isolation. I was so surprised, I almost forgot to answer his question.

"Oh, did I mention the drugs?"

"No."

"When we got to the house, we found the nurse had called the mortuary to come pick up the body. When they moved his pillow, a half-pound brick that looked like solid coke fell out on the floor. The nurse flew into a rage and almost knocked the shit out of me. He would have too, if Al hadn't stopped him."

"You think the roommate was murdered too?"

"Absolutely. I don't give a damn what Doc Baker says. I don't believe in coincidences. One way or the other, it's murder. I can feel it in my bones."

"Drug dealers?"

I shook my head. "I talked to the detectives from Narcotics about that. As far as they know, Morris wasn't a dealer."

Peters snorted. "There are probably a few dealers here in town that Narcotics doesn't know about."

We both work for the same outfit, Seattle P.D., but Homicide and Narcotics aren't always on the best of terms.

It was good to be bouncing ideas off Peters's capable head again. I felt a sudden surge of excitement. Maybe, somehow, we were going to get him back.

"You say these guys were gay, both of them?" he asked. I nodded. "What about the nurse?"

"Riley? What about him?"

"Is he gay too?"

For a long moment I thought about Tom Riley, R.N. The question had never entered my mind until Peters brought it up. "I don't know," I said finally.

"I'm getting to be quite an expert on nurses," Peters observed, with a hint of his old sense of humor. "If I were you, I'd check him out. Maybe it's nothing more or less than an old-fashioned triangle."

"Goddamn it, Peters, I'll bet you're onto something. I'll get right on it."

I was off the chair and out the door so fast I collided head-on with a pretty young physical therapist who was coming into the room to work with Peters. I had seen her several times before. She was quick to laugh and had a ready smile.

"What's the hurry?" she demanded, hands on her hips in mock anger once she had righted herself.

"Get that man jacked up and out of here, would you lady?" I said, wagging a finger at Peters in his bed. "I need him. If he can solve cases lying here flat on his back, Seattle P.D. can't afford to have him out of commission."

Her laughter was still ringing in the room behind me as I hurried down the hallway. In my excitement, I forgot to be tired or hungry. I also forgot I didn't have a car with me.

I dashed out of the hospital and into the parking lot, groping in my pocket for my keys. They were there, all right, along with a whole collection of postcards.

Unfortunately, my Porsche was still safely tucked away in her berth in the parking garage at home. Some days are like that.

You have to take the bad with the good.

CHAPTER 5

IN TOO MUCH OF A HURRY TO WALK OR BATTLE BUSES, I caught a cab for the ten-minute ride to Belltown Terrace, my new building at the corner of Second and Broad. I didn't bother to go upstairs to my apartment. Instead, I took the elevator directly to the residential garage and raced my Porsche up the interminable stack of circles from P-4 to the garage entrance.

Tom Riley had listed his address as being in West Seattle. I took the Alaskan Way Viaduct south and drove across the soaring Spokane Street Bridge. I've always thought the new bridge should have been named in honor of the old Norwegian ship's pilot who broke the old one and was later murdered. His widow was eventually convicted, but I've always fantasized that the killer was really some revenge-minded commuter stuck in the sub-sequent years of traffic jams.

Seattle is a deep-water port, and there are few

places around the city that have readily accessible saltwater beaches. Alki, in West Seattle, is one of those places. It resembles a California beach town far more than it does an ordinary Seattle neighborhood. It comes complete with cruising teenagers, too much traffic, and a constant feud between visitors and residents over the surplus of garbage and the critical shortage of parking places.

Driving there gave me time for reflection. According to Tom Riley, Richard Dathan Morris had been a totally reprehensible character. And by all accounts, Jonathan Thomas had been on the brink of death. So why worry about who killed someone as obnoxious as Morris? And why try to ascertain whether or not Thomas had been murdered or had simply succumbed to the inevitable outcome of his disease?

Why? Because it's my job. Because murder victims are murder victims no matter what, even if they're dying. It's the principle of the thing, pure and simple. If people, no matter how well intentioned, are allowed to kill at will, to rid the land of people they deem unsuitable or to arbitrarily set a timetable to put others out of their misery, the very foundations of our civilization begin to erode.

I've spent most of my adult life working on the premise that murder is murder, that perpetrators must be brought to account in a court of law, and that included whoever killed Richard Dathan Morris and, possibly, Jonathan Thomas.

As I drove, I also kicked myself for not having

been more observant. All Peters had to do was say it to convince me that he was right. And he hadn't even been in Thomas's house. Peters's theory about Tom Riley's sexual preference was what Sherlock Holmes would have termed a brilliant deduction. So what the hell was the matter with me?

The fact that I had missed it was unsettling enough. Had I not seen it because there were no overt signs? Or because I simply hadn't wanted to see it? Was it a case of selective blindness or burying my head in the sand?

As a happily heterosexual male I'm uncomfortable around gays, prejudiced against them. I was propositioned a couple of times when I was younger, and those experiences left a long-term bad impression that I'm only now beginning to sort out.

Over the years, my way of handling that prejudice had been to deal with gays as little as possible. Jim Hunt, the interior decorator who had just finished helping me design and furnish my new condominium, was the first gay I had worked with for any extended period of time. He was a gay without any of the exterior trappings, with none of the supposedly typical mannerisms I had come to expect. In short, Jim was a nice guy who had forced me to come face to face with some of my own deep-seated feelings of intolerance.

Now this series of encounters with Richard Morris, Jonathan Thomas, and Tom Riley was more of the same. They were ordinary people, some good and some bad, just like everybody else.

Tom Riley, if Peters and I were correct, was another homosexual minus the lisping, simpering silliness of the stereotypes. He may have been minus those things, but, I was now convinced, he was gay nonetheless. So now I tried to unravel what possible bearing Tom Riley's sexual preference had on my case.

Had there been some kind of triangle involved? That might account for some of Tom Riley's atypical reactions. Maybe his pronounced dislike of Richard Dathan Morris was symptomatic of old-fashioned jealousy, just as Ron Peters had suggested. Nevertheless, I had a hard time using the word "jealousy" in a male-only context.

I was so lost in thought that I drove straight by the address Tom Riley had given us. I made a U-turn and drove back to it, parking on the street in front of the house.

The place was situated on Alki Avenue itself, far enough east of the lighthouse to be out of the high-rent district. Riley's apartment turned out to be in the basement of a wooden house, living space converted from what had once been a two-car garage. There was a tiny deck outside the sliding glass door with hardly enough room for the single deck chair that sat there in isolated splendor. Only one person at a time could sit on the minuscule deck and view the northern tip of downtown Seattle across Elliott Bay.

As I walked up to the door, I heard someone

inside playing a piano. The tune was an old familiar melody, but it was too much like classical music for me to be able to identify it. When I knocked, the piano playing stopped abruptly and Tom Riley slid open the door. He was cradling his newly adopted blue-eyed cat.

"What do you want?" he asked. His tone of voice, his body language, his manner all said he was not delighted to see me, but then I'm used to that. Being a Homicide detective would never rate high in a popularity contest.

"I've got to talk to you, Mr. Riley. May I come in?"

"Haven't we talked enough already?"

"No."

Reluctantly he stepped aside far enough to let me into the room. Once I was inside and the door was closed, he carefully put the cat down on the floor. The animal crouched on all fours and began scratching his chin on Riley's shoelaces.

"He's not used to the neighborhood yet," Riley explained, looking down at the cat. "I'm worried he might get out and run away."

As I glanced around the room, my first impression was that the place was both small and crowded. It was as though a whole houseful of furniture had been summarily jammed into one or two rooms. Chairs and tables and bookshelves had been crammed together with very little organization or planning.

"You'll have to excuse the mess," said Riley apologetically. "I had hoped to get rid of my extra stuff after I moved here, but I haven't had time."

The piano, a small, beautifully finished spinet, stood just inside the door. On it sat a bottle of Jack Daniel's and a highball glass. It looked to me like Tom Riley was seriously nipping at the hard stuff. Early. It was still well before noon.

"Want a drink?" he offered.

"No thanks. Too early for me."

He picked up the bottle and poured himself a generous drink. Motioning me toward a couch in the middle of the crowded room, Riley sank into a swivel-based rocking chair and placed the half-empty liquor bottle on a glass-topped table between us.

"So talk," he said, downing his drink in a single swallow.

"Drowning your troubles?" I asked mildly.

Riley held up his empty glass and stared pensively through it toward the sliding glass door. The door framed a classic picture of a placid, dazzlingly blue Elliott Bay with the upper end of downtown Seattle gleaming in the background. The Space Needle hovered there like a flying saucer, its supportive tower almost invisible in the flawless sunlight.

"Maybe," he said at last.

"Want to talk about it?"

"Not particularly."

"Mr. Riley, I get the feeling there was far more than a simple nurse-patient relationship between you and Jonathan Thomas."

Raising his head, he looked at me intently, one eyebrow slightly arched. "Do you?"

Riley wasn't making it easy for me. In trying to sort out what had gone on among the three of them, I was already well outside my comfort zone. I had to take better control of the situation, put things on firmer ground.

Without explanation, I reached into my pocket and pulled out the small leather holder that contained both my badge and my ID. It also held the plastic-coated card with the standard Miranda warning printed on it.

Clearing my throat, I began to read: "'You have the right to remain silent . . .'"

Instead of appearing upset, Riley simply poured himself another drink as he listened. Watching me intently, he settled back into his chair as though the words I was reading aloud had nothing whatsoever to do with him. His air was one of total nonchalance.

"So you think I'm the killer?" he asked when I finished. The booze gave his voice a hint of arrogance, a hard edge, that had been absent in our previous encounters.

"The thought crossed my mind," I replied evenly. "Where did you go when you got off from work last night?"

"I came home."

"Did anyone see you?"

"No."

"Was there anyone here?"

"I live alone."

"What about your landlord?"

"My landlord, as you put it, is a widow lady who's blitzed out of her mind by six o'clock every night."

"From what you said earlier, I take it you had a pretty low opinion of Richard Morris."

"That seriously understates the case."

"Why?"

"Because he was a leech and a liar and a miserable excuse for a human being."

"How long had he and Jonathan . . ." I paused, groping uncomfortably for the right word.

"How long had they been lovers?" Riley supplied.

I nodded.

"I don't know. A long time, I guess. If you ask me, Rick Morris saw a likely-looking meal ticket and hung on for dear life."

"Jonathan Thomas had money?"

"His parents are loaded."

"I thought you said they disowned him."

"Jon's grandmother left him some money separately, a trust fund, and the house."

"So the house belonged to him?"

Riley nodded. "Free and clear." He poured himself another drink. "Sure you don't want one?"

"Positive," I told him. This time he didn't down the liquor all at once. Instead, he took a small sip and set the glass down on the table beside the bottle. I had to give him credit. Gay or not, Tom Riley could definitely hold his liquor.

"And Jonathan's parents never came to see him during the time you worked there?"

"Never. From what he told me, that's no surprise. His father's one of those Bible-thumping bigots who claims that being gay is a one-way ticket to hellfire and damnation. And as far as his mother is concerned, what his father says goes."

"What about Richard Morris's mother?"

Riley shrugged. "She came through Seattle a couple of times. I met her. She's a nice enough lady, I guess. A little dingy at times, but with a son like that, who wouldn't be?"

"Tell me about Richard Morris," I said quietly.

"Strictly delusions of grandeur. When I first met him, he was hot to be a cop, an undercover cop. A few weeks later, he dropped that idea completely. It was just as well."

"What do you mean?"

"He was running with the wrong crowd."

"Druggies?"

Riley nodded. "He worked some as a stagehand, but mostly he partied. He dragged home all kinds of undesirable characters at all hours of the day and night."

"Even after Jonathan got so sick?"

Riley nodded grimly. "You bet."

"Drinking? Drugs?"

"Both. Come to think of it, I never actually saw him doing drugs, but there were drugs around."

"And he had money?"

"Always."

"Did he bring anyone home with him last night?"

"There was no one else at the house when I left."

"And you left at eleven?"

"That's right."

"Were there women in the crowd he ran with?"

"A few," Riley answered.

"Any fancy dressers?" I asked, thinking about the bloodstained blue high-heeled shoe.

"Not that I remember."

"What about last night? Was there anything unusual in the way Morris behaved last night?"

"I didn't notice anything out of the ordinary, except maybe . . ."

"Except what?"

"He seemed happy."

"Happy?"

"More like smug. Like he'd pulled off a good one on somebody."

"But you don't know what."

"No."

"And what time did you go back there this morning?"

"Seven-thirty."

"That makes for a pretty long day, from then until eleven at night," I observed. "Were you Jonathan Thomas's only nurse?"

"Yes."

"Every day for five months?"

Tom Riley picked up his glass and drained it.

"Every day," he repeated. "Every single god-damned day."

"That many hours?"

"I didn't turn them all in. I reported the eight I was supposed to, the five days I was supposed to. The rest was on my own time."

"For free?"

He gave me a sardonic grin. "I didn't have anything else to do. Besides, it kept me off the streets."

A short silence settled between us.

"Well," he said at last. "Aren't you going to ask me why I did it? Why I worked all those hours without pay?"

"All right. Why did you?"

He poured one more drink. "Because I have it too," he replied quietly.

For a moment or two I didn't catch on. Finally, I got the message. "AIDS? You mean you have AIDS?"

"Not the disease, at least not yet. I only test positive for the antibodies so far, but I figure it's a death sentence just the same. I've known for a long time. For years. I found out during that initial panic back in '82 and '83 when doctors and nurses were afraid to work with AIDS patients in the hospitals. Remember that?"

It wasn't all that long ago, I thought, recalling my conversation with Doc Baker in the medical examiner's office that very morning. I said, "Yes, I remember."

"It's not as bad now. People are learning that if

you take proper precautions, the disease isn't all that contagious. But it changed my life, you know. I mean I couldn't hang around in bars anymore, I couldn't make that scene and not give a shit about what I might be doing to other people. So I moved here and hid out in work. And I asked to work with AIDS patients. Nothing but. I've worked with six of them so far."

He paused and observed me steadily over the rim of his glass. "They're all dead," he added softly. "One hundred percent."

Once more silence filled the room. The cat wandered in from the bedroom and jumped unbidden into Tom Riley's lap. It circled a time or two before settling comfortably into a ball, purring so noisily I could hear it from where I sat.

Tom Riley glanced from the cat to me. "Any more questions?"

"None," I said, getting up. "I can find my way out."

I did too. I hurried out the door and back to my car.

As I barreled through the milling summertime traffic on Alki Avenue, I thought long and hard about Tom Riley.

From some corner of my random access memory came the words Miss Arnold had drilled into our heads during Senior English at Ballard High School, the words of Rudyard Kipling's immortal poem. They seemed to apply to Tom Riley.

"You're a better man than I am, Gunga Din."

CHAPTER 6

THAT WAS THE SUMMER SOME OF OUR MORE BRIGHT-eyed city fathers decided to rebuild Seattle from the ground up. There was construction everywhere, from aboveground buildings all over the downtown area to the underground transit tunnel beneath Third Avenue.

The accompanying upheaval caused a couple of undesirable results. Number one: it drove a lot of potential shoppers from the downtown retail core and left a large population of panhandlers to feed on a far smaller number of potential soft touches. Number two: it vastly reduced downtown parking.

I had to stop by the department long enough to write my report, but the closest parking garage that wasn't filled to overflowing was five blocks away, five blocks of scrounging, filthy, obnoxious bums. I am not a soft touch, and I didn't knuckle under. One of them told me to have a nice day anyway.

It was good to see the day-shift guys again, the ones Peters and I had worked around for years. With Peters in the hospital, I had temporarily switched to night shift. As usual, Sergeant Watkins, Captain Powell, and a number of others asked about Peters's progress. The patient had made it clear he didn't want visitors, and our coworkers had pretty much complied with his wishes. As far as Peters's condition was concerned, I was the department's main source of information.

Closeting myself in my cubicle, I made short order of writing the mandatory report. Hunger was beginning to assert itself. So was a need for sleep. Given my current schedule, eleven-thirty A.M. was long past my bedtime.

I stopped by the Doghouse on my way home. The Doghouse is a downtown twenty-four-hour restaurant. Timeworn and unpretentious, with duct-taped patches in the carpet, it's one of my favorite haunts. Wanda, my usual waitress, saw me as soon as I came in. When I gave her a thumbs-up signal, she went straight to the kitchen to place my order for two eggs over easy. She came back to my booth carrying a cup of coffee.

"Why so late for breakfast?" she asked. "Working overtime?"

"A little," I answered, although compared to Tom Riley's, my overtime was hardly worth mentioning.

Wanda disappeared and returned with the

crossword-puzzle section of the newspaper. I don't buy newspapers. It's a matter of honor with me, and since moving out of the Royal Crest, I no longer had a next-door neighbor to save the puzzles for me. Wanda had leaped into the breach. She usually had a couple of them put aside for me whenever I came in.

I worked the puzzle while I ate breakfast. I gave myself a pat on the back when I knew that the eight-letter word starting with an *M* that meant threatening was "minatory" not "menacing." Real devotees of crossword puzzles are virtual fountains of useless information.

With the crossword puzzle completed, I sat drinking my last cup of coffee while I thought about Richard Dathan Morris. Riley's comment about him wanting to be an undercover cop was totally out of character. And then there was that bit about the parties. Riley had said there had been drugs present, but he couldn't remember Morris actually using any of them. Unable to make sense of the jumble of information, I gave up and headed home.

It had been only a month since I moved into my new place, and I still wasn't entirely accustomed to living in Belltown Terrace. Intended to be a building of prestigious downtown condominiums, it had, in the course of near-bankruptcy proceedings, become a mostly luxury rental apartment complex instead. Only a careful reading of the documents would have shown my neighbors that J. P. Beaumont was one of their landlords. I kept a pretty low profile about my belonging to the real estate syndicate that owned the entire building. It was bad enough being the owner of the penthouse.

The elevator ride from the fourth level of the underground parking garage to the twenty-fourth floor of the residential tower is a long one. During the ride I still found myself wondering if I really belonged there. And I never put the key in the lock without a twinge of regret that Anne Corley would never be there to share the apartment with me. After all, she was the one who had paid for it.

The place was still brand-new. It still smelled of new paint, new carpet, and new furniture. I had stowed Mrs. Edwards and the girls in a vacant two-bedroom apartment several stories below. When they were home, the two girls delighted in running up and down the intervening stairwells to visit me. When they were around, they always left behind a comfortable clutter of kid stuff that made me feel more at home and less like I was living in a picture from *House and Garden*.

With the girls gone, the place was too clean, too neat, too empty for me to feel at home. Fighting the refugee blues, I headed straight for my old recliner, which Jim Hunt had grudgingly reupholstered in a handsome, pliable leather. It sat off by itself in a small den that had quickly become my favorite part of the huge apartment.

I sat down and took a deep breath. Sitting there

I'm always tempted to wave at the people on the Space Needle observation deck who, no doubt, peer at me through the pay-to-peek telescopes and the huge panes of floor-to-ceiling glass that form the northern wall of my apartment.

Settling gratefully into the old chair's comfortable contours, I let my eyes go shut. I must have fallen asleep. The next thing I knew, the phone at my elbow was jangling me awake. When I reached to pick it up, I noticed that the answering machine underneath it was blinking vigorously, telling me I had messages.

"Hello," I mumbled.

"Hello," a woman answered. "Detective Beaumont?"

"Yes."

"This is Amy again. Amy Fitzgerald. Did you get my message?"

I glanced guiltily at the blinking light. I hadn't liked the machine at the time my attorney, Ralph Ames, gave it to me. Months later, I still wasn't very good about checking it as soon as I came in.

"No," I mumbled. "I just got home. I haven't taken the messages off the machine." The blinking light told me there were three of them. Not only had I not gotten Amy Fitzgerald's message, I didn't have the vaguest idea who she could be. It was a name I recognized but couldn't place.

"It's about Ron Peters," she added.

That joggled my memory. Amy Fitzgerald was someone from the hospital, someone I had met.

"What about him? There's nothing wrong, is there?" I demanded.

"No, but he wants to see you. Right away."

"Do you know what about?"

"Something about Jasmine. He wouldn't tell me any more than that."

I shook my head in disbelief. "He wants to talk to me about a flower?"

"I don't know, Detective Beaumont. He didn't say, but he begged me to call you. If you could just come over . . ."

"Sure," I told her. "I have to shower first, but I can be there in half an hour."

"Thanks so much, Detective Beaumont. I'll tell him you're on your way."

I hung up the phone and pushed the playback button on my answering machine. One message was from Peters's head nurse, one was from a hospital volunteer, and the third was from Amy Fitzgerald, all of them calling with increasingly urgent messages that Peters wanted to see me right away.

Punching the reset button on the machine, I hauled my aching bones out of the chair. I needed sleep. I was dying to sleep. It was easy for Peters to order me over there on the double. He could sleep any goddamned time he wanted to.

No sooner had the thought washed through my head than I was beating myself up for it. He could sleep, all right, but he couldn't do anything else. He couldn't move his arms enough to hold a telephone or feed himself. He was totally powerless, totally dependent on other people for his every need. The least I could do was go to the hospital when he called.

And I'd better not complain about it either.

So I showered and dressed and dragged my weary butt back into the elevator. When I got out my car keys, I realized I had neglected to replace Peters's postcards from Heather and Tracie in my pocket. I didn't go upstairs to get them.

It was two o'clock straight up and down when I pulled into the parking lot down the street from Harborview Hospital. And it was five minutes after that when I walked into Peters's room on the fourth floor.

"What the hell took you so long?" he grumbled when he saw me.

The physical therapist was standing beside his bed, leaning against the wall with one hand casually in the pocket of her long, white jacket and her medium-length light brown hair swinging freely around a slender face. Amy Fitzgerald. That's who she was.

"Come on, Ron. I told you he said he hadn't showered. It took him less time to get here than he said it would."

She came over and took my hand, shaking it in greeting as she smiled up at me. "Don't pay any attention to him. He's a bit cantankerous at the moment. We're all used to it around here."

Glancing back in Peters's direction, she gave him a small wave. "I'll be back later," she said and walked out of the room.

I turned to Peters. He looked pained. "I guess I'm pretty much of an asshole," he said.

"Don't worry about it," I told him. "Everybody is on occasion. What do you want?"

"They're only here for two nights. I thought you'd want to follow up on it right away."

"Who's here? Follow up on what?" I asked. I didn't know what he was talking about.

"On Jasmine," he replied.

"What's that?"

"You mean you've never heard of her?"

I shook my head. "Never."

Peters sighed. "You're hopeless, Beau. Jasmine Day, the singer."

"What about her?" I still didn't know who she was, but I didn't tell Peters that.

"She's playing the Fifth Avenue. Tonight and tomorrow night. That's the show your victim must have been working on when he was killed, the one he was doing the load-in for. Get the paper, would you? It's there on the tray table."

I picked up a newspaper that had been folded open to the entertainment section. The first thing that caught my eye was a quarter-page ad that said, "Jasmine Day is taking the Fifth Avenue by storm." The ad copy went on to say that tickets were still available for her two Seattle "comeback concerts." Pictured was a woman with a face framed by cascades of long, blonde hair. It was almost a Dolly Parton look, except in certain areas where Jasmine Day was somewhat less endowed than Dolly is.

"Who is she?" I asked.

"A pop singer. Had a great rock career going until she got busted for drugs. She's been a patient in Betty Ford's rehab place down in Rancho Mirage."

"That's why they're calling it a comeback concert?"

"That's right. But maybe Betty Ford's cure didn't take. If memory serves, Jasmine Day was into coke in a big way."

Suddenly it began to make sense to me. So that was the connection—that was why Peters had been so frantic to get hold of me.

"And they're only in town tonight and tomorrow night?"

"That's right. I figured somebody should get cracking on it."

"You called that shot. I'm on my way."

I was impatiently punching the elevator button when Amy Fitzgerald caught up to me in the hallway.

"You're not angry with him, are you?" she asked.

"Of course I'm not."

She breathed a sigh of relief. "I was afraid you would be. It's hard for others to be understanding sometimes when people in Ron Peters's condition are so . . . so imperious," she added finally.

"No. Don't worry about it. It was important."

She smiled then, a warm, engaging smile, just as the elevator stopped and the doors opened. "I was happy about it, really," she said. "It's the first time he's shown any interest in anybody but himself."

The door closed before I could tell her that I wholeheartedly agreed.

CHAPTER 7

THE FIFTH AVENUE THEATER SITS ON THE STREET FOR which it was named, just across from the slender, curved base of the Rainier Bank Tower. The box office was open and doing a brisk business when I got there a few minutes after two.

While I waited in line, I studied the life-size posters of Jasmine Day that were displayed around the ticket booth. Huge black-and-white stills showed a lithesome lady of indeterminate age, wearing a skin-tight dress and singing into a handheld microphone. The way her sultry lips grazed the mike was nothing short of provocative.

"May I help you, sir?" The impatience in the ticket seller's voice jarred me out of my reverie and told me it wasn't the first time she had asked.

"Yes. I'm here to see someone with the show."

"We still have tickets for this evening's performance."

"No; I want to see someone with the show, someone who's in charge."

"You'll have to go to the administrative office, if you want someone important," she said icily. "Next."

The woman standing behind me shouldered her way to the window.

"But where do I go?" I asked.

I watched the ticket seller consider whether or not to tell me where I should go and what I should do when I got there. She finally decided against it and simply answered my question. "Down the street to the building entrance. It'll say Skinner Building. Up on the second floor."

Leaving her to sell tickets in peace, I made my way to the front office, which wasn't nearly as plush as the theater itself. It was old-fashioned, functional, and filled with people who didn't seem particularly interested in helping me. If I wasn't there to buy a ticket, I didn't exist.

Eventually I was shown into a small cubicle where an equally small but much younger public relations type was seated at a desk. He reached across to shake my hand and said his name was Dan Osgood. The fact that my business card said Homicide seemed to make him somewhat nervous. He continued to finger the card the whole time we talked, standing it first on one end and then on the other.

"We're really nothing more than a landlord, Detective Beaumont. Westcoast has rented the place, you know—hired their own crew, brought

in their own musicians. Of course, our people are
selling tickets and doing the concessions, but the
production company takes care of everything
else."

"And that's Westcoast Starlight Productions?"

He nodded. "Out of L.A."

"We found one of the stagehands," I told him
quietly. "About dawn this morning, down by the
Burlington Northern Tunnel."

"Dead?" Dan Osgood asked, paling visibly.

I nodded.

"You don't think it had anything to do with
the theater, do you?"

"That's what we're trying to find out. This guy
was from a union local here in Seattle. We found
his union card. He had a paycheck from Westcoast Starlight Productions in his pocket, and
someone at his house told us he was supposed to
work here the night before he died. Who would
he have been working with?"

"On the load-in? Probably the head carpenter."

"Is he from around here?"

"No. He's with the road crew." Osgood pawed
through a stack of papers on his desk, extracted a
piece of yellow legal paper, and ran his finger
down the sheet.

"The head carpenter's name is Alan Dale."

"Any idea where I could find him?"

Dan Osgood glanced at a clock on the wall.
"He's probably backstage now. The tech crew is
having some trouble."

"Can you take me to him?"

Osgood half rose, then sat back down, eyeing me warily. "Is this going to be in the papers or the news?" he asked.

"Not until after we notify the next of kin," I answered. "That'll probably happen sometime this afternoon."

"You mean the murder will be on the news. I know that, but do you have to mention the Fifth Avenue—by name, I mean?"

"I'm a cop," I reminded him. "I don't write the news. I've got no control over how reporters do their job."

Osgood shook his head. "They'll have a fit, you know." He groaned. "The shit's really going to hit the fan on this one."

"Who'll have a fit?" I asked.

"The board of directors. They're a real conservative bunch, you know. They don't like anything out of line, anything controversial. They were reluctant to book this show in the first place, but I convinced them to go ahead."

"What do you mean, reluctant?"

"They were worried about Jasmine's . . . You know . . ." He paused and looked at me as though expecting me to read his mind.

I shook my head. "Her what?" I asked.

"About her reputation," he added.

"What about it?"

"She used to be a rock star, you know, several years back."

Dan Osgood used "you know" the way some

people use "ah." Actually, I didn't know at all, but I nodded, pretending I did.

"About a year or so ago now, she hooked up with one of the surviving big bands. It's taken a while, but she's gradually making the switch to pop, singing a lot of old-time songs from the thirties, forties, and fifties, cashing in on the baby-boomer nostalgia trip."

"And she's doing all right at it?"

Osgood shrugged, a noncommittal gesture that didn't quite measure up to his public-relations position. I rephrased the question.

"How are ticket sales?" I asked.

"So-so," he replied glumly.

"Not that great?"

He nodded. "I told 'em they'd be better off doing one show on Friday night, but nobody ever listens to me. They insisted on two shows or nothing." He looked at me and brightened. "I could give you a comp," he added. "It's a great seat. Front row center."

Osgood took a ticket out of his top drawer and pushed it across the desk toward me. I looked at it without picking it up.

"This couldn't possibly be construed as a bribe, could it, Mr. Osgood?"

His jaw dropped. "Detective Beaumont, of course not! My job is public relations. I mean, you're going to be there, aren't you, talking to people?"

"I suppose so."

"I just thought it would be easier if you had a

ticket. That way, you could come and go as you pleased."

"You mean without having to show my badge."

He shrugged. "Well, actually, that's right. It would create less of a disturbance."

I couldn't argue with his premise. Having Homicide cops wandering in and out of any event does tend to put a damper on people having fun. I picked up the ticket and shoved it into my jacket pocket.

"All right," I said.

"But you'll keep a low profile during the performance, won't you?" Osgood insisted. "You know, we've got another show tomorrow night, and if there's any trouble . . ."

I put up a hand to silence him. "Trust me," I said. "There won't be any trouble. Now take me to see that carpenter guy—what's his name?"

"Dale. Alan Dale."

Osgood led me through a rabbit warren of stairs and hallways, getting us back to the theater without ever leaving the building or having to walk past the crabby lady in the ticket booth. We entered through a door just off stage right.

The Fifth Avenue was originally one of those huge old movie houses that flourished in the days of studio-held theaters. Over the years it had fallen into disrepair and had been scheduled for demolition until a group of civic- and arts-minded types had gotten together under the banner of saving and refurbishing it. The interior is done in a garish Chinese style complete with huge gilt dragons, equally huge crystal chandeliers, and plush red carpets and seats. If I had gone to all that trouble to decorate in such an overblown, nostalgic style, I wouldn't have wanted to book a show that remotely resembled a rock concert either.

All the theater except the stage itself was shrouded in darkness. Onstage, an almost transparent piece of material with a cityscape painted on it hung halfway to the floor. A man stood underneath, peering up into the cavern above and behind the heavy red curtain, shading his eyes from the bare bulb glare of overhead stage lights. At the front of the stage, several people were busy working on what seemed to be a raised platform built over the stage itself, covering the front of it with pieces of gold foil material.

"Can you get it?" The man in the middle of the stage was speaking into the air above him to someone we couldn't see.

"Almost. Almost. Give me a break," a voice answered.

As we stepped up onto the stage, I, too, peered through the glare of lights to see where the voice was coming from. A man clung to a truss some twenty feet above us. With one hand he held himself in place while with the other he struggled with a complex rope connection of some kind.

"That's Ray Holman, the flyman," Osgood explained to me, pointing to the man on the truss. All the word "flyman" did for me was give rise to a whole series of visions of low-grade science-fiction movies. My blank stare must have registered. "He flies whatever parts of the set have to go up and down," Osgood added.

He turned to the man on the stage. "Alan, this is Detective Beaumont from Seattle P.D. He wants to talk to you."

"People in hell want ice water too," Alan Dale replied without looking away from the man above us.

Osgood glanced fitfully at my card, which he still held. "He's with Homicide. He only wants to talk with you for a few minutes."

Alan Dale turned on him then. Jasmine's head carpenter wasn't a big man, but he was tough. Standing on that undressed, empty stage, he was in his element. This was his territory.

"I don't give a shit where he's from or what he wants. I've got a curtain in a little over five hours. I'm not talking to Saint Peter himself until this son of a bitch of a scrim goes up and down like clockwork. We've still got to reweld the track on the revolve."

With that, his focus returned to the man on the truss. "You got it now, Ray?"

"Close," Ray called down. "Almost."

Dan Osgood stuck his tail between his legs and began to slink away across the stage, but I held my ground. When Alan Dale lowered his eyes to the stage, I was still standing there.

"Look," I said, "you've got a job to do and so do I. One of the stagehands who worked here yesterday was murdered last night. I have to ask you a couple of questions about him, that's all."

"Murdered?" Alan Dale appeared mildly interested. "Which one?"

"His name was Morris."

"Rick Morris, that little creep?"

I nodded. "That's the one."

"He's worked for us before. I felt like murdering him myself," Alan Dale said. "I caught the little shit going through one of the trunks instead of unloading it. I fired his ass on the spot. Gave him his check and told him to hit the road."

"Hey, Alan," Ray called down from up above us. "Stop your jawing and try pulling the rope. I think I finally got 'er."

Alan Dale strode away from me to a wall covered with a mass of block-and-tackle gear. He chose one rope seemingly at random, released it, then gave it a long, hard pull. The transparent curtain rose soundlessly into the air until it stopped smoothly at the bottom of the truss.

"Hot dog! Now if we can just get the worm gear working on that goddamned turntable, we'll be in great shape."

Somehow the flyman made it to the stage floor in far less time than I would have thought possible. Maybe he really could fly, but as he walked past us, beads of sweat covered his forehead. He stopped long enough to wipe his face dry with one grimy sleeve.

"Whoever designed this motherfucker ought

to have to put it up and strike it every other day for the rest of his natural life."

With that, Ray stalked toward the back of the stage, where a golden band shell stood cloaked in semidarkness. When he reached it, he turned and called back to Alan Dale. "You coming or not? Drag that welding lead over here."

"I'll be right there." The head carpenter bent over to pick up a welding lead from the floor in front of him, but a voice, calling his name over a backstage intercom, stopped him before he had taken two steps toward the band shell.

"Alan? Alan, are you there?"

Alan Dale sighed, stopped, and turned toward the speaker that was mounted beside the bank of ropes. "Yeah, Ed. I'm here. Whaddaya need?"

"I'm on my way to see Jasmine. She wants to know if you've got the revolve fixed. Did the parts come?"

Alan glanced back at the band shell. "All except the goddamned clutch. The supplier's out of them. He's trying to find one."

"Can you make it work? We don't want what happened in Portland to happen here."

"I can make it work. It won't be great, but it'll work."

"Good," the man on the intercom replied. "I'll tell her."

With a weary sigh, Alan Dale started once more toward the band shell with me right behind him. He stopped me, shaking his head.

"Look, can't I talk to you later? I'm busier'n a one-legged man at an ass-kicking contest. I could talk during the show or after, since we're doing a two-night stand. But right now . . ."

I could see Alan Dale had a problem. So did I. It was almost time to report in to the department for the beginning of our shift. Big Al and I still hadn't taken care of the notification of next of kin, and that had to take priority. We had let it go far too long as it was.

"Sure, that'll be fine, but one more question before I go. You said Morris was going through a trunk. Do you remember which one?"

"Costumes, I think, but I don't really remember. That's not my job. I told Waverly."

"Who's Waverly?"

He jerked his head in the direction of the intercom. "You said one question. That's two. Ask Osgood." With that, Alan Dale left me and headed off, presumably to work on his revolving band shell.

"Who's Waverly?" I repeated when Dan Osgood slunk back up beside me on the stage.

"Ed Waverly. He's Westcoast's road manager."

"And where would I find him?"

"At the hotel, I guess. He said he was on his way to see Jasmine."

"Which hotel?"

"The Mayflower Park, over on Olive. That's where they're staying. Why? Do you have to see him too?"

"I will eventually, but not right now. First I've got to track down two sets of parents so I can tell them their sons are dead."

A sallow look spread over Dan Osgood's high-brow face. I had meant to shock him, wanted to shock him. I don't know why.

I guess the devil made me do it.

CHAPTER 8

I MET AL AT THE DEPARTMENT AND WE MADE A DASH for the freeway, just minutes ahead of afternoon rush-hour traffic on the Mercer Island Bridge. Doc Baker's office had confirmed Jonathan Thomas's ID with his attending physician. Tom Riley had given us Jonathan Thomas's parents' address and told us that Mr. and Mrs. William B. Thomas lived in Bellevue in an area called The Summit.

No one from downtown should ever try to find an address on the other side of Lake Washington without taking along the essentials—lunch, a map, and a compass, for starters. It's not that it's the boonies—it's the burbs, and suburban planners, with the clever little cul-de-sacs they love, should all draw mazes for kids' magazines. In this case, we only had a map. While Al drove us across the Interstate 90 Bridge, I attempted to locate The Summit on my four-year-old map. It didn't exist.

The address said 16318 Summit Drive, so we took the 148th Street exit and stopped at a gas station to ask directions. The young attendant was as obliging as could be. "Sure," he said, pointing to a clear-cut hilltop with only a few lonely, spindly trees and a smattering of rooftops showing on it. "That's it, right up there."

"How do we get there?" I asked.

He shrugged. "Beats me. I can ask my boss."

The boss, a transplant from some corner of the Middle East, barely spoke English, but he communicated clearly enough that he didn't know where The Summit was, nor did he care.

We retreated to the car and attempted, logically enough, to drive to the place. It seemed straightforward enough, since The Summit was clearly visible to us from where we were. It happens to be one of those places you can't get to from here. Three attempts ended in dismal failure, with us wandering blindly through a series of pricey suburban dead ends. We stopped once more and asked directions of a bathrobe-clad lady out walking a pair of golden retrievers. She wasn't able to help us either. That's one of the mysteries about Bellevue. Nobody knows where anything is or how to get there.

We made one more assault, up 150th. This attempt brought us closer than any of our previous forays, but it ended in a necker's knob turnaround blocked by a wrought-iron electronically operated gate. It was apparent that the road beyond the gate led up to the posh development on top of the hill. While we paused to assess the situation, a lady driving a silver BMW opened the gate and drove out. Before the gate could shut again, Al and I scrambled out of our vehicle and sprinted through the opening.

We found ourselves walking just below the crest of the hill. When we topped it, the view was dazzling. To the north was Mount Baker, to the east the forested hills of Snoqualmie Pass, to the south stood the graceful, snow-covered face of Mount Rainier, and to the west lay Seattle, its buildings surrounded by shimmering water against a background of snow-denuded mountains on the Olympic Peninsula.

Al stopped in his tracks and did a complete 360-degree. "What the hell do you have to pay for a view like this!"

"Plenty," I told him, not adding that my own view from the penthouse in Belltown Terrace wasn't much different from The Summit's.

It turned out we were already on Summit Drive. It curved this way and that, meandering like a country road. Except it wasn't. The place was a beehive of activity, with construction vehicles parked here and there around houses in various stages of completion. A backhoe was noisily digging the footings of one while roofers tacked cedar shakes onto the under-layment covered wooden roof of another. No one challenged us as we sauntered along, looking for 16318.

The house would have been difficult to miss. It was huge, a mansion by any standards, situated on a lot that gave it a commanding view from every room, including, I'm sure, bathrooms and closets. The front porch was ablaze with a collection of brass pots filled with brilliantly blooming plants.

Stepping onto the porch, I rang the bell. A few moments later, the door was opened by a dark-haired young woman wearing a maid's uniform. "Yes?" she said questioningly.

I handed her my card. "We're with the Seattle Police Department," I said. "We'd like to speak to either Mr. or Mrs. Thomas."

"Mrs. Thomas just left," the woman said, gesturing toward the road.

"What about Mr. Thomas? Is he home?"

"Yes, but he's busy."

"This is important," I said. "It's about his son."

"I don't have a son," a voice boomed behind her. The young woman started visibly. "It's all right, Sarah. You may go."

With a compliant nod, Sarah retreated from the open door. We found ourselves peering into a rose marble foyer where a thin, stooped man stood at the foot of a curving stairway. I was surprised to find that the source of that robust voice was this frail-looking old man. I saw at once that there was a remarkable similarity between the now-dead Jonathan and his father, William Thomas. Months of wasting illness had aged the younger man until the two men looked more like brothers than father and son.

William Thomas shuffled toward us, leaning

heavily on a gnarled cane, and looked up at us through bushy gray eyebrows. "Who are you and what do you want?" he demanded.

"We're with Seattle P.D.," I repeated. "We were told that you are Jonathan Thomas's father."

"Was," he corrected bitterly. "No more." He reached out as if to close the door. I caught it with the toe of my shoe and edged into the doorway.

"We're with Homicide, Mr. Thomas. Your son is dead. We came to tell you."

It was a brutal way to break the news, but I wasn't of a mind to be especially kind. You don't find most parents denying their child's very existence when you come to notify them that something has happened to said child.

"Dead?" he asked stupidly. "Did you say dead?"

I nodded. William Thomas reached out a bony hand and grasped my jacket lapel, shaking me with surprising vigor. "Did he repent?" he asked. "Did he pray for forgiveness of his sins?"

"I don't have any idea. I'm sorry."

Thomas turned from me and shuffled away from the door, shaking his head.

"What a waste," he mumbled. "What a terrible, shameful, sinful waste."

We followed him into a magnificent sunlit living room. He sat down at the end of an opulent sofa, using the arm of the couch as well as the cane to ease himself into a sitting position. He was still shaking his head.

"It's God's scourge," he said, reaching for a white Bible that lay on a polished cherrywood end table beside his couch. He moved the book into his lap, stroking it with his hand, letting his fingers trace the pattern of the gold-embossed lettering. "For the wages of sin is death," he continued as though we weren't in the room.

"You knew your son was ill?" I asked.

He started at my question. "Ill? You call that ill? That's not an illness. It's a pestilence, visited on the wicked, on those who have willfully turned their faces from the Lord."

William Thomas looked across the room and stared out the huge window at the expanse of city and mountain at our feet. His rheumy old eyes were reddened, but there were no tears of sadness. His hand, resting on the Bible, trembled with some inner tremor. The old man may have disowned his son, but he wasn't letting him go to the devil without a fight.

"I don't believe Jonathan died of AIDS," I said quietly.

Slowly William Thomas swung toward me, an almost electrical charge of interest crossing his face. It was as if I had thrown him a lifeline. "You what?"

"Detective Lindstrom and I are with the Homicide squad," I said. "We're investigating your son's death as a possible murder."

"You think he was murdered?" Thomas asked.

I nodded. "We'd need you to request an autopsy to verify it, but . . ."

"He didn't die of AIDS?" he asked incredulously, having to verify over and over what I'd said, as if he hadn't quite heard me correctly the first time.

"That's what we think, but because of the nature of your son's illness, the medical examiner is reluctant to do an autopsy. You or someone in your family will have to request it."

Forgotten, the Bible slipped to the floor as the old man used the crook of his cane to pull a telephone within reach. "Who do I call?" he demanded. "I'll do it now. This very minute."

I read him Dr. Wendell Johnson's number. His hand shook violently as he punched the numbers. He sat impatiently, drumming his fingers on the table, as he waited for the call to be answered. "This is Jonathan Thomas's father," he said into the phone.

Evidently, in the space of a minute, Jonathan Thomas was no longer disowned.

"I want to talk to the doctor," William Thomas continued. There was a pause. "That's all right. I'll wait," he said.

While William Thomas sat on hold, an oppressive silence settled over the room. I looked around at the expensive, tasteful furnishings—the gleaming wooden tables; the burnished brocade of the sofa and chairs; the elegant pieces of crystal set here and there; the lustrous, broadleafed plants.

It struck me as ironic that Jonathan Thomas, shut out of this house while he lived, was being welcomed back as a prodigal son only after he was dead. It was a hell of a price to pay. I wondered where, in the Good Book, it said that murder was more acceptable than AIDS.

Maybe it wasn't in the Good Book at all, but it certainly was in William B. Thomas's mind. More macho, maybe, and less dishonorable.

"This is Jonathan Thomas's father," he said again into the phone. "I understand you were treating my son. Yes, yes. I know. Two detectives are here with me now. They said they need an autopsy, that I should call you to request it."

Again there was a pause. "What do you mean, it isn't necessary? It is if I say so, and I want one."

Dr. Johnson used every means at his disposal to attempt to dissuade the old man, but Jonathan's father held on like a bull terrier. From hearing his side of the conversation, it was clear we were offering a cause of death that wasn't AIDS, and William Thomas wasn't letting it out of his grasp.

At last the doctor agreed, and Thomas turned to us in triumph. By then I understood why Jonathan had preferred to spend his last days in a squalid little house on Bellevue Avenue rather than in this sumptuous mansion.

His father was a bigot of the first water.

"They'll do it," Thomas said to us. "Tomorrow morning, probably. Is that soon enough?"

I nodded. "That's plenty of time."

Big Al cleared his throat. "When did you disown your son?" he asked.

William Thomas's eyes shot from me to Al. "Why do you ask that?"

"We're trying to put together a background profile."

The answer evidently satisfied him. "A year and a half ago," he replied. "On Christmas Eve. He said he had something to tell us, that he had to be honest with us. It almost killed his mother. We were better off not knowing."

"Did you know his . . ." I stopped and re-arranged what I was going to say. "Did you know his roommate?"

"Richard? Sure, we knew him. They had been friends, we thought, since college. We didn't have any idea . . ."

"You didn't understand the real nature of their friendship?"

"Absolutely not. Not until that night."

"And what happened?"

"I threw him out of the house, right then."

"This house?"

He shook his head. "A different house. Over in Sahalee. We got rid of it. I couldn't stand to stay there afterward."

"You said you knew about his illness."

"That's why he told us."

"Because he was dying?"

Just then the front door opened and closed. Moments later a middle-aged woman wearing lime green sweats and trendy Reebock running shoes entered the room. Carrying an armload of dry cleaning, she stopped cold when she saw us.

"I didn't know you were expecting anybody," she said.

"I wasn't, Dorothy. Come sit here by me."

He patted the seat next to him. Obediently she came to his side. Dorothy Thomas was a good twenty years younger than her husband. I put her age at about fifty-five, although if she'd had the help of a good plastic surgeon, she might have been older.

"These men are policemen," William Thomas was saying. "They've come to talk to us about Jonathan."

"Jonathan?" Unconsciously, her left hand went to her throat, the huge diamond on her ring finger glittering in the sunlight. "Is something the matter?"

"He's dead," Thomas told her.

She looked into her husband's face, her eyes wide, but she didn't fall apart. She didn't give way to whatever it was she was feeling.

"May God have mercy on his soul," she whispered.

I suspected that God would probably come across with a hell of a lot more Christian charity than either one of Jonathan Thomas's pious parents could muster.

When we finally left, I was relieved to be outside that heartless shell of a house, happy that we had to walk some distance to the car. It gave me a chance to let off steam.

"Could you do that?" Al asked me as we walked.

"Do what? Throw my kid out of the house when I knew he was dying?"

Al shook his head.

"I don't think I could, either," I told him. "Not even if he was as queer as a three-dollar bill."

CHAPTER 9

WHEN WE GOT BACK TO THE DEPARTMENT, WE CON-
tacted the Bellingham police and asked them to
dispatch officers and notify Richard Dathan Morris's mother. Back in our cubicle, I finished my
part of the paperwork and rested my head on my
hands while I waited for Al to complete his.

I closed my eyes for a moment, hoping the fa-
tigue would somehow magically disappear. It
didn't, and for good reason. A glance at the clock
on the wall told me I was well into a second
twenty-four-hour period with no sleep.

"Let's go get some coffee and some food," I told
Al. "In that order. I'm ready to drop."

On the way back downstairs, we stopped off at
the Washington State Patrol crime lab to see what,
if any, progress they were making. My old friend,
Janice Morraine, had been assigned the high-
heeled shoe.

"My preliminary analysis says the blood and hair we found on the shoe match that of the victim. We've taken some prints off the shoe, but no prints with blood on them. The blood has been smeared though."

"The killer was wearing gloves?" I asked.

"Probably. It's a fairly expensive shoe, by the way. Ferragamo, size 8½B. And it's seen some real hard use."

"What kind of shoes?" I asked.

"Ferragamo. They're manufactured in Italy. I've got people tracking the batch number."

"Think you'll have any luck?"

Janice shrugged. "Your guess is as good as mine, but the color is so unusual that I'm hopeful. My source over at Nordstrom says it's possible they're custom-made."

"Anything else?"

"Doc Baker says he discovered some trace evidence on the victim. Some hair. We'll have that tomorrow morning. We also sent investigators back up to the parking lot above where the body was found. They picked up some material, but we don't know yet whether or not it's related."

"You'll keep us posted?"

Janice glowered at me. "Of course not. Everything we find out we're marking top secret and burying in a file drawer! What do you think?"

"Just checking, just checking," I told her.

Big Al and I drove down to the waterfront and elbowed our way through the tourists to Ivar's

Clam Bar. We both ordered clam chowder and coffee. We took our food to the outdoor tables and ate while watching ferry traffic come and go.

"Storm's blowing up," Al commented, sniffing the air.

"How can you tell?"

"Can't you smell it?"

I sniffed, filling my nostrils with creosote-laden salty air that told me nothing. Looking up, I could see both the moon and winking stars.

"You wait and see," Al said. "It'll be raining by morning."

Back at the department there was a call waiting for us from Bellingham. Their officers had been unable to locate Mrs. Grace Simms Morris. Through talking with neighbors, particularly the one who was feeding her parakeet, they had determined that she was out of town. She had taken a short trip down the Oregon coast and was expected to return to Bellingham by Sunday evening at the latest. The neighbor had added that Mrs. Morris would probably stop off in Seattle for a day or two to visit her son.

That information didn't leave Big Al and me much option but to go back to the house on Bellevue Avenue East. As far as we could tell, it was undisturbed. There were no lights, no open doors or windows, nothing to indicate anyone had been there since Tom Riley had taken the cat and abandoned ship.

"You got any bright ideas?" Big Al asked.

"Let's leave a note for her to call us," I suggested.

Al reached for one of his business cards, but I stopped him. "Don't use that. It says Homicide on it." I rummaged through my wallet and found a bank deposit slip with my name and telephone number on it. "We can leave this. If she calls my number and I'm not there, she'll get an answering machine, not the department."

Big Al nodded in agreement. We left a note on the door asking her to call me, nothing more.

We were on our way back down the hill headed for the Fifth Avenue Theater when dispatch came through with an urgent summons for Al. Molly, his wife, wanted him to go with her to Children's Hospital, where their four-year-old grandson had been taken by ambulance for an emergency appendectomy.

Al dropped me off at the theater entrance. The doors were just opening. I flashed the complimentary ticket Dan Osgood, the P.R. man, had given me and was one of the first people inside the lobby. A program hawker was busy unwrapping a stack of programs. I bought one, thinking it might give me a little more in-depth information about the people connected with the show than I would find in the free program provided by the theater.

I tracked down the house manager and told him I wanted to talk with Alan Dale, Ed Waverly, or Dan Osgood. He took my name and ticket location and told me he'd pass along the message. He said he doubted that any of them would have time to see me before the curtain, but that he'd see what he could do. I had no choice but to settle into my front-row center seat, read my programs, and wait for the theater to fill up around me.

The glossy color program consisted mainly of action shots of Jasmine Day, singing and dancing in front of a series of lavish sets and backdrops. The color photos did more to show her vitality than the black-and-whites I had seen earlier outside the theater. Those had been sexy, sultry, inviting. These were also sexy and inviting, but there was a subtle addition, an exuberance and enthusiasm that was somehow lacking in the others.

I read all the bios carefully, particularly those of people whose names I recognized. Alan Dale came from Oakridge, Oregon. His credits were primarily in drama, both off and on Broadway. This was his fifth show with Westcoast Starlight Productions.

Ed Waverly, the director and road-show manager, had been with Westcoast for a number of years. He originally had been with the New York City Ballet as a dancer, choreographer and director before signing on with the Westcoast company.

I read Jasmine Day's bio with special interest. She had been born in Jasper, Texas, a town only some fifty miles from Beaumont, where my own father was born. For years I had threatened to go to Texas and track down my father's people and let them know of my existence, but I had never gotten beyond the map-studying stage. That was how I knew about Jasper, Texas, and that was *all* I knew about Jasper, Texas.

The article said Jasmine had begun her career by singing in church and Sunday school and had gone on to become a rock star. Now she had moved away from her rock background and was hitting the big time again, only this time in an adult, easy-listening format. I thumbed through the book again, studying the pictures closely. I didn't know about the easy-listening part, but she sure as hell was easy on the eyes.

The theater was gradually filling up and the house manager still hadn't come back with a message for me. I finally got up and went looking for him, entering the plush lobby just as the lights blinked their five-minute curtain warning. When I found him, he was behind a counter, busy passing out hearing-aid equipment to a group of blue-haired little old ladies. I waited in line impatiently until he finished with the LOLs.

"Remember me?" I asked when I finally reached the counter.

"Of course I remember you, Mr. Beaumont. I took your message backstage, but they're all up to their eyeballs right now. They said they'd try to see you during intermission, after the show, or tomorrow sometime."

They could stall me, they could put me off, but they wouldn't get rid of me. "I'll try intermission," I told him, but he didn't hear me. He was already turned to the next person in line and was reaching down to lift the equipment to the counter.

I hurried back to my seat. To my surprise, the cavernous theater was only a little over half full, but the audience was far different from what I expected. Dan Osgood's and the bio's descriptions of Jasmine Day as a rock-star-gone-pop had led me to believe I'd be rubbing shoulders with black-clad, spike-haired, rock-loving punks. Instead, I found myself seated among well-dressed, lavender-haired ladies, some of them escorted by dutiful but mostly bored husbands, with nary a black leather jacket in sight.

The curtain was just going up as I sat down. The opening act was an impressionist who billed himself as PeeWee Latham. He did a creditable job of imitating all the presidents from FDR to Reagan. His material was good enough to tickle the funny bones and occupy the interest of his over-the-hill audience, but when he started wandering through Hollywood personalities, he lost me. Sitting still in the warm theater combined with my loss of sleep to put me under, I faded into a nodding stupor.

I was too far gone to force myself awake as applause escorted PeeWee off the stage. I continued to doze, dimly aware that the orchestra I couldn't see had struck up an enthusiastic overture. The music was a comfortable mixture, made up of bits and snatches of old, familiar tunes. It lulled me further down into my restful slumber.

A crash of cymbals at the end of the overture made my eyes snap open abruptly.

Around me, the theater was completely dark,

with only the green exit signs glowing dimly near the doors. Suddenly, a splash of blinding spotlight illuminated the center of the stage.

The cityscape scrim I had seen earlier in the day covered the stage, and in front of it, captured in a brilliant circle of spotlight, stood a woman with her back to the audience, a woman in a long satin, nearly backless, dress. A vivid, vibrantly blue, dynamite dress.

Long blonde hair fell in casual ripples across bare shoulders. She stood there in a provocative, sway-hipped stance, her body undulating gently in tune to the music. A microphone was cradled lightly in one hand, and her arms hung loosely at her sides.

She was wearing gloves—long, white gloves that ended well above her elbows. One slim, well-formed leg was thrust out from a long slit up the side of the satin skirt, and her toes were tapping in time to the beat. She was wearing heels, incredibly high, shiny black spike heels.

Jasmine Day had yet to turn to face her audience, but already I, along with every other red-blooded male in the audience, grasped that she was a very beautiful woman. There was an almost palpable sucking in of middle-aged paunches and a visible straightening of shoulders as the men in the audience came to full attention.

The orchestra's introduction ended. With cat-like grace, Jasmine Day swung around to face us, her motions fluid and easy. Raising the microphone to her lips, she began a sultry rendition of

Frank Sinatra's hit "My Way." She sang with the mike almost against her lips, yet there was no fuzzing of the consonants. Her voice had a bell-like clarity and a resonance that made every word, every syllable fully understandable, even in that cavernous auditorium.

As she sang, the mane of her blonde hair framed her face, shifting and shimmering under the stage lights. Her eyes, a wide, opaque blue, never seemed to blink. The dress, a wonder of engineering, clung to every curve of her body, with no visible means of support except those shapely curves themselves. I was close enough to the stage to note that the golden tan on her legs was smooth, bare skin, not nylon. There was no hint of panty line under the sleek material of her dress.

She stood on the stage with her legs spread as far as the taut material of her skirt allowed, belting out the song as though her very life depended on it, pouring herself into the music until she and it were one. When that song finished, it was as though the audience had been holding its collective breath. Around me people broke into ecstatic applause. This was the kind of music they had paid good money to hear, and Jasmine Day was giving them their money's worth.

The performance was electrifying. Jasmine Day danced and sang, her voice swelling over the sixteen-piece band that backed her. Each song was accompanied by sets that, through Alan Dale's technical wizardry, flowed on and off stage without a pause or hitch.

The first act was pure pleasure for me. Unfortunately, pleasure isn't my business. When the curtain came down for intermission, it was time for me to go to work.

I headed backstage. A security guard stopped me before I even made it to the top of the steps.

"No one's allowed back here."

I was attempting to talk my way around him when Dan Osgood appeared behind the security guard's shoulder.

"It's all right," Osgood said. "You can let him through."

Grudgingly, the guard let me pass.

"Thanks," I said to Osgood.

I had spotted Alan Dale and several other people near the band shell. As I started in that direction, Osgood fell into step beside me.

"Enjoying the show?" he asked. I nodded. "She's something else, isn't she?" he continued.

"Better than I expected."

Osgood was still congratulating himself on his good taste when we reached the turntable. The band shell sat like a gigantic wedding cake, balanced on what seemed to be a single metal leg that disappeared into the raised wooden platform beneath it. Alan Dale was walking around the turntable checking the bolts underneath, followed by a slightly built, balding man. I recognized Ed Waverly from his picture in the program.

"You're sure it'll work?" Waverly asked.

Alan Dale stopped and turned on him, looking

as though he wanted to bash Waverly over the head with his wrench.

"Look, Ed," Dale said with an air of forced tolerance. "I told you it would work, and it will. This'll do for tonight and tomorrow. The clutch will be waiting for us when we get to Vancouver. We can fix it when we do the load-in there. Meantime, we're leaving the safety plate off so if something does go wrong with the track, it won't be so hard to fix it."

I turned to Osgood. "That's Ed Waverly, right?"

Osgood nodded. I turned back, intending to introduce myself to the road-show manager, but he was already halfway across the stage. Instead I caught Alan Dale's eyes. "Can you talk to me now?"

"How about tomorrow morning?" he asked. "Say ten-thirty or so at the Mayflower?"

There was no point in alienating him. "Sure," I said and went looking for Waverly. I was too late. He'd already gone back out front, where there were people waiting for him. Frustrated, I decided to try talking to Jasmine Day herself.

To my surprise, I discovered that once I was backstage, no one questioned my presence or my reason for being there. I wandered off toward the dressing rooms. There was a small common area where the musicians were already lounging. I made my way through the crush to a door with a removable plastic nameplate that said, in an elegant script, *Jasmine Day*. I knocked.

"Who is it?"

I opened the door. Inside, Jasmine Day had changed from the blue dress into a black silk jumpsuit. She was standing with one foot on the seat of a chair, lacing up a high-topped boot that ended just below her knee. She glanced at me over her shoulder and returned to the boot.

"If it isn't Sleeping Beauty," she said.

"I beg your pardon?" Thinking she must be speaking over my shoulder to someone else, I glanced behind me. No one was there.

She finished lacing the second boot and turned toward me, tying and smoothing a heavy gold belt around her waist.

"Call it morbid curiosity," she said, sauntering past me. She walked up to a light-studded dressing-room mirror, wiped a smudge of mascara from her cheek, and applied a fresh coat of lipstick.

"I don't understand," I said.

"Oh?" she replied, checking the line of lipstick. "You're sitting in one of the road manager's comps, front-row center. Divine right of kings and all that. I always check during PeeWee's act to see what I'm going to be stuck with after the show. I checked on you, just before I went on. You were sawing logs."

An embarrassed flush crept up my ears. She saw it and laughed.

"You're blushing. This the first time you've been caught sleeping in a theater?"

Before I could answer, there was a knock on the door behind me. It swung open, narrowly missing me. I moved out of the way. A stagehand stuck his head into the dressing room. "Five minutes, Miss Day," he said.

She nodded and turned back to me. "So who are you?" she asked. "An old crony of Ed Waverly's?"

I had been reaching for one of my cards. I dropped it, letting it fall back into my jacket pocket.

"I know Dan Osgood," I replied.

She shrugged and gave me an openly appraising once-over. "Well, at least you're under seventy and not half bad-looking, for a change. So where are you taking me for dinner?"

That caught me off guard. Dinner? The flush got worse. My nose probably could have glowed in the dark. I didn't remember mentioning dinner.

"It's a surprise," I mumbled, amazed by my own quick thinking. Being around beautiful women usually paralyzes both my tongue and my brain, in that order.

She laughed aloud at that. "I like surprises," she said. There was another quick knock on the door. "I've gotta go," she added, darting past me on her way out of the room. She paused momentarily with her hand on the doorknob.

"What's your name?"

"Beaumont. J. P. Beaumont. My friends call me Beau."

She smiled. "All right, Beau. Pick me up at the hotel about half an hour after the show."

She hurried out and left me standing there in the dressing room, feeling like I'd just been picked up and put down by a very selective tornado. I looked around me. The blue dress was slung carelessly over a brass-framed dressing screen. Two black shoes lay side by side in front of the screen, discarded and forgotten where Jasmine Day had hastily kicked them off.

Behind me, the door opened and a woman almost as wide as the doorway itself marched purposefully into the room. She took one look at me and stopped cold. "What the hell do you think you're doing, mister?" she demanded.

"I was just . . ."

She waddled over to me and stuck her face close to mine. "You were just nothing! Get out of here before I call the cops."

I got moving. She didn't have to tell me twice.

CHAPTER 10

THE NAP I HAD TAKEN DURING PEEWEE LATHAM'S ACT now served me in good stead. I didn't sleep at all during the second act. Neither did anybody else.

The act opened with the revolving band shell turning and moving forward just to the right of center stage, bearing with it the sixteen-piece backup orchestra.

From the other side of the stage, a golden grand piano moved smoothly to center stage. On it, draped in a lush blues singer pose, lay Jasmine Day.

From the moment she appeared, Jasmine had the audience's rapt attention. The skin-tight jumpsuit revealed everything and nothing. No hint of excess flesh wiggled under the sleek material. When she slid gracefully off the piano to sing her second number, she looked ten feet tall and bulletproof. It was funny; she hadn't seemed nearly that tall or imposing when she was standing next to me in her dressing room.

Jasmine was nothing short of a human dynamo. She threw every ounce of her body and being into the songs she sang, and the audience loved it. Halfway through the set though, in a distinct change of pace, she brought out a simple wooden stool and sat down to talk.

She told us how glad she was that her stay at Betty Ford's rehabilitation center had given her a chance to shake the drugs that had been destroying both her life and her career and how grateful she was for the enthusiastic response audiences all over the country were giving her new show. This show. The one she was sharing with us.

It was a homey little chat, relaxed and ingenuous, and it accomplished just what it was calculated to do: it put an already friendly audience even more squarely in Jasmine Day's corner. J. P. Beaumont included.

I'll confess that my mind wandered a little near the end of the show. I was worried about where I'd take Jasmine Day for dinner and how I'd explain my relationship with Dan Osgood if the question came up. I'm still not sure why I was so reluctant to tell her I was a cop. In retrospect I chalk it up to male pride, to wanting to preserve the illusion that she was going with me by choice rather than by necessity as a side effect of my job.

As soon as the curtain rang down for the last time, I dashed home to change clothes before the appointed meeting with Jasmine Day. I made two phone calls from my apartment. One was to the department, leaving word for Al, if he called in from the hospital, that I was going on surveillance and would be in touch with him later. I didn't divulge the exact nature of that surveillance. Call it a sin of omission.

The other call was to the Canlis Restaurant up on Aurora Avenue. I made a late dinner reservation for two.

After a hasty shower, I put on clean clothes and was in front of the Mayflower Park Hotel just at ten-thirty.

The Mayflower Park isn't one of Seattle's brand-name hotel giants. It's smaller and more personal than the Sheratons and Westins of the world. In the course of the last few years, it has been totally refurbished, making it long on quality but without quite the snob appeal of some of the other downtown hotels.

I walked inside the cool, brick-floored lobby and liked what I found. The lobby was comfortably furnished and quiet except for the occasional sound of muted laughter that drifted in from Oliver's, the candlelit hotel lounge off to the right of the registration desk.

An efficient young desk clerk greeted me cheerfully.

"Jasmine Day," I said.

"Oh, are you Mr. Beaumont?" the clerk asked.

"Yes."

"Miss Day left word for you to go on up to her

room. Sixth floor. To the right after you step off the elevator and all the way to the end of the corridor."

As I stepped into the elevator I felt like an imposter, as if I had no right to be there, but Jasmine was the one who had assumed we were going to dinner. I decided my best strategy was to shut up and enjoy it.

I knocked on the door at the end of the corridor. It was opened by Jasmine Day herself. She was wearing a variation on a man's white racer-backed tee shirt, except that it had an intricate rhinestone design bordering the neck and shoulders. The shirt came down to her knees and was cinched in just above her hips by a loose-fitting gold lamé belt.

Her long legs were encased in a pair of very close-fitting tights that ended just above well-formed ankles. Her shoes, three-inch hooker heels, were made of delicate gold lamé straps.

Jasmine Day tossed her head impatiently, loose blonde hair shimmering across her shoulders. "Well, are you going to come inside, or are you going to stand out there gawking all night?"

Hastily I went inside. "Sorry, I didn't mean to be rude."

Jasmine Day shut the door behind her. She leaned against it for a fraction of an instant looking up at me. "That's all right," she said resignedly. "I suppose I should be used to it by now."

Briskly, she walked past me into the room. Near the window was a seating area made up of two plush apricot chairs and a matching couch. Between them, on a glass coffee table, sat a single cup of coffee. She picked it up and took a sip, studying me carefully over the rim of the cup.

"So you're a friend of Dan Osgood's," she said noncommittally.

I made no reply to her comment. I glanced around the room uneasily. It was evidently a suite. There was nothing in sight that remotely resembled a sleeping area. A round conference table in one corner was buried beneath several bouquets of flowers as well as a basket of fruit and an unopened bottle of champagne.

"Fans," she explained. "I guess they enjoyed the show."

She had finally given me a conversational opening I figured I could handle. "So did I," I ventured. "You throw everything you've got into your performance."

"Not everything," she said evenly. "There are some things I hold back."

The coffee cup rapped sharply against the glass-topped table as she set it down. "That's why I wanted to talk to you here before we went to dinner."

She motioned me toward the unoccupied chair opposite her. I moved mechanically toward the chair, conscious of her unblinking eyes riveted on my face, aware of the almost hypnotic effect her voice had on me.

"We have to go over the ground rules," she said quietly.

"Over what?"

"The ground rules." She smiled, seeming to enjoy my obvious discomfort. "You see, every so often the guys who end up with Ed Waverly's comp tickets think it's a package deal, that if we go to dinner, I'll be dessert."

"Miss Day, I . . ."

She held up a hand, effectively silencing me. "So this is what we'll do. We'll go have a quiet little dinner someplace. You talk and I'll listen, or vice versa. Then you bring me back here and I'll come up to my room alone, all right?"

"Right," I said, nodding in agreement.

Jasmine Day smiled brightly in return, revealing a dazzling array of perfectly formed, straight white teeth. "Good," she said, "but just in case you forget, there's one more thing I should mention."

"What's that?"

"There's a brown belt hanging in my closet. It doesn't have anything to do with my wardrobe."

It was a moment or two before her hands-off-or-else meaning soaked into my thick skull, but I finally got the picture.

"Let's go, then," I said abruptly, getting up. "Our dinner reservation is for ten forty-five. The kitchen closes at eleven-thirty."

As we rode down in the elevator, Jasmine Day casually reached out a hand and took my arm. I suddenly felt as if I was caged up with a lioness who had momentarily sheathed her claws. It didn't improve my already limited ability as a conversationalist.

"So what do you do, Mr. Beaumont?" she asked.

For whatever reason, I still didn't want to tell her I was a cop. "I work for the city," I hedged somewhat lamely.

We were outside near the car by then. "You must be doing all right," she commented, idly running a finger along the edge of the Porsche's open sunroof while she waited for me to unlock the door.

"Not bad," I replied.

It was small-talk time, and I've never been good at small talk. Instead, I concentrated on driving. I put the 928 through its paces, cruising down Olive and up Sixth Avenue to Aurora, skimming through traffic lights just as green turned amber.

As we glided effortlessly up the long, steep hill on Aurora, I glanced in Jasmine Day's direction. Her face was impassive in the intermittent glow of streetlights.

"Do you always drive this fast?" she asked.

I eased up slightly on the accelerator. "Not always. Only when I'm nervous."

She laughed then, a lighthearted, breezy laugh. "So I make you nervous? That's refreshing for a change. Most men think they're God's gift to women."

I turned off Aurora into the Canlis Restaurant's covered portico, where valet-parking attendants were eager to assist us. Two young men in white lab coats leaped to open our doors. One relieved me of my keys in exchange for a ticket, while the other gave Jasmine Day a hand getting out of the car. I was fully conscious of the envious looks that followed us through the door.

Once inside, we were shown to a small candlelit table next to a window. A waiter appeared almost as soon as we were seated. Cautioning us that the kitchen would be closing in less than forty-five minutes, he suggested that we order our food at the same time we ordered drinks.

Jasmine opted for straight tonic while I asked for a MacNaughton's and water. We ordered Canlis salad, prepared at our table, and Hawaiian grilled steaks, medium rare. When the waiter left with our order, Jasmine turned her attention to the window.

"What's the big black spot down there?"

"Lake Union," I said, looking out and down at the dark smudge of unlit water with its border of reflected lights. Off to the left we could see the northern tip of the Aurora Bridge, while in the other direction, toward the east, headlights winked across the I-5 span at the far end of the lake.

I played tour guide. "The bridge you see way down there, the tall one, is where the freeway crosses the Montlake Cut. That leads into Lake Washington. Have you ever been in Seattle before? Do you know anything about it?"

She turned away from the window and rested her chin on her hand, regarding me seriously. "I did a concert at the Coliseum once, back in the old days. I opened for The Living Dead. Ever hear of them?"

I shook my head.

"That doesn't surprise me. The band broke up several years ago after the drummer OD'd and the lead singer got sent up for dealing."

The waiter returned to place our drinks in front of us. Jasmine Day remained silent until he was well out of earshot. "I guess I'm lucky that I lived long enough to grow up. A lot of the singers and musicians I started out with didn't make it this far."

I took a sip of my drink and leaned back in my chair, wondering how old she was. Thirty maybe, if that. "How did you get out of Jasper?" I asked.

She smiled, a quick, amused smile. "I started out singing solos in the First Baptist Church when I was seven years old. I've got a whole flock of relatives back in Texas who'd be more than happy to tell you that it's been all downhill ever since. They're convinced I'm going to hell in a handbasket."

"Are you?"

She shrugged. "Maybe. Anyway, Mary Lou Gibbons sang her heart out at weddings and funerals and potluck dinners and saved her money so she could get the hell out of Jasper."

"And you're Mary Lou Gibbons, of course," I said.

"You bet. Little Miss Goody-Two-Shoes. Or at least that's who I was supposed to be. I sang hymns in church. I taught myself rock out in the garage where nobody could hear me. When I was sixteen, I bought myself a one-way ticket to New York."

"And the rest is history."

She nodded. "That's right."

The waiter returned, pushing a cart with the salad ingredients carefully assembled on it. Next to a large wooden bowl lay a copy of the souvenir program from Jasmine Day's concert. The waiter leaned close to her.

"Excuse me, madame," he said apologetically, "but the woman over there wanted me to ask if you would mind autographing her program. She said they've just come from your show and she loved it."

"I'd be delighted," Jasmine said, picking up the program. She nodded slightly in the direction of the lady three tables away, who gave her a tiny, self-conscious wave.

The waiter handed Jasmine a pen. She thumbed through the program until she found her picture. Then, instead of signing it, she got up, walked over to the table, and chatted with her embarrassed but delighted fan. Jasmine signed her name with an expansive flourish and returned the program to its owner.

Meanwhile, watching the transaction, I took a long pull on my MacNaughton's and wondered what the hell I was doing there.

Jasmine returned to the table smiling. "It's always nicer if you can sign it to them personally," she said.

The waiter was obviously conscious of Jasmine's attention as he created our salads. There was an almost electric sensuality about the lady, and the waiter was no more immune to it than I was.

"So how did Mary Lou Gibbons become Jasmine Day?" I asked, once the waiter had served our individual salads and walked away.

"On my back."

It was a no-nonsense reply, and it left no room for misinterpretation. It caught me off guard, with a mouthful of salad. A large piece of romaine lettuce went down the wrong way and stuck crosswise in my throat. I choked and coughed, trying to jar it loose.

"I take it that's not a career path you approve of," she said mockingly.

I didn't say anything in return because I still couldn't talk.

"I slept my way to the top once," she said quietly and added in a determined tone, "This time, I'm doing it right."

That statement was open to interpretation, but I didn't have nerve enough to ask.

CHAPTER 11

TIRED AS I WAS, WITH THE LENGTH OF TIME I'D GONE without sleep, drinking even one MacNaughton's was a big mistake. Drinking two was downright stupid. Halfway through the meal, the drinks hit me. Hard.

My mind wandered. It was all I could do to hold up my head, to say nothing of my end of the conversation.

Jasmine didn't seem to mind. In fact, I don't think she even noticed. I did my best to listen while she talked.

It was as though someone had pulled a plug and her life's story came tumbling out. She told me anecdotes about growing up in the conservative confines of Jasper, Texas. There were tales of some of her wilder exploits from the heavy-metal rock days. She also told me about her six-week stay at Rancho Mirage.

I was doing my best to listen, concentrating on

every word, but eventually my eyes must have glazed over.

She stopped abruptly. "Am I boring you?" she demanded.

"No, not at all. I didn't sleep last night. I just hit the wall."

She started to push back her chair. The waiter, hovering solicitously nearby, hurried to pull it out for her and help her to her feet. "Let's go then," she said.

I guess there's a certain similarity between being drunk and being uncoordinated. If the truth be known, I was probably a little of both. As we walked toward the door, I misjudged the height of a carpeted step, tripped, and almost fell. Eventually I righted myself and went on with as much dignity as I could muster, but I was aware of the questioning glance Jasmine Day cast over her shoulder in my direction.

Outside the almost deserted restaurant, my Porsche sat waiting by the door, its powerful engine purring contentedly under the hood. As I handed the attendant my parking ticket and a tip, Jasmine walked to the driver's door and got in. She was sitting there with both hands resting easily on the steering wheel when I turned to get in.

"Hey, what's this?"

She leaned out the window and smiled up at me. "I make it a point never to ride with someone who's had too much to drink."

The trio of parking attendants were observing this small drama with undisguised amusement.

Rather than make it worse, I clamped my mouth shut, walked around to the other side of the car, and got in. If Jasmine Day really did have a brown belt hanging in her closet, there was no sense arguing with her about it. I had no intention of fighting her for the keys.

I slammed the passenger's door shut just as she finished readjusting the seat. Considered in retrospect, maybe Jasmine was right and I was drunk, because that capable action on her part plucked me good. It had taken me months to master all eight of those goddamned complex seat controls.

Instantly I wasn't the least bit sleepy anymore. Or drunk either, for that matter. I sat there doing a slow burn while blood pounded angrily in my temples. Who the hell did she think she was, assuming that I was drunk! Where did she get off, taking away my car keys! Driving my car!

"Which way do we go?" she asked.

Tersely, I directed her out of the parking lot, around the winding underpass that goes under the south end of the Aurora Bridge, and back up the hill to southbound Aurora Avenue.

"You're not a very happy drunk," she commented mildly.

"I'm not drunk, I'm tired," I snapped, noticing all the while that she drove my Porsche with disgusting competence.

"Drunk or tired, either way you shouldn't be driving. Where are we going?"

"The ground rules, remember? Back to your hotel."

"Rules were made to be broken," she replied.

I was still mulling over that enigmatic remark when she asked, "Where do you live?"

We were just turning right off Aurora onto Wall. I pointed toward Belltown Terrace, its late-night high-rise lights winking above the surrounding smaller buildings. Instead of turning left onto Fifth Avenue, which would have taken us directly back to the Mayflower, Jasmine headed down Wall toward Belltown Terrace.

Grudgingly, I directed her through the zigzag maze necessitated by downtown Seattle's one-way traffic grids. She eased the Porsche through the parking-garage doors, down the series of ramps, and into its assigned parking space without missing a beat.

So Jasmine Day had driven a Porsche before. Big deal!

With the car safely tucked away, Jasmine switched off the motor and dropped the car keys into my outstretched hand.

"I had fun tonight," she said quietly. "Thanks."

I grunted in reply and got out of the car.

"May I walk you to your door?" she asked.

I'm from the old school. The tables were turning a little too much, and I didn't like it. "How come?" I answered stiffly. "Do I look as if I need it?"

"Maybe," she answered, grinning.

I shrugged. "Suit yourself," I said. "We'll call you a cab from my apartment." It was hardly an engraved invitation.

We stopped in front of the locked door that opens into the garage-level elevator lobby, where I proceeded to fumble incompetently with my keys.

"You know," she said. "I think I like you. You're an interesting combination of old-fashioned machismo with just a hint of an ego problem."

I finally managed to insert my key in the lock and turned to look at her as I pushed the door open. She was grinning up at me. Not smiling—grinning. Impishly. I looked away and punched the Up elevator button.

The elevator doors slid open and we got in. It's a hell of a long way from P-4 to the twenty-fourth floor when you've got less than nothing to say. I glared at the pattern in the carpet so I wouldn't have to talk to her or look at her. I was sure she was laughing at me, and I didn't know what to do about it.

"Penthouse?" she asked as the elevator door opened on my floor to let us out.

I nodded.

"You never mentioned that before," she said.

"You didn't ask."

We went inside the apartment. As I reached to turn on the lights, I noticed the red message light on my answering machine was blinking furiously. I was torn between ignoring it and playing back the recorded calls. I chose to ignore it. Jasmine and I didn't know one another well enough for her to listen in on my messages.

Jasmine walked through the spacious living room to the wall of windows, where she stopped to look down. One of the windows was open. Twenty-four stories below, at the rear of the building, a few late-night cars were visible both on First Avenue and on Broad. We could hear them too, but only distantly. She turned from the window and examined the room, nodding in transparent approval.

"This is very nice," she said. "Quiet too. Not exactly the Kmart school of interior design."

I didn't know if that was a compliment or if she was making fun of me. "Glad you like it," I said.

Moments later Jasmine Day solved my answering-machine dilemma by asking to use the bathroom. I directed her down the hall to the first door on the right. As soon as the bathroom door shut behind her, I made a dash for my machine.

The first few calls were hang-ups. I skipped over those. Then there was a call from Al Lindstrom, saying that although the surgery on his grandson was over, there had been complications and he would probably be at the hospital most of the night. In other words, I shouldn't expect to see him at work on Friday.

Al's message was followed by several more hang-ups. Then there was a call from Peters. His voice sounded as if he was talking to me from the bottom of a tin can, and he said he'd call back in the morning.

Finally, at the very end, a woman's voice came

on the machine. Her words were clipped and impatient. "Mr. Beaumont, this is Grace Simms Morris. Since you left a message for me to call, the least you could do is be there to answer your phone. I've tried several times. Now I'm going to bed. I had planned to stay with my son, but he must be out of town. I'm at the Executive Inn tonight. Room 338. If I don't hear from Richard by noon, I'll be going on home to Bellingham late tomorrow afternoon."

I scribbled some notes on a pad I keep near the phone. After stuffing the notes in my jacket pocket, I pushed the erase button, leaned back in my chair, and closed my eyes to listen to the soft whir of the machine.

Wind blowing in my face woke me up. A forerunner of Big Al's promised storm, a stiff breeze was blowing in off Puget Sound through the still-open window. The lights in the room were turned off, but as I got up to close the window and go to bed, my way was lit by the hazy glow of moonlight reflected off low-hanging clouds.

Half asleep, I tried to remember exactly how the evening had ended. Had I ever called for a cab to send Jasmine Day back to the Mayflower Park Hotel? Had I turned out the lights, or had she?

I shed my tie, jacket, and shoulder holster, leaving them hanging, in that order, on a chair at the dining-room table. I kicked off my shoes and padded down the hall in my stocking feet. After stopping off briefly in the bathroom, I stripped and headed gratefully for bed. The red numbers on my clock radio said 3:45 as I slipped my feet under the covers.

"So you finally decided to come to bed," a voice said softly.

The mattress dipped slightly as someone on the other side of my king-size bed turned toward me.

If I were ever going to have a heart attack, it would have been then, that very moment. I had thought I was totally alone in my apartment—I wasn't. Someone was there, not only in my apartment but in my bed.

Jumping to my feet, I frantically groped behind me, fingers searching blindly for the switch on the bedside lamp. At last I found it. With a click, the room was awash in light.

On the other side of the bed, leaning sleepily on one elbow, was Jasmine Day, or at least someone who looked vaguely like Jasmine Day. Her long, blonde hair was gone. The lady in my bed had hair cut as short as a 1950s crewcut.

"What happened to your hair?" I croaked.

Jasmine gestured toward the dresser. I looked. There, indeed, was the familiar mane of blonde hair, perched on what I recognized as the silver cocktail shaker from my bar.

"What are you doing here?" I demanded.

"Waiting for you," she answered. "I figured you'd come to bed eventually. Do you want to get into bed or not?"

Suddenly self-conscious, I got into bed and pulled the covers up to my chin. I lay there, holding the covers with a death grip, staring up at the ceiling.

"You asked about my hair. Does it shock you?"

I glanced over at her without answering. She was lying on her belly, chin resting on her arms, with the golden curve of one naked breast pressed hard against the firm surface of the mattress.

"When I was in the seventh grade back in Jasper, one of the kids in our class, Bruce Cantwell, got cancer. The treatment made all his hair fall out. I came up with the brainy idea that everybody else in class should shave their heads. I was the only one who actually did it. My mother pitched a fit. She made me wear a wig until it grew out. For a long time, I forgot how good it felt to wear my hair that short.

"Last year, while I was in treatment, I remembered. So I cut my hair off. It's like a disguise now. People expect me to look a certain way. When I go out without a wig, no one knows who I am. I get my anonymity back. I can walk down the street and be Mary Lou Gibbons and nobody knows who's there."

She moved toward me on the bed. "Are you mad that I'm here?"

"Surprised," I answered.

"So you don't mind?"

I was smart enough to see that any reply I might give to that question would be treacherous, so I kept quiet. Her hand reached out, tentatively touching my shoulder. A solid sheet of gooseflesh spread from her fingertips over the entire length of my body.

She inched closer to me. Now I could feel the warm, supple softness of her body against mine, hip to hip, breast nudging gently against a rib. I was conscious of the noisy thump-a-thump of my own heartbeat. I turned to look at her. Jasmine Day's finely molded face was only inches from mine, her blue eyes intense and watchful in the bright light while her fingers traced an absentminded pattern on my upper arm.

"Maybe I'm nothing but a sexist at heart," she continued, smiling a little. "I'm used to being pursued. If a man wants me, I don't want him. It's as simple as that. I'm not used to being sent packing in a cab."

Deftly, she pried the covers loose from my fingers, lay my arm flat on the bed, then nuzzled into the curve of my neck.

"Besides," she murmured, her lips grazing the sensitive skin over my collarbone, "I wanted to get to know you better."

And so she did. It took a little encouragement on her part, but eventually I rose to the occasion.

Jasmine Day didn't seem to have any complaints.

Neither did I.

CHAPTER 12

IT SEEMED ONLY MOMENTS LATER WHEN I OPENED MY eyes, drawn awake by the smell of newly made coffee. Jasmine Day, wearing nothing but one of my oversized shirts, stood beside the bed holding a tray. On it sat a coffeepot and two clean cups.

"How do you like your coffee?" she asked.

"Black and strong."

"Good," she said. "Me too."

Holding the tray level, she eased her way back into bed and settled against the pillow I held up for her. She filled the two cups and handed one to me.

"Good morning," she said.

For a time we said nothing else. We each sat there with our respective cups in hand, thinking our own private thoughts. It's tough going to bed with a stranger. There's nothing much to talk about the next morning when you wake up.

I stole a furtive glance at her. Without makeup,

Jasmine Day's eyelashes, eyebrows, and short hair were all the same tawny golden color, the texture of the individual hairs fine and delicate. No, I decided, there was nothing masculine about the haircut. It showed off the fine molding of her smooth skull and accented the firm set of her chin and high cheekbones. There was nothing dykish about Jasmine Day's looks any more than there had been anything dykish about her behavior in bed a few hours earlier.

"It's raining," she said suddenly.

The sound of her voice startled me. I jumped, slopping some of the hot coffee on my bare chest. I mopped it up with a corner of the sheet. She watched me do it.

"Am I still making you nervous?"

"You'd better believe it."

She laughed. "Well, I won't for very much longer. I'm scheduled to do two talk shows today. We tape one this morning and do a live one this afternoon. I've got to go back to the hotel to get ready. Would it be too much trouble for you to drop me off, or are you still determined to send me home in a cab?"

I glanced at her and could see she was laughing at me. "I don't hold grudges," I said. "I'll be happy to give you a ride."

"And can I use your shower?"

"Sure. Help yourself."

She refilled our cups, put the tray down on the foot of the bed, then got up and walked toward the bathroom. I watched with considerable interest while she gathered up her clothes. My shirt was long on her, but not quite long enough. When she bent over to pick up her purse, the view was tantalizing.

My response was classic and predictable. I lay on the bed, drinking my coffee and arguing with myself about it while I heard her turning on the water in the shower and adjusting the temperature. Finally, I made up my mind. After all, she had started it. So what if it was a case of mistaken identity? She was the one who had put the idea in my head, who had said ground rules were made to be broken.

I got up and tapped gently on the bathroom door. She opened it a crack and peered out at me through a cloud of steam.

"May I come in?"

She smiled. "That's up to you." She reached out a bare arm and clasped it around my neck, pulling me into the room with her.

One of the things I had marveled about when I bought the penthouse at Belltown Terrace was the massive sunken tile bathtub and shower in the master bathroom. I had wondered about it, but in the few weeks I had lived there, I'd had no chance to field test it the way Jasmine Day and I did that morning, with the needle points of hot water stinging our naked bodies and thick steam boiling up around us.

Later, as we dried off, I gave her an appreciative

flick on her water-dotted rump with my damp towel. "That is undoubtedly the best shower I've ever taken," I said.

"Not bad," she replied.

As she began to rummage through her purse for makeup, I heard the phone ring. When I answered it Peters was there. He still sounded as if he was talking from the bottom of a large tin can, but he seemed cheerful, more like his old self, more like the man who had been my partner until his neck got broken.

"Look, Beau. No hands."

"What do you mean, no hands?"

"The phone. It's a speakerphone with an automatic redialer. All I have to do is press one button, and it dials you up. We've programmed in twelve different numbers, and nobody has to hold it for me. It's a present from Ralph Ames."

That figured. Ames, my attorney and friend from Phoenix, is a gadget freak, particularly when it comes to phone gadgetry. He was the one who had forced me to accept an answering machine in my house, and I was well aware of his own automatic redialer. I suspected I wasn't nearly as grateful for my answering machine as Peters and the rehabilitation floor at Harborview were for Peters's handless phone. Ames had somehow found a way to give Peters back a small measure of independence.

"Did I wake you?" Peters asked.

"No," I told him innocently, not mentioning

Jasmine Day. "As a matter of fact, I just got out of the shower." I glanced at the clock. It was already after eight and I was supposed to be at the May-flower to meet with Alan Dale by ten. "I'll have to leave in a little while though," I said. "Got an appointment downtown."

"I wanted to catch you before you left, to find out if you had seen the review."

"Review? What review?"

"Of last night's concert in this morning's *P.I.*"

The *P.I.* is short for Seattle's morning paper, the *Seattle Post-Intelligencer.* Peters knows all about my antipathy toward the media in general and news-papers in particular. While we worked together, his daily briefings were all that had kept me informed of current events.

"So tell me about it," I urged.

"I'll read it to you," he said. " 'Over the last three years, Westcoast Starlight Productions has brought some real dogs to town. Their shows have been pretentious, overdone, and undersold. So when advance publicity said Jasmine Day would be "taking the Fifth Avenue by storm," I was one of the nonbelievers, one who said it would never happen. Not nohow. Not noway.

" 'I'm writing this to tell you I was wrong. I'm serving up a whole column of crow for breakfast this morning.

" 'There's good news and bad news here. The bad news is that the Fifth Avenue Theater was only half full when knockout Jasmine Day strutted her stuff last night. The good news is that there still should be plenty of tickets available for tonight's performance. It deserves to be a sellout.

" 'Miss Day is someone whose considerable talents as a vocalist and a dancer were concealed during her druggy, heavy-metal rocker days. Her versatility and dynamic voice effortlessly overcame not only Westcoast's hokey staging but also the Fifth Avenue's stubborn sound system. Lots bigger names in show biz have cracked their front teeth on that one.

" 'The big-band sound of Hal Gordon's orchestra would have overwhelmed a lesser performer, but it was Jasmine Day's show from beginning to end.

" 'They say that most rock stars cross that magic-thirty age barrier and disappear forever. Kids won't listen to them after that. Jasmine Day is thirty-two. I, for one, am glad the teenyboppers are done with her. Now the rest of us get to have her.

" 'In the course of the concert, Miss Day stepped aside from her music long enough to give a courageous, frank talk about drugs, what they've done to her life, and how she's put her life and career back together after her bout with cocaine. It's a talk that's timely and inspiring. Surprisingly, it doesn't detract from the music.

" 'So if your Friday night is looking dull and dreary, go see Jasmine Day. She really has taken the Fifth Avenue by storm.' "

Peters stopped reading.

"I guess he liked it," I said.

"I'll say."

"I liked it too," I added.

" 'Too,' " Peters echoed. "You were at the concert?"

"It was terrific."

"Oh," he responded. There was a pause. Then he said, "Did you pick up any leads?"

"A couple. I'll be following up on those later this morning."

"What about the nurse? Was I right about him?"

"On the money, Peters. You called that shot one hundred percent. He's gay as a giggle. Except I don't think it was a triangle. The nurse is on his way to developing AIDS too. He took care of Jonathan Thomas as a sort of penance."

The silence on the other end of the line lengthened.

"Hey, Peters. Are you there?" I asked.

"I'm going to hang up now," he said.

"What's the matter? Did I say something wrong?"

In answer, I heard a click and then a dial tone. I called the hospital back and asked for Peters's extension. The switchboard operator told me his line was busy.

I was still puzzling over what I might have said that offended him when the bathroom door opened and Jasmine Day walked into the bedroom.

"I thought I heard voices."

"It was the phone. A friend of mine called to read me a review of your concert last night."

She made a face. "I try not to pay any attention to reviews. It's too hard on my ego."

"This one wouldn't be. The guy loved it."

"Oh," she said and finished cinching her belt tightly around her waist. "Is there anything here to eat? I'm famished."

"The deli downstairs makes a reasonable breakfast, and for a sizable enough tip they'll even deliver."

"Do it," she said, heading for the door leading to the living room. "Scrambled eggs, hash browns, bacon, toast, and orange juice."

It's no coincidence that I know the deli's telephone number by heart. As soon as the bedroom door closed behind Jasmine, I picked up the bedside phone and dialed. I ordered breakfast. I even broke down enough to ask them to bring a *P.I.* along with the food.

I left the bedroom and went into the living room, where I found Jasmine curled up on the window seat looking down at the steady rain falling on Puget Sound.

"It's really dreary out there," she said.

"It's not so bad. If you asked most people who live here, they'd tell you they love the sun, but they don't mind the rain. If they did, they'd leave."

I walked over and sat down on the window seat beside her. Something was wrong. She seemed distant, remote. The casual teasing air was gone.

She took a sip of coffee without looking up at me. "How come you carry a gun?" she asked quietly.

Looking at the dining-room table and chairs, I saw my shoulder holster still hanging on the chair, exactly where I'd left it when I went to bed. When I thought I was going to bed by myself.

The jig was up. Jasmine Day had me dead to rights.

"I'm a police officer," I said.

"Not a friend of Dan Osgood's."

"No. I'm with Homicide. I was there investigating a case."

"A murder?"

I nodded, but she wasn't looking at me. "One of the local stagehands. He died early in the morning after he finished working on the set."

"After the load-in?"

"I guess that's what you call it. You didn't know anything about it? Nobody told you?"

She looked up at me then and gave a small shrug. "I'm the star. Ed tries to protect me, tries to keep those kinds of things away from me so I won't get upset. But how did you end up with a comp? With that particular comp," she added.

"I talked to Dan Osgood earlier in the day. He knew I planned to come to the performance to talk to people. He offered me the ticket. Said it would make it easier to come and go as I pleased."

"And how did you get to my dressing room?"

"I went backstage during intermission, but I couldn't talk to anyone. They were all busy, working on that band shell thing. I wandered over to your dressing room planning to ask you a question or two . . ."

"And I jumped to the wrong conclusion."

I nodded. "I was about to hand you my card when you said what you did about going to dinner."

"You don't understand. I always go to dinner after the show with whoever has that seat. It's been that way the whole tour."

"But why?"

"Why? Because the people are usually friends of Ed Waverly's, that's why. Because I owe him. Because when nobody else would give me a break, when nobody else was willing to back the new me, Ed Waverly said yes. He got Westcoast to take me on. I'd go to dinner with the devil himself if Ed Waverly asked me to."

I reached out and let my hand rest on her knee. "Couldn't we pretend that my having the tickets wasn't Ed Waverly's idea all along?"

She sat looking down at my hand for a long moment and I thought it was going to be all right. Then she picked up my hand and removed it from her leg.

"I don't think so," she said, getting up. "You lied to me. I'm going to get my hair. You'd better go ahead and call me that cab."

She stalked across the living room and down the hall.

"But, Jasmine . . ." I began. She didn't answer

me, didn't even pause. "Easy come, easy go," I said to myself as I watched her walk away.

About that time the phone rang. It was the delivery boy from the deli, calling from downstairs, asking to be let in through the security door so he could bring breakfast upstairs. I had barely put the phone down when another call came through. I recognized Watty Watkins's voice. He's the day-shift sergeant with Homicide.

"Sorry to bother you so early, Beau," he said, "but I thought we should let you know we just had a call from the medical examiner. He says Jonathan Thomas died of a massive cocaine overdose. The doc who did the autopsy is screaming for us to arrest the nurse."

"Leave Tom Riley out of this," I said.

"Look, Beau, this is a whole new ball game. I've assigned a team of detectives. You're working one case; they're working the other. They've sealed off the house, and the crime-scene team is on its way over."

"I'm telling you, Tom Riley had nothing to do with it."

"And I'm telling you that the day-shift guys are going to conduct their own investigation and draw their own conclusions."

The doorbell rang. "Hang on, Watty, someone's at the door."

I hurried to answer it, paid for the food and the newspaper, put the tray down on the table, and returned to the phone.

"I'm back," I said.

"From your report, I see that you already notified Thomas's parents. What about Morris's mother? You ever get hold of her?"

"I'll be talking to her today."

"Good. The media has been bugging Arlo Hamilton to release the victim's name, but we're waiting on notification of next of kin." Arlo is Seattle P.D.'s public information officer.

Jasmine came down the hall. The wig was firmly in place. She dropped her purse and shoes on the parquet floor near the door and then stood, one hand on her hip, regarding me from across the room.

"Look, Watty," I said. "I've got an appointment at ten o'clock. I'll stop by and talk to you after that, all right?"

Hurriedly, I put down the phone and went to the door, where Jasmine was standing on one foot, pulling on a shoe.

"Jasmine," I blurted. "I meant to tell you—"

"Did you call me a cab or not?"

"No. Let me give you a ride."

"I'll walk if I have to." She started to bend down for her other shoe. I beat her to it, picked it up, and handed it to her. In the process, I looked at the shoe, a finely crafted sandal. The manufacturer's name was written on the instep-Ferragamo. The size was inked into the heel strap. Size 8½B.

With that, she slipped on the sandal, turned,

and walked out the door. I didn't try to stop her.
There was no point.

I stood there, thunderstruck. I heard the elevator come and go without moving. Finally, I shook myself out of my stupor. There had to be thousands of pairs of Ferragamo shoes in the Seattle area. Hundreds in size 8½B.

"Don't jump to conclusions," I told myself. I hurried out to the elevator. It was slow coming, and by the time I got down to the lobby door, she was gone.

I went back up to my apartment. The food was sitting on the table getting cold. I didn't bother to touch it. My appetite was pretty well shot. I wondered if I'd ever get it back.

CHAPTER 13

I drove to the department with my mind in turmoil. Ferragamo, size 8½B. I tried to convince myself that the evidence was strictly circumstantial, but I couldn't. I don't believe in Santa Claus or blind coincidence. Cops who do don't live very long.

Sergeant Watkins was deep in conference with Captain Powell. I hung around outside the fishbowl until they broke it up and Watty came outside.

"How's it going, Beau?" he asked. "You look beat."

"Thanks," I told him. "Nothing like a vote of confidence. I'm shot to shit."

"Did you get the message from Janice Morraine? She's evidently got something for you. She called a few minutes ago and raised hell because you weren't available."

"I hope you reminded her that I work swing shift," I said.

"So does she," Watty returned.

Some arguments are winnable and others aren't. This one wasn't. Without bothering to go to my desk, I took a quick hike down the back stairway to the crime lab on the second floor.

I found Janice Morraine there in the lab, hunkered down over her microscope.

"How's it going, Jan?" I asked.

She straightened up, rubbing her back. "Depends. If you're asking about my sex life, it doesn't. If you're asking about work, we're making progress."

"Work," I said. "Did you get that trace evidence from Doc Baker?"

She patted her microscope. "Yup. It's right here."

"And what is it?"

"It's a hair," she said. "A nice, long synthetic blonde hair. Top quality," she added. "It's so good, it was impossible to tell it wasn't real until I got it under the microscope. The crime-scene investigators picked up one just like it from the Pike Place Market parking lot yesterday afternoon. All we have to do now is find that wig. It must be a beaut."

There was a sick feeling in my gut that said I might know the exact whereabouts of that very wig, that when last seen it had been firmly attached to the head of Jasmine Day as she walked out of my apartment and slammed the door shut behind her. I didn't let on.

"You're sure they match?"

"Of course I'm sure. Synthetics are a hell of a lot easier to match up than natural fibers."

"Thanks, Janice," I said, backing away from her table. "You've been a big help."

"Any time," she said with a smile. "That's what I get paid for."

Back upstairs, I found a message waiting for me from one of the guys on night shift. He had taped it to my phone so I would be sure not to miss it. Reverend Laura Beardsly of the Pike Street Mission wanted me to drop by and see her as soon as possible. The message was marked urgent.

The Pike Street Mission is only a block from the Pike Place Market and six blocks from the Mayflower Park Hotel. There was just time enough to go see Reverend Laura before my scheduled meeting with Alan Dale. At nine-fifteen, I pulled into a thirty-minute parking place on First Avenue in front of a defunct office-supply store. Two minutes later, I was pushing open the alley entrance to the Pike Street Mission.

Reverend Laura Beardsly has been the director of the mission for several years. She's lasted longer than any of the do-gooders who have preceded her. They mostly burned themselves out trying to rescue ungrateful wretches who didn't particularly want to be rescued.

Reverend Laura, a raw-boned, plain-looking woman, has built quite a following among Seattle's street people. She has a reputation for helping people when they want help, without unnecessary moralizing or haranguing. And she has brains enough to leave them alone the rest of the time. I first met her when Peters and I were working a bum-bashing case where a college student got his rocks off by setting fire to drunks in downtown alleys.

It wasn't an auspicious beginning, but in the period of time since then, Reverend Laura had established a good working relationship with the department in general and with Peters and me in particular. When she hollered, we listened.

Reverend Laura's mission, housed in what used to be one of Seattle's seedier taverns, seemed to be thriving, at least from a user's point of view. I knew the overnight shelter was usually full even though the treasury was not. The mission's telephone had long since been disconnected for nonpayment, which is why I couldn't phone, why it was necessary to stop by in person.

The "born-again" tavern occupies the subbasement of an office building. It opens, by means of a steep, narrow stairway, onto a stretch of alley that fills up with rats and drunks every night as soon as the sun goes down.

Reverend Laura, impervious to her surroundings, lives there twenty-four hours a day, sleeping on a simple cot in a room behind the chapel. Another room, off to the side of the chapel where the former establishment ran an illegal card room, has been converted into a six-cot dormitory where homeless derelicts can bed down for the night. The spartan accommodations are free and available on a first-come, first-served basis.

A tinkling bell above the chapel door announced my arrival. Reverend Laura hurried down through the chapel to meet me, her work-roughened hand extended in greeting. Her buck-toothed smile was one of genuine welcome.

"Hello, Detective Beaumont. Thank you for coming," she said. "I was afraid she would change her mind."

"Who would change her mind?" I asked.

Reverend Laura didn't answer. Instead, she turned and hurried back the way she had come. I tagged along behind her. When we reached the door to the bunk room, she stopped and opened the door.

"It's time," she announced in a businesslike tone that brooked no nonsense.

Inside, the group of ragged derelicts who had spent the night were busy gathering their meager possessions for yet another day on the street. Reverend Laura waited beside the door as they shuffled out one by one. Only when the last one had made his way down the aisle and out the door at the back of the chapel did she turn and continue on her way, leading me past the spare wooden pulpit at the front of the room and into her own private living quarters.

People who send their cast-off clothing to St. Vincent de Paul or who mail checks once a year to the Salvation Army pat themselves on the back for their generosity without ever being sullied by the grim realities of poverty. The donors to that kind of sanitary, twice-removed charity never see or touch or smell the recipients. Especially smell.

Reverend Laura, on the other hand, lives in the trenches next to her charges. At that very moment, her room reeked of the unmistakable odor of unwashed destitution.

At first glance, I thought the windowless room was empty, that the "she" Reverend Laura had mentioned had made a break for it and disappeared. On one side of the room a narrow, neatly made cot was pushed against a bare brick wall. On the other side sat a desk, an old, metallic green office discard, covered with several stacks of books and a disorderly scatter of papers.

In the middle of the room stood a single dilapidated chair, a small table, and an ancient floor lamp with a fringed antique shade. The dim glow of the lamp's single bulb provided the only light in the musty, darkened room.

Reverend Laura followed me into the room and closed the door behind her. She moved past me into the shadows beyond the glow of the lamp.

"He's here, Belinda," she said gently. "The man I told you about. You must talk to him. Come on. He won't hurt you."

As my eyes adjusted to the light, I noted two shapeless lumps huddled against the far wall, near a door that presumably opened into a basement corridor of the office building above us.

Drawn out by Reverend Laura's coaxing voice as well as by her guiding hand, the two lumps moved in concert, slowly emerging from the concealing shadows into the light.

The first lump turned out to be approximately a grocery cart's worth of bulging plastic bags. The second figure was that of a woman, bulky and shapeless under multiple layers of clothing. I knew her on sight, even without her usually ever-present grocery cart. I had seen her a hundred times before, but I had had no idea her name was Belinda.

For years she'd been a fixture in the sheltered plaza under Seattle's monorail station. Depending on the direction of the wind and the rain, she and her cart with its collection of treasures could be found huddled against the wall of Nordstrom's downtown clothing store or under the monorail entrance ramp itself. The ragged woman in her shapeless brown coat and scarf had stood out in a stark contrast to the well-dressed career ladies hurrying to buy lunch-hour shoes or purses in trendy downtown department stores.

But construction of Seattle's new Westlake mall had temporarily closed the monorail station. A high, impenetrable chain-link construction fence now locked her out of her favorite haunt. Driving past once, I had noticed she was no longer there, but I didn't know what had become of her, what new territory she might have staked out for herself. Now here she was, approaching me tentatively like a gun-shy dog, keeping the grocery cart strategically positioned between us.

"This is Detective Beaumont," Reverend Laura explained. "He's working on that case, the one you told me about. He needs your help."

Belinda's age was as indeterminate as her shape. She could have been fifty-five, she could have been seventy. Weathered, wrinkled cheeks collapsed over a dentureless mouth, but her eyes, set in grimy skin, were birdlike sharp and bright. They darted nervously from Reverend Laura's face to mine. Had the minister's sturdy frame not been blocking the way, I'm sure Belinda would have broken and made a dash for the door.

As it was, I moved carefully and reassuringly toward her, holding out my hand over the cart. Belinda's limp fingers were cold and damp to the touch.

"Hello," I said. "I'm Detective Beaumont. My partner, Detective Lindstrom, and I work homicide together. If you have information that would help us, we'd appreciate whatever . . ."

Belinda turned away from me and fell against Reverend Laura, clutching fearfully at the younger woman's blazer.

"But what if he doesn't believe me?" she wailed. Her tongue tripped over toothless gums, making what she said slurred and difficult to understand. "What if he says I'm crazy, that I'm seeing things again? I don't want to go back to that place. Please don't let them send me back."

"Shh. No one's sending you anywhere, Belinda," Reverend Laura reassured her. "I'll see to it, but you must tell them what you saw night before last. Tell Detective Beaumont what you told me."

Taking the old woman by her shoulders, Reverend Laura turned her around bodily until she was once more facing me.

"She was so pretty," Belinda said.

"Who was pretty?"

"The woman. When I opened my eyes and saw her, it scared me. I thought she was a vision. An angel, maybe. I used to see angels all the time. That's why they put me in the hospital."

"And where did you see her, this pretty woman?" I asked, trying to keep my voice gentle so I wouldn't frighten the bag lady further.

"I got here too late to spend the night," Belinda went on, one hand tentatively motioning toward the redbrick wall of Reverend Laura's monastic room. "The cots were all full, so I couldn't stay. It wasn't raining, so I decided to sleep down by the market."

She paused as though searching for words. I felt my heartbeat quicken. A pretty woman. A blonde wig. The market. I kept my voice even, but it took tremendous effort. "What time was that?" I asked.

Belinda shrugged. "Ten. Eleven. Maybe later. I don't know. There's a place down there by the parking garage, near that gravel parking lot. I go there sometimes when the weather's nice. I fell asleep. When I woke up, she was there."

"Who was?"

"The lady. This pretty lady with long blonde hair and a long dress and long white gloves and high heels. She was standing there by the stairway, waving at someone who was coming up the stairs to the parking lot from the waterfront."

Long white gloves too. I let the air in my lungs out slowly. "Could you see who was coming up the stairs?" I asked.

Belinda shook her head. "No, but it was a man."

"How do you know that?"

"Because I saw him when he got to the top of the stairs."

"Is the parking lot lit?" I didn't remember if there had been lights there or not, and I wondered how Belinda could have seen things in so much detail.

Belinda glared at me impatiently. "It was a full moon," she said. "Anyway, this woman waved at him like she was waiting for him, and I could hear him coming up the steps toward her. She leaned down then. She took hold of the handrail and leaned down and reached for her shoe like she had a rock in it or something."

She stopped. "Then what happened?" I asked, urging her to go on.

"So I saw him, but only for a second. When he reached the top where I could see him, the lady straightened up. She had taken both shoes off. All of a sudden she went after him, pounced on him like she was a cat and he was a mouse. For a minute I thought they were both going to fall back down the stairs, but somehow he got away from her. He tried to run, but she grabbed him by the knees and pulled him down. The next thing I knew, she was on top of him, pounding on him with the shoe. He tried to fight her off, but it was like . . . like . . ." Belinda hesitated again.

"Like what?" I insisted.

"You'll think I'm making this up."

"No. Just tell me what happened."

"It was like she was too strong for him. And too quick. I thought it would never end," Belinda added.

"Go on," I said.

"All of a sudden he got real still, but she kept beating on him. Kept hitting him. I could hear it. It was awful, like somebody pounding meat to tenderize it." She shuddered at the memory, and her whole body trembled.

"But she didn't know you were there?"

"No. I held my breath. I didn't want her to hear me, to know where I was hiding. Pretty soon she stopped and got up. She looked around like she was checking to see if anyone saw her. First she looked up toward the market, then back down toward the water. When she couldn't see anybody, she started pushing him."

"Pushing?"

"Rolling, I guess. Toward the fence. There's a fence there, to keep people from falling off the cliff. It's pretty tall, but there's a hole under it, a hole big enough to crawl through. She shoved him under it. He rolled down the hill and kept on rolling until I couldn't see him anymore. I don't know why he didn't get hung up in the fence."

"What happened then?"

"She took off."

"Which way did she go?"

"Down the stairs. The same way the man came up."

"What did you do?"

"For a while, I didn't do nothing. I was scared. I was afraid she'd come back and find me."

"So you waited?" Belinda nodded. "How long did you wait?"

"I don't know. Finally, when I was sure she was gone and not coming back, I got my stuff and left. I went down Western. It's easier than going back up the hill with the cart."

"Are you the one who called 911?" I asked.

Belinda gave a sharp, involuntary intake of breath. She drew away from me, shrinking against Reverend Laura. "How'd you know that?" she demanded.

"I didn't know, I just guessed. It's easy to get to the ferry terminal from the lower end of Western, and that's where the 911 call came from. Why didn't you leave your name?"

"I was afraid."

"Afraid we'd think you'd done it?"

She shook her head. "Afraid you'd think I was crazy. Delusions, that's what they called it years ago when I used to see things. This isn't that, is it?"

"No," I assured her. "The woman you saw was

real enough. And the man you saw is dead. Is there anything more you can tell us about her or him?"

"Not really. I only saw her from the back, and after he got there, it all happened too fast."

"Would you recognize her if you saw her again?"

Belinda shook her head. "I don't know. I don't think so."

"Did she say anything to him?"

"No. Not a word."

"What did you do after you called 911?"

"I was still scared. I didn't know if I did the right thing or not. I worried about it all day. Finally, last night, I came here to talk with Reverend Laura. She told me I should tell you."

"Reverend Laura was right, Belinda. We needed this information. It helps us know who we're looking for. You're sure you never caught sight of her face?"

"Positive."

"What color was the dress?"

"I don't know. A real pretty blue or green. I couldn't tell in the moonlight."

"And you say she was wearing gloves?"

"Long ones. Old-fashioned ones. The kind that come up over the elbows."

"Right, I know the kind. Do you remember anything else?"

"No. Nothing."

I took my pencil and notebook out of my pocket. "What's your address, Belinda?"

Belinda moved closer to Reverend Laura's sheltering arm. "I don't have one," she said plaintively.

Reverend Laura patted the older woman's shoulder reassuringly. "You can use this address," she said to the bag lady quietly. Then to me she added, "I'll have her stay here with me for the next few days in case you need to reach her."

"Your last name, Belinda?" I continued.

She shrank close to her protector. "I . . . I . . . don't remember," she stammered.

I waited, but it was no use. If Belinda had a last name, she had long since forgotten it or blocked it out. I closed my notebook. It was par for the course. Every once in a blue moon, you have a real-live eyewitness to a homicide. Even though Belinda couldn't remember her own name, she was one of that rare eyewitness breed. I was sure that what she had told us would help me arrest Jasmine Day for the murder of Richard Dathan Morris, but I wasn't at all sure it would help get us a conviction.

Defense attorneys make mincemeat out of totally reliable witnesses. And Belinda was decidedly not one of those. Not if she couldn't remember her own last name.

CHAPTER 14

BY THE TIME I LEFT THE PIKE STREET MISSION, I WAS already late to see Alan Dale. Instead of going straight to the Mayflower Park Hotel though, I drove through the misting rain to my place at Second and Broad. I parked on the street and hurried up to my apartment. I found the Jasmine Day souvenir program on the kitchen counter right where I had left it.

Turning on the fluorescent kitchen light, I held the glossy program up so I could examine the cover photo. Sure enough, what I didn't want to see, what I dreaded seeing, was right there—Jasmine Day in a long blue dress with elbow-length white gloves. The long blonde wig was there, along with something else. Shoes. Blue high-heeled shoes. Cobalt blue shoes that matched the cobalt blue dress. Ferragamo, size 8½B.

"Shit," I muttered aloud as I sank into my old

recliner, my thinking chair. Forgotten, the program dropped onto the table beside me.

One by one the ugly pieces were falling into place. Bit by bit, the puzzle was coming into focus. The only thing missing was motive. What was the deadly connection between the stagehand and the star?

Cocaine. That had to be the answer.

The lab had confirmed it was a brick of cocaine we'd found in Jonathan Thomas's pillow. That was the only thing that made sense. Clearly, Jasmine Day wasn't the squeaky-clean reformed addict she had pretended to be during her second-act inspirational chat. And I found myself doubting that anything she'd told me later that evening had been the truth either. So, if she was involved with the cocaine, was she buying or selling? Was she dealing or using? And who else was in on it with her?

In the long run, the answers to those questions weren't important. Her involvement with drugs was nothing but an unsavory backdrop to the rest of the story. My focus had to be on only one issue, murder, and how Jasmine Day was tied in with Richard Dathan Morris and Jonathan Thomas.

In that regard, Jasmine Day was my prime suspect. My only suspect.

I used to think that as I got older it would be easier to turn off personal connections, but it doesn't work that way. I had to force myself to lock away all memory of what had gone on between Jasmine and me. I had to blot out all remembrance of what had gone before and concentrate on the job at hand.

With a sigh, I finally dragged myself out of the chair and went into the bedroom. I knew what I had to do.

For a time I crawled around on my hands and knees, going over the carpet inch by inch. Eventually my patient search paid off. In the bathroom, on the floor near the sink, I discovered what I needed. A hair. A single long, blonde hair. I rummaged in several jacket pockets before I found a stray glassine bag to put it in.

That done, I headed out for my tardy appointment with Alan Dale.

I found him drinking a solitary cup of coffee in Clippers, the Mayflower Park's elegant little hotel restaurant. He was sitting next to the window watching a busy remodeling project in the Times Square Building just across the street on Olive.

Clippers was a brightly lit, open room. It's probably eminently suited to graceful dining, but it wasn't so hot for my purposes. I needed dark, not light. I needed seclusion. I needed a place where I could ask Alan Dale some pointed questions without having to worry about whether or not someone was listening over my shoulder.

"Sorry I'm late," I apologized, sitting down at the marble-topped table. "I got tied up."

He looked up at me as I sat down across from him and nodded without humor. "I'll bet you did," he said.

Before, when I had tried to talk to him, Alan

had been busy, hurried. His answers had been clipped, but there had been none of the undercurrent of hostility that was distinctly present now. I put myself on guard.

"You said you had questions," Dale said. "Let's get 'em over with."

Obligingly, I pulled out my notebook. "How long have you worked for Westcoast Starlight Productions?" I asked.

Dale shrugged impassively. "Two and a half years, I guess, give or take."

"And didn't you tell me that Richard Morris had worked for you before?"

"Three shows that I've been on and a couple of others Ray knows about."

"But you didn't like him."

"I don't have to like any of the local hands. I don't get paid to like 'em. I just have to get the job done. Morris always seemed to have his head up his ass, like he was really somewhere else. I complained about him, but he had a lot of pull with the locals here. Complaints or not, he still got called out every time we brought a show through town."

"And this time you fired him?"

"That's right. It was the first time I caught the little sucker red-handed. I told Ed at the time that as far as I was concerned, he'd never work for us again."

"You told Ed Waverly."

"That's right."

"Would he have gone along with that?"

"You bet."

"Were any of the other local hands friends of his?"

"Probably, but I don't know for sure. I've had my hands too full with tech problems to worry about my stagehands' social lives."

"What about Jasmine Day?"

"What about her?" His clipped question in answer to mine alerted me.

"Did she have any connection with Morris?"

"No."

Alan Dale had given me a categorical answer. Truth is hardly ever that absolute. I looked at Alan Dale closely, and he met my gaze without wavering.

"Have you ever worked with her before?"

Dale shook his head. "I was doing Broadway-bound bus-and-truck shows on the East Coast when she was into heavy-metal concerts at this end of the world. Those two lines don't cross very often."

"So how long have you known her?" I asked.

"A month and a half."

"Can you tell me anything about her?"

"Why do you want to know?"

"What's she like to work with? Temperamental? Hard to get along with?"

"When things are going fine, she's fine, but when there's trouble . . . You saw me working on that worm-gear drive, right?"

I nodded. "Well, that son of a bitch stuck on me in Portland. It got all bound up and busted the track right in the middle of the second act, with the orchestra half on and half off the stage."

"So what happened?"

"We had to stop the whole goddamned show while the tech crew came out and bodily turned the orchestra until it was pointing in the right direction. After that, we went ahead and finished the show. As soon as it was over though, all hell broke loose."

"Jasmine pitched a fit?"

"Are you kidding? I thought she was going to tear me limb from limb. She could do it, you know. She's a brown belt."

"So I've heard," I observed. "Is there anything about her behavior that you'd classify as erratic?"

Dale looked at me. For the first time, a slow grin spread over his face. "You haven't spent very much time around show people, have you?"

I shook my head. "No."

"I didn't think so. They're mostly erratic. They wouldn't be in the business if they weren't."

"Have you heard any rumors about her, like maybe she might be messing around with drugs again?"

The grin was gone as suddenly as it had appeared. "No." Dale's answer was emphatic. "Absolutely not. If somebody told you that, I'd say they were trying to cause trouble. Jasmine may be screwed up in some ways, but I'd lay odds she's clean. She's worked too hard to get that way, personally and professionally."

I tried coming from a different direction. "So you think she deserves what's happening now—on the tour, I mean."

"The success?" He snorted. "Believe me, it's been bought and paid for."

There was a hard edge in his voice, and I wasn't sure what lay behind it. "What do you mean by that?"

"Do you have to ask?"

I felt the blood rushing to my ears. Alan Dale had landed the blow fair and square. No, I shouldn't have had to ask. I knew the answer, from Jasmine Day's own lips.

I went looking for more innocuous territory. "What exactly does a head carpenter do?"

"I'm a jack-of-all-trades, the one who keeps everything running. If it breaks, I fix it. If it wears out or just disappears, I get a new one."

"In other words, you're in charge of everything," I said.

"Everything," he agreed. "Particularly on this show. I'm double-carded, both IATSE and Actors Equity. I'm head carpenter and stage manager, both."

"You handle costumes?"

He nodded. "Including costumes, if it's something Bertha can't handle. It helps keep expenses in line."

"Who's Bertha?"

"Bertha Harris. The head costumer. We call her Big Bertha for obvious reasons. She's been in the business forever, and she's one of the best."

"Didn't you tell me the other day that Morris was messing around with one of the costume crates? Isn't that why you fired him?"

"Trunks," Dale corrected. "One of the costume trunks."

"Did you ever figure out what he was looking for?" I asked.

"Sure; that was easy, once Bertha told me what was missing."

"What?"

"One of Jasmine's costumes, complete with dress, wig, and a pair of shoes. The last pair of shoes, by the way. One of the heels on the next-to-last pair broke off in Portland. We just got in the replacement this morning."

"Where from?"

"A shop in Beverly Hills. Rodeo Drive Shoe Salon. They've been good about keeping Jasmine's shoes in stock in case we do run into problems."

"So let me see if I've got this straight. Later, after you caught Morris going through the costume trunk, you found one whole costume had disappeared?"

"That's right."

"Any idea what he'd want with a woman's evening dress?"

Dale shrugged. "Someone told me they spotted him down at the Edgewater. He wasn't wearing it then, but he could have changed into it later."

"The Edgewater. The hotel down on the waterfront?"

"Right," Dale answered. "The one where you can fish out your room window."

I remembered the matchbook with "The Edgewater Inn" on it, the one we'd found under Richard Dathan Morris's body. I was genuinely puzzled. "What for?" I asked. "Why would he go there?"

"You mean to tell me you live right here in the city and you don't know about what's going on under your very nose?" Dale asked.

"I guess not."

"They've got a follies there. The whole cast is made up of female impersonators. When I heard that, I figured Morris must have lifted the costume before I caught him. My guess is he hid it somewhere and came back to get it later. He probably wanted to play dress up."

"But was he wearing the costume when whoever it was saw him at the Edgewater?"

"No."

"And you didn't go?"

Dale shook his head. "There are a few of us on this show who aren't AC/DC. I happen to be one of them."

"Who saw him there, then? At the Edgewater. Do you remember?"

"It was one of the local guys, but I don't know which one. I see so many, they all look alike. I'd know him if I saw him, but I don't remember his name. I can get it for you tonight, if that's soon enough."

"That would be a big help."

The waitress brought the bill. I took it and paid

off both our coffees. "Is that all?" he asked as the waitress walked away. "I should probably go back to my room and grab a quick nap if I want to be on my toes tonight."

"Did I understand you to say that a replacement pair of shoes came today?"

"That's right. Via Federal Express. They brought them right to my door."

"Your door? You mean here in the hotel?"

"Where else?"

"Could I see them?"

The hostility that had gradually drained out of his voice came back all at once. "Why?"

"I just want to see them, that's all."

I followed Alan Dale out of the restaurant, through the lobby, and up to his room on the eighth floor. His room was definitely not a suite. On the table sat a bulky, unopened Federal Express envelope. He tossed it to me. "What's this all about?" he asked.

Instead of answering, I tore open the outer envelope. A crimson shoe box dropped onto the table. Inside the box, under a covering layer of tissue, a pair of bright blue shoes lay nestled together. Ferragamo stilettos, size 8½B.

They were duplicates of another shoe I'd seen before, although these didn't have any bloodstains on them.

I replaced the lid on the box and handed it to Alan Dale. "Thanks," I said. "You've been a big help."

"Think nothing of it," he replied.

When I left the head carpenter's room, I went back down to the lobby and asked the desk for Ed Waverly's room. I was told he and Miss Day had just left the hotel in a limo on their way to an appearance on a local television talk show. They weren't expected back until sometime after four. I tried checking on the rest of the cast and crew, but they had gone, as a group, on a ferry ride.

I left my name and my number at the department for Ed Waverly. It was time for me to go on duty, although I felt as if I'd already been at work for a long time. All day and all night.

Before heading for the department though, I went to the bank of pay phones near the desk and called the Executive Inn. I was told Mrs. Morris was out and I should try again later. At least she hadn't checked out. I was remiss in not being more aggressive about tracking her down, but there are only so many hours in a day, I told myself.

On the way up to the fifth floor of the Public Safety Building, I stopped off at the crime lab. I wanted to turn in the glassine bag containing the hair from my apartment.

I found Janice Morraine standing in the elevator lobby next to a knee-high metal ashtray, smoking a cigarette. Janice is the only smoker in the crime lab, and she's exiled to the lobby whenever she needs a fix.

"You're here almost as much as I am," I said.

"That's nothing to brag about," she retorted.

With no further comment, I handed her the

bag from my pocket. She opened it and peered inside.

"What is this, another sample from our ubiquitous blonde wig?"

"What do you mean, ubiquitous?"

"Bill Foster, one of the other criminologists, just gave me one from that other crime scene. The one up on Capitol Hill?"

"Jonathan Thomas?" I asked.

"I don't remember the name. The OD up on Bellevue. The guy with AIDS. All I can say is," Janice added, "this must be one very busy lady."

"She's busy, all right," I replied grimly.

"Where did it come from?"

"I'd rather not say."

Janice Morraine gave me a long, appraising look before she bent down to snuff out the butt of her cigarette in the ashtray. We've worked around one another for a long time—years, in fact. Janice Morraine probably knows me better than she ought to.

"That's just as well," she said. "There are some things I'd rather not know." She dropped the glassine bag into her lab-coat pocket. "Anything else?"

"Not at the moment."

"I'd better get back to work," she said.

Janice Morraine walked away, leaving me standing there alone in the hall wondering if I was as screwed up as she seemed to think.

I didn't much like the answer I gave myself.

CHAPTER 15

SERGEANT WATKINS WAS GUNNING FOR ME WHEN I stepped through the doorway on the fifth floor. "Beau, Captain Powell wants to see you, pronto."

That kind of summons to Captain Powell's fishbowl is much the same as being twelve and getting sent to the principal's office. One look at the captain's face told me he was kicking ass and taking names.

When I walked into his office, Captain Larry Powell was sitting at his desk, thumbing through a thick stack of papers in front of him.

"What's up?" I asked.

"Shut the door," he replied without looking up. I knew right then I was in deep shit. I shut the door and waited.

"What the hell have you been doing with your time that you haven't bothered to notify Richard Dathan Morris's next of kin?" he demanded.

The best defense was to go on the attack. "Look,"

I said. "There are only so many hours in a day. We've been tracking her. The neighbors said she was out of town. They weren't able to say where she'd gone. I finally left a message for her last night, but I still haven't been able to make a connection."

Powell finally looked up at me. "Doug and Larry did," he said. Detectives Doug Manning and Larry Hicks worked Homicide on the day shift; obviously, they were the team Sergeant Watkins had assigned to the Jonathan Thomas case.

"How come?"

"Because she showed up this morning at the crime scene on Bellevue, that's how come. When she found out what had happened, they had to call an aid car for her."

"So where is she now—in a hospital? I tried calling her hotel a little while ago, and she wasn't there."

"Don't waste your time looking for her now. In other words, what you're telling me is that you knew where she was staying last night, but you didn't bother to get word to her."

"Look, Captain," I said. "There wouldn't be a murder for Doug and Larry to investigate if Big Al and I hadn't spent half the day battling the system and tracking down Thomas's parents to get their agreement on the autopsy. If it weren't for us, someone would have gotten away with murder in this town."

I was hot now. I hadn't exactly been lying down on the job. I felt as if I'd been living and breathing Richard Dathan Morris for days.

"Not only that," I continued, "most of the people involved in this case will be leaving Seattle tonight as soon as Jasmine Day's concert is over at the Fifth Avenue Theater. They're on their way to Vancouver, B.C. When I finish up with the people who are leaving the country, I'll get around to the people who aren't." With that, I turned on my heel and started out of the room.

"And Al is off tonight?"

"Yes, he's off tonight. His grandson had emergency surgery last night. The kid almost died. Big Al spent the night at the hospital with his wife. Of course he's not coming in."

"Great—" Powell began, but I slammed the door behind me, cutting off whatever else he might have said. I ran into the night-shift Homicide squad leader, Lowell James, in the corridor on my way back to my desk.

"What's going on?" he asked. "How come Powell had you in the fishbowl? I heard he's mad enough to chew nails."

"He needs a fucking Ping-Pong ball," I snapped. "And I'm it."

James followed me to my desk and leaned against a corner of it, crossing his arms. "Maybe you'd better tell me what's going on."

"Powell is ripped because I didn't notify Morris's next of kin before his mother showed up at another crime scene and found out on her own."

"Have you talked to her yet?"

"No. And I never will, if people don't get off my case and give me a chance to go to work."

James uncrossed his arms and backed away from my desk. "I can take a hint," he said. "Don't let me stand in your way."

He started away from my desk but stopped long enough to say, "By the way, I guess you heard the results on the Thomas autopsy. You were right. It was a cocaine overdose."

"I know," I said and let it go at that.

As soon as Sergeant James left, I picked up the phone and dialed the Executive Inn one more time. They said Mrs. Morris was in but that she wasn't taking calls, not from anybody. I went down to the garage and checked out a car to pay her a personal visit.

The desk clerk at the Executive Inn wasn't the least bit happy about telling me where Mrs. Grace Simms Morris's room was. "Something terrible has happened to that poor woman," the clerk said. "She wants to be left alone."

I held my identification so the clerk could read it. "I know what's happened to her," I said. "That's why I have to talk to her."

Reluctantly, the clerk picked up the phone and dialed a number. "This is the desk, Mrs. Morris," she said apologetically. "There's a detective down here who insists on seeing you."

The clerk listened for a moment, then looked at me. "Are you with the DEA?" she asked.

I had already shown her my identification,

which said I was with Seattle P.D., not the Drug Enforcement Agency, but evidently that hadn't sunk in. "I'm with Homicide," I answered. "I'm investigating the murder."

She repeated what I'd said to Mrs. Morris. "All right," the clerk said finally, setting the phone down. "She says you can go on up. It's room 338, just to the right of the elevator."

When I got off the elevator, the door to room 338 was already standing open. A woman was waiting in the doorway.

My first impression of Grace Simms Morris was that she was maybe forty-five years old. Her skin was smooth and translucent. Later I was forced to revise that assessment upward when she told me she had been thirty when Richard, her twenty-seven-year-old only child was born. Evidently Grace maintained her fragile beauty with the help of a skilled plastic surgeon.

Grace Simms Morris was a well-preserved, small-boned woman with a head of champagne blonde hair that couldn't have come from anything but a bottle. She was dressed in a rose-colored suit that was simply but elegantly cut. That kind of simplicity doesn't come cheap. Grace Simms Morris had money.

"You're sure you're not with the DEA?" she demanded in a breathless, little-girl rush of words as I stepped off the elevator.

"I'm sure," I assured her, showing her my ID. She held it up close to her face and read through a pair of narrow reading glasses perched on her nose. Studying her as she read, I admit I was somewhat shocked. From what the clerk and Captain Powell had said, I expected to find Mrs. Morris hysterical, at the very least. She was far more indignant than tearful.

"I don't understand why they're doing this," she said.

"Why who's doing what?" I asked.

"Why the DEA is pretending they don't know who my son was or what he was doing."

"What was he doing?"

"Working for them," she snapped.

A door opened down the hall and two people walked toward the elevator. Quickly Mrs. Morris pulled me into her room. "I don't want anyone to overhear," she whispered conspiratorially. "Maybe they still have to keep it a secret because they haven't made all the arrests yet."

You could have knocked me over with a feather. "Your son was working for the DEA?" I must have looked as incredulous as I sounded.

"Of course he was, although that Mr. Wainwright said it wasn't true."

"Who's Mr. Wainwright?" I asked.

She shook her head. "I don't know. He's someone at the DEA office here in Seattle. I tried to talk to him, but he gave me the brush-off. I don't like it when men treat me that way."

Mrs. Morris walked away from me. She settled herself on the edge of the bed gracefully, smoothing her skirt over her knees. Then she motioned me toward the room's only chair.

"This is very hard for me, Detective Beaumont," she said. "I'm all alone, and Richard was my only child. I tried to get Mr. Wainwright to understand that."

"Understand what?"

Mrs. Morris seemed to talk in circles. We weren't getting anywhere.

"Detective Beaumont, since my son was a law-enforcement officer who was killed in the line of duty, I want to plan a fitting law-enforcement funeral for him. You know, with the uniformed officers carrying the casket, that kind of thing. But how can I if his supervisors don't have the common decency to come forward and tell what happened?"

"Mrs. Morris, what exactly was your son doing, do you know?"

"He was working undercover, of course."

"But you knew about it?"

"Richard told me everything. We were very close."

"What about his roommate—did he know about it too?"

Mrs. Morris shrugged. "I don't know. I suppose Jonathan knew. We never discussed it.

"He was so happy," she said suddenly, and just as suddenly she dabbed at her eyes. "He was finally getting to do what he'd always wanted to do. You know, he wanted to be a police officer from the time he was little."

"Is that so?" I ventured.

"For a long time I thought it was just a stage.

You know, most little boys go through a period when they want to be a cowboy or a doctor. I thought that eventually Richard would grow out of it, but he never did."

"For some of us it takes longer," I said.

Mrs. Grace Simms Morris smiled at me thinly through her tears. "You know, Rich would have loved you," she declared.

Knowing what I did about Richard Dathan Morris and his sexual preference, I wasn't sure what to make of that statement. For a few moments the two of us sat uncomfortably in the room, the cop from Homicide and the victim's mother, with nothing to say to one another. Finally, I broke the silence.

"You said he told you everything. Did he tell you what he was doing for the DEA?"

Suddenly, Mrs. Morris sat up a little straighter. My question had given her son the credibility he'd been denied elsewhere. "Cracking a drug ring, what else?" she answered huffily.

"He told you that?"

"He said it had something to do with cocaine, lots of it, and the theater. But that's all he said. He wouldn't tell me any more. He said it would be too dangerous for me to know more than that. I was very proud of him and glad to help him too."

"Help?"

"I kept some things for him. He sent them to me, and I put them in my safety deposit box in Bellingham."

"What kind of things?"

"Envelopes. I didn't look inside them. I'm not a prying mother. He just said he wanted me to keep them in case . . . in case . . ." She broke off.

I was impatient, but I managed to keep quiet until she regained her composure and could go on. "In case something like this would . . ."

For several minutes she sobbed brokenly. Finally, she got up, walked over to the dresser, and looked at herself in the mirror. Carefully she wiped a rivulet of mascara off her cheek.

It occurred to me that Grace Simms Morris was careful to maintain her appearance under even the most trying circumstances. I wondered if other kinds of appearances were equally as important to her.

"Did you know Jonathan Thomas?" I asked.

"Of course I knew Jon. He was a wonderful young man. It was so tragic what happened to him."

I thought for a moment that she was referring to his murder. She soon disabused me of that notion. "I can't understand why they don't keep better track of the people who donate blood these days, but I guess it could happen to anybody."

"People who donate blood? You mean Jonathan Thomas contracted AIDS through contaminated blood?"

Grace Simms Morris gave me an arch look. "Why, of course. How else would he have gotten it?"

How else indeed!

"Jon and Rich were very devoted to one an-other," she continued. "Such good friends."

"Friends?" I asked.

"The very best of friends," she assured me openly. "From the time they met in college. Why, that must have been ten years ago now. Time seems to fly these days, doesn't it?"

I nodded, but I didn't answer. Talking with Mrs. Morris was like stepping into quicksand. If Richard Dathan Morris hadn't seen fit to come out of the closet with his mother while he was alive, I didn't want to be the one to bring him out now that he was dead. I didn't have much respect for the dead, but I did for the living.

"You said he sent you envelopes to hold for safekeeping. When did he start doing that?"

She stopped to think for a moment. "Several months ago, I don't know exactly. I'll be able to tell for sure when I get them out. The envelopes all have postmarks on them."

"I'm sure you're not the prying type, Mrs. Mor-ris, but mothers have ways of knowing things, even things they're not supposed to know. Don't you have some idea about what might be in those envelopes?"

She smiled. "You mean like knowing what's in your Christmas present before you ever un-wrap it?"

"Yes."

"You're right. Rich said that he never could sur-prise me. I don't think he would have sent me drugs. That would have been illegal. I think he sent me information, things he didn't want to fall into the wrong hands. But I don't know who to give them to now."

"Did you tell that man at the DEA about them?"

"Mr. Wainwright?" I nodded.

"Certainly not. Why should I? He was rude to me. I'll show them to you, if you want me to."

"What exactly did this Mr. Wainwright say to you?"

"It wasn't so much what he said as how he acted. He treated me like I was a crazy old woman who didn't know what I was talking about. He said he was certain there was no one here in Seattle working as a CI." She paused. "Do you know what that means?"

"A cooperating individual," I explained. "An informant."

She pulled herself up straight. "Why, that louse!" she exclaimed. "Imagine him calling my son that. An informant. Rich was a hero, Detective Beaumont. He wasn't an informant."

I didn't take the trouble to explain the finer points of law enforcement to Mrs. Grace Simms Morris. I stood up and handed her one of my cards. "If I came to Bellingham next week, would you be willing to show me what's in the safety deposit box?"

"Certainly, Detective Beaumont. I'll be happy to. You mean you'll come even if the DEA won't?"

I nodded and her face crumpled. "Thank you," she said.

"Would you like me to try talking to the DEA for you?" I asked.

"If you think it would help," she said.

"It might," I said, but I didn't much believe it. I've dealt with more than my share of grieving mothers in my time. I figured Wainwright at the DEA must have done the same.

CHAPTER 16

WHEN I GOT BACK TO THE CAR, I SAT FOR SEVERAL MINutes pondering. On the one hand, I had to agree with Tom Riley's assessment of Grace Simms Morris as a dingy broad with a case of motherly selective blindness. But still, what she had said about her son had the ring of truth to it. At least she believed it was the truth.

That took me back to Richard Dathan Morris, the victim. Was he a narc working for the DEA as his mother claimed, or was he the lowlife described by Tom Riley? Or did the answer lie somewhere in between? Without knowing more about Morris, without understanding what had made him tick, it was impossible to get a fix on the relationships of all the other characters in the drama.

If Morris had indeed been working for the DEA, and if he had somehow uncovered Jasmine's involvement in a cocaine ring, that would have been a reason to waste him. That's the way things work in the drug trade. Narcs and dealers play that way. For keeps.

My mental gymnastics were taking me nowhere. I still didn't know enough about any of the players to make a sound judgment. Turning the key in the ignition, I decided to head for lower Queen Anne Hill and the local office of the DEA. Why not check with Wainwright myself? Maybe he'd tell me something he couldn't or wouldn't tell a murder victim's mother.

I was there by four-fifteen, standing in an outside office trying to work my way past the agent of the day. When I told Roger Glancy what I wanted, he was more than a little reluctant to take me to the agent in charge.

"Look," Glancy said, handing me back my ID, "do we have to go over all this again? Somebody else was just in here raising hell about the same thing."

"Who? A woman?"

Glancy nodded. "She looked nice enough to begin with, but by the time she left, she was pitching a fit all over the office, just about bouncing off the walls and screaming bloody murder. She claims it's all our fault that her son is dead."

"Maybe it is," I said quietly. "Now, are you going to let me see Wainwright or not?"

"He's busy."

"Interrupt him."

Reluctantly, Glancy got up and led the way down a short hallway and past a secretary's desk.

He stopped in front of a door with a polished brass nameplate on it that read B. W. WAINWRIGHT, AGENT IN CHARGE. Glancy knocked.

"Come in," someone called from inside.

Glancy led the way into B. W. Wainwright's private office, where an affable-looking man in his mid-forties was seated behind a large desk. Wainwright, sandy haired and wearing tortoise-shell glasses, looked more like an accountant than a drug buster, and the papers on his desk were arranged in precise, well-organized stacks.

"This is Detective Beaumont of Seattle P.D.," Glancy was saying.

Wainwright pushed the glasses up on top of his head and rubbed his eyes wearily. "I wasn't aware we had an appointment."

"We don't," I said. "I stopped by because I need your help."

"With what? You working a narcotics case?" he asked.

"Homicide," I answered. "Drug-related."

"Show me one that isn't."

"It's about Richard Dathan Morris."

"Not him again."

"What do you mean, again?"

"I just finished having a run-in with his mother. She's got some wild idea that he was working for us."

"Was he?"

"No."

"You're sure?"

"Yes, I'm sure, Detective Beaumont. I happen

to be in charge here. I know who works for us and who doesn't."

I noticed the condescension in his manner of speech, the hint of arrogance that said he was wasting his time talking to me, a lowly detective from a municipal police department. It set my teeth on edge, the same as it must have done to Mrs. Grace Simms Morris.

"You mean, as the agent in charge, you not only know all the agents under you but all the local CIs as well?"

Our eyes met and held, each of us assessing the other. "That's precisely what I mean," he said, levelly. "We have to keep pretty close tabs on our confidential informants. Otherwise they end up dead."

"Richard Dathan Morris is dead," I reminded him. "Isn't there a chance that someone down the chain of command might have taken on another informant without letting you know about it?"

"No. No chance. I run this outfit, Detective Beaumont. Make no mistake about it. Those who don't play by the rules, by my rules, don't stay."

"And there's no record of Richard Dathan Morris in your personnel files."

"No."

"Did he ever apply to work for you?"

"Not so far as I can tell. I looked through the inactive application files after Mrs. Morris left here, but I didn't see any mention of him."

"So once she left your office, you did at least check."

"Detective Beaumont, Mrs. Morris is a woman under a great deal of stress. I checked, but just so I could tell her honestly that we showed no record of her son in this office. None whatsoever."

"Doesn't it seem a little unusual for someone like Mrs. Morris to come up with that kind of story?"

"Are you kidding? It happens all the time. Parents don't want to think their kids are involved with drugs. They'll come up with any harebrained rationalization to make it look like what is, isn't."

"How do you explain the envelopes, then?"

Wainwright frowned. "What envelopes? She never mentioned any envelopes."

Of course she hadn't mentioned them, because B. W. Wainwright had acted like a turkey, had treated her exactly the same way he was treating me. I said, "The ones Richard Dathan Morris sent to his mother before he died. The ones she keeps in her safety deposit box in Bellingham."

"She didn't say anything to me about that."

"She didn't think you'd believe her."

"Did she tell you what's in the envelopes?"

I shook my head. "No. And I didn't have time to go look at them today either. I've got my hands full as it is, and my partner's off today. I told her we'd come up next week and take a look."

"In other words, you think there's something to the story."

"Yes. Mrs. Morris said envelopes, not packages. She seems to think her son sent her information—

names, dates, places, deals. Things he needed held for safekeeping."

Wainwright nodded slowly. "I suppose that's possible, but if he wasn't working for us, who was he working for? Seattle P.D., maybe?"

"I'll check that out. If he wasn't connected to you or to our department, he might have been freelancing and stumbled into something big, something he couldn't handle."

"Freelancing is dangerous," Wainwright said.

"Dangerous, hell," I told him. "In this case, it was downright fatal. Twice."

"You mean the roommate? I heard about that."

I nodded. "I was the one who found the cocaine in his pillowcase."

"Then you're also the one who insisted on an autopsy. That was good police work."

"Thanks," I said, but I wanted to get back to the subject at hand, back to Richard Dathan Morris and his mother. "What are you going to do about Mrs. Morris?"

Wainwright looked clearly affronted. "Do about her? I'm not going to do anything about her. Not one blessed thing! Look, Detective Beaumont, you and I are in pretty much the same business. Do crackpots ever call you up and give you information that isn't worth a plugged nickel?"

"Occasionally."

"Believe me, that's what we're dealing with here. In spades. I'd bet money on it. Mrs. Morris lost her son in a drug deal gone sour. She wants desperately to paint him as a hero so she can feel better and look people straight in the eye, so his death won't seem like such a waste. I'm willing to let her believe whatever she wants to believe, but I'm not squandering one more minute of my agency's time or resources on this scam."

"Any other ideas, then?" I asked. "If he wasn't working for us and he wasn't working for you, who was he working for?"

"Another dealer. They're like sharks. Big fish eat little fish. It happens all the time."

Wainwright got up and showed me to the door. The interview had come to a close. "Thanks for your help," I said, holding out my hand.

"It was nothing," Wainwright said. "Any time."

That was certainly true. I wasn't much more in the know after my interview with B. W. Wainwright, but the conversation had given me food for thought.

Supposing Richard Dathan Morris had been freelancing, supposing he had found something big. The package of coke we'd found in Jonathan Thomas's pillowcase wouldn't have been worth much more than $25,000 on the street. What if Morris had stumbled into a conspiracy, into something much larger and more complex than that one simple package of cocaine? What if he had unearthed a major distribution network? Who else would be involved? Who else, that is, besides Jasmine Day?

It was time to beard the lioness in her den, time to have a little heart-to-heart chat with the lady.

After all, now that she knew I was a cop, I might just as well go ahead and be one.

I headed back downtown. Afternoon traffic was moving at a snail's pace. The closest parking place to the Mayflower Park Hotel was several blocks away. I didn't call ahead to announce my visit, not even from the lobby phone. There was no sense in giving Jasmine any advance notice.

I had a fleeting sense of déjà vu when I found myself once more pausing outside her door on the sixth floor, once more knocking for admittance.

"Who is it?" she called.

"Detective Beaumont," I answered. This was, after all, an official visit.

The door flew open without the slightest delay. Mary Lou Gibbon was the one who opened the door. The trademark Jasmine Day wig was no-where in evidence. The face before me was distorted into a mask of cold fury.

"Why, you no-good son of a bitch! You have the nerve to show up here? The brass-plated balls to come knocking on my door like you owned the goddamned place?"

She was wearing something like a pair of powder blue silk pajamas and matching high-heeled sandals. The angry face that looked up at me had been scrubbed clean of all makeup, creating an incongruous mixture of innocence and rage.

"May I come in?" I asked. "I have to talk to you."

"About what?"

"Drugs," I said. "Cocaine in particular. And Richard Dathan Morris."

"You're the one who did it, aren't you!"

"Did what?"

"Started the rumors."

"What rumors?" I asked, genuinely puzzled.

"Westcoast's pulling out of the tour. Tonight's the last concert."

"Pulling out?"

"Yes, goddamn it. Pulling out. It's over. Finished. The deal I made with Ed Waverly was that I keep my nose clean. Word got back to California that one of the stagehands was killed and that drugs were involved. They pulled the plug on me just like that."

Tears welled up in her eyes. "Get out of here, you asshole. Get away from me."

The tears got to me. They always do. The man and the cop in J. P. Beaumont went to war, the man's natural tenderness toward a woman he's bedded battling with the cop's revulsion toward someone who may be capable of cold-blooded murder. The cop won.

"I've got a witness who places you at the scene of the crime," I said. "Someone who saw you do it."

"Saw me do what?" she asked.

"Look, Jasmine, this isn't some simple little possessions scrape that your lawyer can bail you out of and nobody will be the wiser."

"What are you talking about?"

"The night of the load-in, what did you do?"

"I was here in my room, the way I always am the night before a show. I worked out, I got a good night's sleep."

"Was there anybody here with you? Anyone who saw you and would be able to say you didn't leave the hotel all night?"

She looked at me, frowning, a puzzled expression on her face. The feigned innocence made me furious.

"Jasmine, this is murder. Homicide. I came here to talk to you, to give you a chance to give yourself up and maybe turn state's evidence. Once all the facts are known, maybe there's a possibility of a plea bargain, maybe there were extenuating circumstances—"

I never saw it coming, never noticed when she slipped noiselessly out of the sandals. The ball of her foot cleared my face by a hair's breadth and crashed through the wall board next to me. The wall splintered with the force of the blow.

"Next time, it'll be your face," she snarled. "Now get out!"

The next thing I knew, we were standing in the hallway.

"Jasmine . . ." I began.

"Don't worry about the damage," she said icily. "It'll be a pleasure to pay for it. You're trying to set me up, aren't you? What is this, blackmail? Is that what you're trying to pull?"

Alan Dale came hurrying down the hall. "What's going on?"

"He's trying to set me up, to frame me for murder."

"He's what?" Dale demanded.

"It's not bad enough that he's gotten Westcoast

to cancel the rest of the tour. Now he's trying to frame me for murdering that stagehand, the one who died the night of the load-in."

"You'd better get the hell out of here," Dale growled at me. "If I see your ugly face again, I'm liable to flatten your nose or break your balls."

He took Jasmine's hand and led her away from me, back into her room. The door closed. For a long time, I stood looking at it. I had just seen a spectacular display of deadly force. Jasmine Day's brown belt was more than empty words, and she could easily have coldcocked me if she wanted to.

I looked up and down the hall, embarrassed that she had caught me off guard. No one was there. Luckily, no one had witnessed my humiliation. That was some small comfort anyway.

What would happen now? I wondered. I had blown it, told her she was under suspicion. Now what would she do? Would she run or not? There was no way to tell.

Just then the door opened and Alan Dale stepped back into the hall.

"I told you to get the hell out of here," he said.

"Tell her not to leave town," I said.

"Tell her yourself," he retorted. "If you're tough enough."

Dale turned away from me and walked down the hall. Making no move toward Jasmine's door, I stood there watching him go as I tried to assess the damage to my ego.

At least it wasn't fatal. I'd probably get over it. Eventually.

CHAPTER 17

I DROVE BACK TO THE DEPARTMENT, FEELING UNEASY. Something was eating at me, nagging away at the back of my mind. I was so lost in thought that when I saw the familiar face across the crowded lobby of the Public Safety Building, I didn't move quickly enough to duck out of sight.

The face belonged to none other than my old nemesis, Maxwell Cole.

Max is an ex-boyfriend of my ex-wife, which is the nicest thing I can say about him. We were in college together, in the same fraternity. He's nursed a grudge against me ever since I waltzed Karen, my first wife, out from under his nose and straight down the aisle.

Usually, once those teenage romantic rivalries are over, they're over. It's kid stuff, and it goes away. Unfortunately, Max and I run in the same circles. His work as a columnist for the *Seattle Post-Intelligencer* and mine as a police officer continually throw us together. We get in each other's way, on each other's nerves. Besides which, I don't like him. I'm sure the feeling's mutual.

I wasn't happy to see his overstuffed, walrus-like form thumping through the crowded rush-hour lobby. He hailed me from across the room.

"Hey there, J. P. How's it going? I was just coming upstairs to look for you."

"I'm busy," I returned. I punched the button and watched impatiently as the light showed the building's sluggish elevator stopping on every floor on its way to the lobby.

"All I want is the answer to one question. Who's the blonde?"

"What blonde?"

"That's not nice, J. P. Here I am, coming to you to do my civic duty, and you hold out on me. Is that any way to treat an old pal?"

"What civic duty?" I asked. "And what blonde?"

"Come on now. You dicks aren't the only guys with sources on the streets. I happen to have some informants of my own. You tell me what you know, I'll tell you what I know."

The elevator door opened. I waited while the crowd drained out; then I got on and pushed the button for floor two. I wanted to stop by the crime lab and talk to Janice Morraine before I went on up to my cubicle on the fifth floor.

Max followed me onto the elevator without pushing any buttons of his own. He was evidently going wherever I went. "You're working the Burlington Northern homicide, aren't you?" he asked.

I gave a noncommittal shrug. When we reached the second floor, I got out and Max tagged along.

"Somebody told me you were the one screaming for an autopsy on that queer up on Bellevue, the one who died of an overdose instead of AIDS."

"So?"

Max grinned, a knowing smirk that waggled the ends of his drooping handlebar mustache. "I've been doing a little detective work of my own, J. P. I heard through the grapevine that you interviewed a bag lady about that shoe-wielding killer, a blonde in a long blue dress."

That got me good. I don't like it when newspaper reporters tell me things about my cases that they're not supposed to know. "How'd you find out about that?"

"The bag lady's got more than a couple of screws loose, J. P. She blabbed her story to anyone who'd listen before you and Reverend Beardsly managed to lock her up in the Pike Street Mission."

I moved toward him menacingly. "Max, if you so much as breathe a word . . ."

The remainder of my threat went unfinished. Max sprang backward, holding up one soft, white hand to protect his equally soft, flabby face. "So she was real."

"If you know what's good for you, Max, you'd by God better not leak word of this. You'll jeopardize the entire investigation."

"Who said anything about leaking? I came here to give you some information."

"What kind of information?"

"About the blonde."

"What about her?"

"I've located another witness who saw her."

Another witness? Maybe one who would prove to be more reliable than Belinda? One who had also seen the fatal struggle in the parking lot? The noose seemed to be tightening around Jasmine Day's pretty little neck. My pulse beat faster in my throat, and I felt a sense of rising excitement like a trailing hound catching a scent.

"Where?" I demanded. "Down by the tunnel? In the parking lot?"

Maxwell Cole enjoyed his brief moment of triumph. He wanted to bask in it, to rub my nose in it. He pursed his lips and shook his head. The movement sent his thick glasses sliding down his nose. He shoved them back into place.

"Are you going to tell me who she is or not? I've got a hunch, but I want to know for sure."

"This isn't *Let's Make a Deal*, Max," I reminded him. "It's a homicide investigation. If you knowingly withhold information, I'll personally see to it you go to jail. You can count on it."

Maxwell Cole suddenly looked uneasy. He'd never make it playing poker. His face gives him away. "You wouldn't do that, would you?" he whined.

"Try me."

"Up on Bellevue," he said.

"What?"

"My witness saw the same blonde up on Bellevue, right in front of the house where the other guy died. Same blue dress, same long gloves, same blonde hair."

"What time?"

"Around one or so. That squares with what the medical examiner's office says was the approximate time of death."

I took out my notepad. "Who's the witness?"

"An LOL who lives down the street."

"What's this little old lady's name, and what exactly did she see?"

"Her name's Mavis Davis."

I must have looked dubious.

"Honest to God, J. P., that's her name," Max continued. "I didn't make it up. She's got this ugly little mutt named Gordy, an old dog. Gordy's been sick. The other night, he had to go for a walk. Late. While she was waiting for him to do his job, she saw a cab stop in front of the house on Bellevue. A woman in a long blue dress got out."

"What kind of cab?"

"She didn't say."

"So what happened?"

"She said she watched the woman get out of the cab, pay the driver, and go inside the house."

"That's it?"

"That's it."

"Did the cab go or stay?"

"It left."

"Did she say what kind of cab?" I asked again.

"No. Only that it was green."

"How did you find her?"

"I was up there poking around, trying to find an angle, and I just stumbled into her. It was blind luck. She was out walking her dog. Again. He's still sick."

I couldn't recall the name Mavis Davis surfacing in any of the apartment buildings Big Al and I had visited the previous morning, but then we must have talked to seventy-five people while we were searching for a possible witness.

"Where does this woman live?" I asked.

"Just off Harvard, a couple of blocks north."

"What's her number?"

"Wait a minute. You haven't told me about the blonde."

"And I'm not going to. What's the number?" He gave it to me finally, under protest, and I wrote it down.

"Is it Jasmine Day?" Max blurted suddenly.

"What makes you think that?"

"Just a hunch, that's all."

Maxwell Cole doesn't have a modest bone in his body. His diffident answer was totally out of character. I had made the connection between Jasmine Day and Richard Dathan Morris, but I wanted to know how Max had done it. If there was another trail leading to Jasmine Day, I was going to check it out myself.

"Bullshit!" I told him. "You got the idea somewhere, Max. It's a long jump from a witness seeing an unidentified blonde in a blue dress to accusing a particular blonde of murder, especially if the blonde is a famous singer. I want to know who put that notion in your head, how you made the connection."

Max backed away from me. "Why should I tell you? You won't help me."

"I'll help you, all right. I'll keep you from going to jail. Now tell me where you got your information."

Max blinked and looked puzzled. "Does that mean it isn't her?"

I didn't answer, but Max jumped to his own conclusions. "If it isn't her, why did someone call me and say it was?"

"Someone called you? Who? When?"

He shrugged. "I don't know who it was. Just an anonymous tip. You know, people think newspaper people can actually do stuff. A guy called late this afternoon, right when I got back to the office after talking with that Davis woman."

"What did he say?"

"Just that Jasmine Day was under suspicion in two drug-related murders. I talked it over with my editor. He said the story was too hot to print without some sort of official confirmation. Libel, you know, and all that. So I came looking for you."

"He said two?"

Max nodded. "That's right."

So someone was passing out inside information, someone who knew Jasmine was under suspicion in the Jonathan Thomas case before we knew she was.

"But why'd he call you?" I asked.

Max shrugged. "He said he thought maybe it was something I'd be interested in putting in my column."

"He said that on the phone?"

"Sure."

"What days does your column run?"

"Tuesdays, Thursdays, and Saturdays," Max answered. He looked annoyed, as if he thought I should have known that vital information without having to ask.

"And this guy asked for you by name?" Max nodded. "What have your columns been about this week?"

I'm sure Max thinks every word that drips from his fingertips is golden. He was probably shocked to know that I had no idea what tub he'd been thumping on.

He answered grudgingly. "Tuesday's was about the judge in Tukwila who's got three DWI convictions. Thursday's was all about overcrowding in the jail. Tomorrow's is about people stealing parking meters from downtown Seattle."

My radar came on with a little warning pip. I don't like it when murder trials are conducted in the newspapers, especially when the trial is in full swing before a suspect is even arrested. This smacked of a frame-up to me, of someone wanting to put Jasmine Day so firmly in front of our noses that we wouldn't look beyond her.

Part of making a successful frame-up work is to make it seem plausible, to get people to buy the story. How better to do that than to engage the help of the local media? You get them to do your job for you, have them print the story for you so it will seem logical and reasonable.

Maybe you could engage a local cop too, if you could find one dumb enough to fall into the trap. That brought me up short. Was somebody using both Max and me as fall guys? I didn't like the possibility, but it was there all the same.

If that was the case, who was behind it? Max's description of that week's column material didn't sound like such hot stuff to me. It didn't sound like something that would capture the imagination of someone who had just blown into town. What would make an outsider think that someone writing columns about stolen parking meters or DWIs might be interested in solving a murder?

They wouldn't. If someone was indeed trying to frame Jasmine Day, it had to be somebody local, someone who knew Maxwell Cole well enough to be sure he would snap at the bait.

"I don't know who the blonde is," I said, "but you can bet I intend to find out."

I turned and headed for the crime-lab door, knowing full well that Maxwell Cole couldn't follow me inside. Don Yamamoto, head of the Washington State Patrol Crime Lab, had thrown Max out long ago, telling him to get lost and not come back.

"J. P., you're lying to me," Max protested over my shoulder. "You come back here and tell me the truth."

The funny thing was, if I had known the truth right then, I might very well have told him.

Inside the crime lab, I found Don Yamamoto himself seated in a small, cluttered private office. Stripped down to his shirtsleeves, with a knotted tie hanging loose around his neck, he was poring through papers from a disorderly jumble of file folders strewn across the desk in front of him. Standing up when I tapped on the glass window of his office, he came toward me holding out his hand.

"I wondered when you'd show up, Beau. Did you get Jan's message?"

I shook my head. "I just got in. I haven't been upstairs yet."

"She had to leave early. She called upstairs looking for you just before she went off duty."

"I've been out."

Yamamoto smiled. "That's okay. I don't suppose she'll mind if I jump the gun and give you the news first. She did a first-rate job. She got hold of the import/export company that deals with the shoe manufacturer and traced the shoes to a—"

"Don't tell me, let me guess. To a shoe store in Beverly Hills."

Don Yamamoto frowned. "If you never got Jan's message, how'd you know that?"

"Just lucky, I guess. Go on."

"Anyway, when she found out the customer's name, she ran a few of the prints we found on the shoe through our new fingerprint identification system. We got a match."

"Of course you did. They're her shoes."

I've known Don Yamamoto for a number of years, and I've never seen him flustered. But he was this time. It showed all over.

"You know about Jasmine Day, then?" he demanded. "About her priors? Jan got one of the guys upstairs to run a check on her."

"Jasmine doesn't make a secret of her past," I said. "Were any of her prints bloody?"

"No, but . . ."

It was too easy, the finger was pointing too clearly. My warning pip got stronger. "No buts, Don. The killer was wearing gloves."

Don looked at me and shook his head. "You mean to tell me you don't think she did it? There's the wig and the shoes and the prints, but you still don't think it's her?"

When he said the word shoes, everything that had been bothering me came into focus. The shoes. The killer had used the shoes to pummel Richard Dathan Morris. Jasmine wouldn't have needed shoes as a weapon, wouldn't have stooped to that, not when she had a perfectly good foot handy.

A flood of relief rushed through my body. I hadn't wanted it to be her, and now I was sure. Jasmine hadn't killed Richard Dathan Morris, but who had? Someone wearing her costume, the one Morris had stolen.

I came back to the present to find Don Yamamoto staring at me, waiting for me to answer.

"Something about it doesn't seem right to me,"

I mumbled. "I don't like it when all the pieces fall into place without a fight."

It sounded half-assed and feeble, but it was better than blurting out what was really going through my mind and admitting to Don Yamamoto that the real reason I knew Jasmine hadn't done it was that I had seen the lady in action, and she'd scared the living shit right out of me.

Don Yamamoto scratched his thinning black hair and shook his head. He looked as if he didn't much believe me, and I didn't blame him. On the surface it didn't sound very plausible to me either.

"A frame-up?" he asked with a scowl. "Maybe it's time to think about early retirement, Beau. The benefits are real good."

"Piss up a rope," I told him and left the crime lab. Neither one of us was going to change the other's mind.

I was excited as I went up the three flights of stairs to my office. I felt I'd stumbled onto something important, but I didn't know what to do with it or how to come up with some corroborating evidence. I sat down in my cubicle and stared briefly at the wall, trying to decide what to do next.

I was torn. Part of me wanted to go and try to talk with Jasmine Day, to see if she knew of any enemies in her past or present who might be out to get her. The other part of me wanted to talk to Mavis Davis and find out what she had to say.

Mavis Davis won the toss. I started for the garage and ran smack into Sergeant Lowell James. "I was just looking for you, Beau. What's happening? I've gotten no report from you."

"I'm on my way to interview a woman on the Morris case," I said. "A new witness." I told him about Mavis Davis, neglecting to say that she actually was a witness in the wrong murder. I convinced myself it was a case of careful editing rather than outright lying.

"Where'd you find her?" he asked.

"Maxwell Cole turned her up and came by to tell me."

"You're shitting me. Maxwell Cole? The Maxwell Cole from the *P.I.*?"

"That's the one."

Sergeant James shook his head. "Will wonders never cease?" he said.

I started on down the hall. "Remember," Sergeant James called behind me, "I want a full written report before you go off duty tonight, understood?"

"Right," I answered. "You'll have it."

I wondered what it would say.

CHAPTER 18

IT WAS SIX O'CLOCK WHEN I FOUND MAVIS DAVIS'S house just up from the Harvard Exit Theater. The only reason I was able to find a parking place was that the movie didn't start for another hour.

The house was a tiny place, unfenced but with wrought-iron bars on every window and door. As soon as I rang the bell, a small dog started yapping inside, the hoarse, rasping bark of an old, frail dog.

A tiny peephole window opened in the door just at eye level. "Who is it?" a woman asked sharply.

"Miss Davis? I'm Detective J. P. Beaumont with the Seattle Police Department." I held my identification up to the window so she could see it.

"What does it say?" she asked. "I can't read it."

"It says I'm a detective with the Seattle Police Department. I'd like to talk to you."

"I suppose you talked to that other man, the one who was here earlier."

"That's right. Maxwell Cole from the *P.I.* gave me your name and address. May I come in?"

She sighed. "Oh dear. I told him I didn't want to get mixed up in any of this. I should have kept quiet."

I felt awkward, leaning over to speak to her through the small opening. And it was difficult to understand her, since the dog was still carrying on its earsplitting yammering in the background.

"If I could just speak to you for a few minutes, Miss Davis, it would be very helpful. I have to ask you a few questions about what you saw."

"*Mrs.* Davis," she snapped. "I haven't been 'Miss' for a long time."

The peephole window slammed shut. A moment later, I heard her begin working her way down the door, unlocking a series of four dead bolts before the knob finally turned and the door opened.

Instantly the dog darted out, making a dive for my nearest ankle. Mrs. Mavis Davis grabbed him and scooped him up into her arms on the second attempt. By then he had only grazed my sock. The dog was an ugly, dun-colored miniature poodle with wildly protruding eyes and several missing teeth.

When I first saw her, Mavis Davis was also toothless, but once she had retrieved her dog, she held him with one arm, reached into her apron pocket with her other hand, and popped a pair of dentures into her mouth.

"Shh, now," she said to the dog. "It's all right, Gordy. This man is a policeman. He isn't going to steal anything."

Gordy remained unconvinced. He continued to bark.

Mavis Davis stepped to one side and motioned me into the house. As I walked past, Gordy made another lunge for me. This time he grabbed for my elbow. The only thing that saved my jacket was the dog's lack of teeth. The woman sat down in a rocking chair and patted the dog lovingly.

"Gordy worries about me, you see," she said fondly. "We live here alone. He's my only protection."

Other than raising an ungodly racket, I don't know what good the dog could possibly have done her. He grew quiet finally, and lay in his owner's lap, glaring menacingly at me.

I looked around the room then. It was filled with old-fashioned furniture covered with fancywork and doilies. In the corner sat an old cabinet-style radio that probably hadn't worked in years.

Keeping one restraining hand on the dog, Mavis reached over and picked up a skein of yarn and some crochet work from a nearby table. Next she perched a pair of narrow-lensed reading glasses on her nose. Resting her needlework project on the dog's back, she begin crocheting, peering at me from time to time over the upper rim of her glasses. She was a scrawny woman, in her seventies or so, with narrow, angular features and a hooked nose.

"So what do you want, Mr. . . . ?"

"Beaumont," I supplied. "Detective Beaumont. I want to talk to you about what you saw night before last."

"You mean when I was out walking Gordy?"

"Yes."

" 'Twasn't much. Just a woman getting out of a cab, late at night. Happens all the time."

"Except this time she was going into a house where a murder took place a short time later," I said. "Did you get a good look at her?"

"I already told that other man. She was blonde, and she was all dressed up too, in a long blue dress, white gloves, and no shoes."

"She was barefoot?"

"If you're not wearing shoes, young man, then you're barefoot, seems to me," Mavis answered crossly.

"Tell me exactly what happened."

"Gordy woke me up about twelve-thirty. He used to make it through the night without needing to go out, but he's been sick lately. Getting old, maybe, just like me. When he has to go, he has to go. So we went out. I had my bag and my pooper scooper. It's the law, you know."

I nodded. "Yes, I know," I agreed.

"Anyway, he has this favorite place, so we went there. It's on the parking strip, a block or so the other side of Harvard. I was standing waiting for him to finish when the cab drove up."

"Drove up where?"

"To that house, the little one there between

those two big apartment buildings. Do you know the one I mean?"

"Yes, go on."

"Anyway, this woman got out of the backseat. I noticed her because you don't often see people that dressed up in this day and age. You just see kids with long hair and ragged clothes or jeans, and nothing matches."

"What about the woman?"

"Oh, yes. She got out of the cab, went up to the window, and paid the driver, and then went into the house."

"You say she went into the house? Was the door open?"

"No."

"So how did she get in?"

"She had a key. I watched her unlock the door and go inside."

"Did you see anything else?"

Mavis Davis shook her head. "No. By then Gordy was finished, so I cleaned up after him and we came home. I was cold."

"What time was that?"

"About a quarter to one, maybe. I wasn't sleepy anymore, so I stayed up and worked for a while. It was two or so before I went back to bed." She smiled. "It doesn't matter what time I go to bed, since we can sleep as late as we like, right, Gordy?"

Gordy gave a miniature growl in reply. He had never taken his ugly eyes off me.

"Do you know the name of the cab company?" I asked.

Mavis shook her head. "I take the bus most of the time, or I walk. I don't pay any attention to taxis. All I know is it was green."

"Light green or dark green?"

"Oh, you know, that funny light green chartreuse color."

I did indeed know. That could only be one of the Far West taxis.

"And you say she walked up to the window to pay her fare."

"That's what I said," Mavis answered.

That struck me as odd. I've been in lots of cabs with women, especially when I lived at the Royal Crest and went places with my neighbor Ida and some of her retired pals. They always paid the fare while they were still in the cab, passing the money to the driver before they got out.

"Would it be possible for me to use a phone?" I asked. "Maybe I could call the cab company and get a line on the driver."

Mavis shrugged her shoulders and nodded toward the kitchen. "It's out there, on the wall. The light's just inside the door."

The moment I stood up, Gordy had another fit. I don't know how anyone could keep, much less love, a dog as obnoxious as that.

I went into the kitchen and found both the phone and the phone book. I called Far West Cabs. The fact that it was that particular company was a stroke of pure luck. Years before, I had been assigned the case of a Far West cabbie who was murdered and dumped in Green Lake. I had broken the case within days and sent the cabbie's wife's boyfriend to Walla Walla on a charge of second-degree homicide. The wife ended up spending some time in the slammer as well.

Ever since, any help I needed from Far West came through on the double. This was no exception. The dispatcher on duty was the same one who had been there the night before.

"This is Detective Beaumont," I said. "I'm working a case and need some help."

"You bet," he replied. "If we've got it, you can have it."

"It's about a fare from the night before last. Actually sometime after midnight, I don't know where she was picked up, but a Far West cab dropped her off in the one-thousand block of Bellevue Avenue East sometime after midnight, so it was really very early in the A.M. yesterday. A barefoot blonde, wearing a long blue dress and white gloves."

"Oh, him," the dispatcher said. "We're looking for him too."

"Pardon me?" I asked, sure that I hadn't heard correctly.

"I said we're looking for him too. He left one of his shoes in the cab."

"A blue shoe?"

"That's right. I've got it right here in the lost-and-found."

"But you said 'him.'"

"Sure I said 'him.' The driver picked him up at the Edgewater. All those drag queens go down there for the female-impersonator acts. The drivers don't much care to pick 'em up, if you know what I mean, but a fare's a fare."

"It was a man?"

"That's what I said."

"Go check the shoe," I ordered. "Is it a Ferragamo, size 8½B?"

The dispatcher was off the line for a moment or two; then he came back. "You must be psychic, Beaumont. That's what it is, size 8½B. What do you want me to do with it?"

"Hang onto it until somebody from the department comes to get it. Unless the owner shows up. In that case, call 911 and have somebody come pick him up."

"No shit?"

"No shit. This guy's a killer. He's two up on us already."

The dispatcher whistled. "This is serious, isn't it? Anything else I can do to help?"

My mind was leaping from one direction to another. It was a frame. The killer, disguised as Jasmine Day, had first murdered Richard Dathan Morris, then taken a cab to the house to murder Jonathan Thomas. Why? And how had he left there?

Supposing he had gone there in search of cocaine—coke Morris had either stolen or planned to sell. There had been plenty of time for the killer to make a leisurely search. After all, he knew Morris wasn't coming back.

So the killer searched the house, but maybe he

had been squeamish about touching the sick man's bed. Maybe that's why he hadn't found it. Or maybe Jonathan Thomas woke up and recognized him.

The light came on. That had to be it. If Jonathan Thomas had recognized whoever was there, that explained why he had to die. The killer might not have been willing to risk letting Jonathan's disease run its natural course. If Thomas had recognized him and told the nurse, Riley would have listened, would have believed him, and would have told someone else.

"Hello, are you there?" The dispatcher interrupted my train of thought. "I said, is there anything else I can do to help?"

"Yes, there is. Do you know the other dispatchers, the ones who work for other companies?"

"Sure."

"Call them. See if anyone went to that same address later that night and picked up someone else. If so, find out where they took him. Can you do that?"

"No problem."

"How long will it take?"

"Maybe fifteen minutes or so. There aren't very many of us at that time of night."

"Look," I said, "it's important. If you could check it out and get back to me here, I'd really appreciate it."

I gave him Mavis Davis's telephone number. When I hung up the phone and turned around, Gordy was there in the kitchen doorway, standing with one front paw poised in the air, eyeing me distrustfully. The moment I stepped away from the phone, he started barking again, so hard that he literally bounced up and down with every bark.

Mavis came to the doorway and grabbed him up again. "Are you finished?" she asked.

"No. I've left word for someone to call me back here, if it's all right with you. What you told me is really important. We're having it checked out right now."

"Checked out. You mean you don't believe me?"

"It's not that. I've found the cab company that brought . . ." I paused. "That brought her to the house," I said carefully. "Now we have to see if anyone else picked her up and took her away later on."

"You mean she didn't live in that house?"

"No."

Mavis shook her head disapprovingly. "You know, in my day, young women weren't allowed to go gallivanting around town at all hours of the day and night. It's no wonder they get into such trouble nowadays, is it?"

"No," I agreed. "It's no wonder at all."

She offered me coffee. I accepted, grateful to have something to do while we waited for the phone to ring. It was actually only ten minutes later when the call came through. Mavis answered it and then handed the receiver to me.

"This is Larry down at Far West," the guy said. "This Detective Beaumont?"

"Yes."

"Well, a Yellow Cab picked a guy up from there about three-thirty yesterday morning. Took him to 6886 Greenwood Avenue North. I talked to the driver. He remembers him real good."

"How come?"

"The guy wasn't wearing any shoes."

"Larry, thanks. I've gotta run."

My hand shook with excitement as I pressed down the receiver button. I was finally getting somewhere, making progress. I dialed direct to Sergeant Lowell James's desk in the department.

"Where've you been, Beau? We've got people looking all over for you."

"Never mind that. I'm onto something. Where's the *Cole's*?"

Cole's is a reverse directory that makes it possible to locate people by address or phone number rather than by last name. It's a bill-collector's bible. It's good for detectives as well.

Sergeant James went off the line momentarily. "I've got it," he said when he returned. "Now, what's the address you want?"

I gave it to him. Greenwood Avenue North, number 6886. While I waited for him to look up the information, I entertained myself by tapping a pencil impatiently on the wall beside the phone. The noise set Gordy off again. If he'd been my dog, I would have strangled him on the spot.

"Got it," Sergeant James said. "The name's Osgood, Daniel P. Osgood."

"Holy shit!"

"Who is he? What's going on?"

"Get me a backup team and get them there pronto. I'll meet them at that Greenwood address in . . ." I paused long enough to look at my watch. "In fifteen minutes."

"Who is Daniel P. Osgood?"

"The man who killed Richard Dathan Morris and Jonathan Thomas."

"The man? I thought we were looking for a woman."

"Look, are you going to get me some help or not?"

"They're on their way," Sergeant James told me.

"Me too."

I hung up the phone, thanked Mavis Davis for her help, and dashed for the door with Gordy right on my heels.

I didn't look back to see whether or not the door slammed on his nose. It was supposed to.

CHAPTER 19

I TURNED THINGS OVER IN MY MIND AS I DROVE TO Osgood's address on Greenwood North. It was beginning to make sense, all of it. I remembered how Dan Osgood had acted the first time I met him, how he had turned my card over and over in his fingers, how he had blanched when I mentioned visiting the murder victim's parents. I had seen it then, but it hadn't registered. It did now.

Osgood had to be the local connection between whoever was importing the coke and Richard Dathan Morris. He was also the connection between Morris and the Fifth Avenue Theater, the one who had arranged the work calls, who had seen to it that Morris worked the Fifth Avenue shows.

Was it possible that someone connected with Westcoast Starlight Productions was the supplier? If so, who was in charge? Who called the shots?

To begin with, there was Jasmine Day, the one I was supposed to think was it. But planted evidence aside, Jasmine didn't have the necessary continuity. This was her first tour with Westcoast. I wanted to believe that she was nothing more than a pawn, unlucky enough to be in the wrong place at the wrong time. But a dangerous pawn, I cautioned myself, remembering the hole in the wall beside my head. A nitroglycerine pawn.

So who else was there at Westcoast? Most of my dealings had been with Alan Dale, the head carpenter/stage manager. He had claimed to be the one who fired Morris for poking around where he shouldn't have been. Had he fired him first and killed him later? Dale had seemed more than slightly upset when I implied that maybe Jasmine was back on drugs. I remembered him glaring at me in the hallway outside Jasmine Day's room. Was there something else going on between them, something more than the obvious professional relationship?

Then there was Ray Holman, the guy on the truss high above the theater stage whom Osgood had called the flyman. I had seen him working, but I had heard very little from him. He had seemed to be a taciturn man with his head always buried in some piece of equipment or other, someone who was always around but who blended into the woodwork. What was going on behind that silent, workaholic mask of his?

And then there was Ed Waverly. What about him? He was the one Jasmine credited with giving her a chance when nobody else would, the one who had been willing and able to put together a tour for her when she came out of treatment and wanted to change career directions. Waverly didn't seem like such a hot prospect to me, but I couldn't afford to ignore anyone.

That left Bertha, Big Bertha the costume lady, as the only other permanent member of the company I had spoken to directly. Big Bertha had been formidable enough when she had chased me out of Jasmine's dressing room during intermission the night before, but it looked to me like she spent a hell of a lot more time pushing food than pushing drugs.

The upshot was that when I hit Greenwood Avenue North some fifteen minutes later, I had made zero progress. I still had way more questions than I had answers.

My two backup detectives were already in place and waiting for me. So was Sergeant Lowell James. In one hand he held a bona fide search warrant with Dan Osgood's address filled in in the appropriate blank. James never told me how he managed to get a search warrant that fast, and I never asked.

The sky had cleared, although the ground was still wet. It was one of those early summer Seattle evenings when it seems like afternoon will go on forever. Greenwood Avenue is enough of an arterial so that no one paid any attention to the extra two or three cars parked here and there along the street within a block or two of 6886.

Detectives Hawkins and Maynard, the backup team, circled the block to cut off any chance of an exit through the rear door, while Sergeant James and I cautiously approached the front. It was a modest white frame house with a small front porch. There was no fence and no shrubbery, only a narrow patch of grass badly in need of cutting.

Sergeant James stood to one side while I moved to the door. With my hand raised to knock, I paused. From inside the house came the sound of a woman weeping. I listened for a moment or two, then tried the old-fashioned bell button next to the door. Nothing happened. There was no ring, and the sound of weeping continued unabated. After waiting a moment or two longer, I gave a sharp rap on the wooden door frame. The weeping ceased abruptly, and the hardwood floor creaked as someone came to the door.

The woman who swung open the door was in her late twenties or early thirties. Her appearance was disheveled. She wore a pair of faded jeans and a paint-splattered sweatshirt. Her nose and eyes were red, her face was wet, and her shirt showed damp spots where tears had dripped off her face onto her clothing.

"What do you want?" she asked.

"Police," I answered, peering over her shoulder to see if there was anyone behind her in the room. There didn't seem to be. "We're looking for Daniel Osgood." I handed her the search warrant.

Her hand clutched it. She crumpled it without bothering to look at it and backed away from me into the room.

"He's not here," she answered.

"Do you know where he is?"

She shook her head from side to side. New tears coursed down the wet paths on her cheeks. "He's gone. He left me for good."

"You mean he moved out?" I asked.

I motioned Sergeant James into the house. He came through the door cautiously. He, too, glanced warily around the room before moving forward. While he crept from room to room making sure there was no one else in the house, I turned to the weeping woman.

"I begged him not to go," she said. "I told him that I forgave him, but he said he was going all the same."

"Forgave him for what?"

She looked down at her hands, and her lower lip trembled. "There's another woman," she said. "I suspected for a long time, but the other night I knew for sure. He came home late. I could tell he had showered. His hair was still damp. He had used some other kind of soap, and he smelled of perfume."

I couldn't help feeling some compassion for her. This was a woman with blinders on. If she was devastated by the idea that her husband was messing around with another woman, I wondered what would happen to her when she figured out he was a drug-dealing murderer to boot.

"Do you have any idea where he would have gone?" I asked. "Relatives? Friends?"

She shook her head. "I suppose he went to

work. There's a show down at the Fifth Avenue Theater. He couldn't afford to lose his job."

"What did he take with him?"

"Just a suitcase."

"Only one?"

"That's all I saw."

"What was in it?"

"I don't know. He was just zipping it up when I came into the bedroom. He didn't expect me home from work that early. He was going to leave me a note. He wasn't even going to tell me good-bye." She burst into tears again.

"How long ago was this?"

"Two hours ago, about."

Just then Sergeant James came back into the living room. He was shaking his head. Hawkins and Maynard trailed behind him. "There's nobody here," James said.

Hawkins was carrying a crumpled paper sack. "Have a look at this, Beau." He held it up and I looked inside. I caught a glimpse of blue material.

"The dress?" I asked.

Hawkins nodded. "And a pair of white gloves," he added. "He didn't even bother to ditch them in somebody else's dumpster."

"He didn't think we'd follow him home," I said.

I turned to the woman again. She was blowing her nose, attempting to regain her composure. She seemed oblivious to what Hawkins had said.

"What's your name?" I asked.

"Julia," she whispered. "Julia Osgood." Her answer was almost inaudible.

"I'm correct in assuming you're his wife?"

"Yes."

"And you had quarreled?" I asked.

Julia Osgood nodded slowly. "I told him I was sick and tired of him coming and going at strange times. I told him I wanted a husband who was a real husband. I wanted to wake up in bed at night and find him there."

"He was out late often?"

"He works nights whenever a show's in town, but the night before last he didn't come in until it was almost light." Julia Osgood looked down at her hands. Her lower lip trembled. "I didn't worry about the partying, but knowing he had been with someone else . . ." Her voice trailed off.

It wasn't so much that Dan Osgood had been *with* someone else. He had actually *been* someone else. But I wasn't prepared to go into that with Julia Osgood. Not right then.

"And you think he may have gone to work, even though he packed a suitcase and was leaving home?"

"Dan doesn't miss work," Julia declared. "He prides himself on that."

"What kind of car does he drive?"

"A Honda Accord. But it's in the garage; it broke down. The transmission went."

"So when he left, how did he go?"

"He called a cab."

"Do you know what kind?"

She nodded. "I watched him from the window. It was a Yellow Cab."

I turned to Sergeant James. He was shaking his head. "I'll bet he skipped," I said to him. "We'd better check with the theater. If he's not there, we'll issue an APB."

Something seemed to click in Julia Osgood's head. She looked quickly back and forth between Sergeant James and me. "An APB? An all-points bulletin? For Dan? Why?"

"Mrs. Osgood," I said. "We're conducting a homicide investigation here. We have to ask your husband some questions."

"Homicide?" Her eyes widened. She groped behind her for a chair and lowered herself into it. "You think Dan's involved in a murder?"

"Possibly. And drugs too."

She looked at me directly. "Oh," she said. It was an acknowledgment, not a denial. "He told me he was getting out of it. He promised."

"Out of what?"

"Cocaine. He used it sometimes."

"Did he sell it?"

"No."

"Are you sure?"

There was a pause, a long pause, and then a much smaller "No."

Sergeant James was standing near the door. "Come on, Beau. We'd better go."

I nodded. If Osgood was trying to make it out

of the country, there wasn't a moment to lose. I turned back to his wife. "Would you be willing to give us a statement?" I asked.

"I suppose so," she answered.

"Then you'd better come with us. Sergeant James can take you down to our office. You shouldn't be here by yourself."

"Dan wouldn't hurt me," she said.

There was a good possibility she was wrong about that, but I didn't argue the point. "Maybe your husband wouldn't hurt you, Mrs. Osgood, but some of his associates might. I'd rather you went along with Sergeant James. I'd feel better."

Julia Osgood nodded slowly, got up, and picked up a purse from a small table near the front door. On her way out she paused as she passed by me.

"I love him, you know," she said quietly. "I'm glad you caught him. Even when I knew he was using, I couldn't bring myself to turn him in. Do you understand that?"

I nodded. I did indeed understand.

Julia Osgood turned away from me and followed Sergeant James out of the house. Maynard and Hawkins were standing by the door, awaiting instructions.

I looked around the room. A gold-framed wedding picture of a smiling Julia and Daniel Osgood sat on a wooden mantel over the fireplace. The picture was several years old. The happy, smiling people in it were a few years younger, but neither one of them had changed very much. I plucked the picture off the mantel and handed it to Detective Maynard.

"That's him," I said. "I know what he looks like; you don't. Get copies made of that and paper the airport with them."

They headed out. I took the opportunity to use the phone. First, I called the Port of Seattle office, to let the port police know what was up. Next, I called the Washington State Patrol Crime Lab and requested a crime-scene team to come to the Greenwood North house and go through Dan Osgood's home with a fine-tooth comb. My next call was to Larry at the Far West Cab Company. For the third time that day, I put him on the trail of a fare. I think he was getting tired of playing that game. So was I.

It didn't take long, since we knew both the company and the time and point of origin. I waited on hold until Larry came back to me. "They dropped him off at the back entrance of the Fifth Avenue Theater at five thirty-seven. Does that help?"

"You bet it does."

My last call was to the Fifth Avenue. I asked to speak to the house manager.

"This is Detective Beaumont," I told him when he came on the line. "I don't know if you remember me from last night or not."

"Sure, I remember. What can I do for you?"

"I'm looking for Dan Osgood. Is he around?"

"I don't know. Let me check." He was away from the phone for several minutes. Finally he came back. "Nobody's seen him today. He must not have showed up for work. Is there a message, if I see him?"

"No," I said. "No message."

Julia Osgood had left the search warrant lying on the table by the door. I handed it over to the crime-scene investigators as soon as they got there. Since we were going by the book for a change, I had to flaunt it. I think it took the crime-lab guys by surprise.

By the time I got to the airport, the port police had already made copies of the wedding picture. They, along with Detectives Maynard and Hawkins, were working their way through the ticket counters and gates, handing out copies of the picture to all ticketing agents and to the security guards at the various concourse entrances.

They had done a hell of a job of coordinating. If Dan Osgood had been there, I'm sure we would have found him. But he wasn't. No one had seen him. We all compared notes. The consensus was that, if Dan Osgood was flying out of Seattle, he hadn't gotten to the airport yet.

Leaving Maynard and Hawkins to work with the port police, I drove back to Seattle alone. So near and yet so far. I was frustrated. Instinct and logic said Osgood would try to make a break for it, and with his car out of commission, the airport was our best bet.

I wanted to be there when the net closed in on him. I wanted to make the arrest personally. It's an occupational disease with detectives. We all want that, to be on hand when the quarry's brought to ground.

But in this case, there was another overriding consideration: Dan Osgood hadn't been working alone. And whoever his accomplice was, it had to be someone connected with Westcoast Starlight Productions, someone who, at that very moment, was down at the Fifth Avenue Theater working Jasmine Day's concert.

I glanced at my watch. The search at the airport had taken longer than I realized. It was nearly nine. The first act would be nearly over. Almost time for intermission. Almost time for Jasmine Day to meet whoever might be sitting in that front-and-center seat.

I felt a little stab of jealousy then, an unreasonable pang because I wasn't sitting there and somebody else was, somebody else who would be going out with Jasmine Day after the show, and later . . .

I didn't let myself think about later. There wasn't any point in it.

CHAPTER 20

THE MARQUEE LIGHTS OUTSIDE THE THEATER WERE brightly lit. I pulled over beside the curb and stopped, leaving the car, with its emergency flashers blinking, sitting in a passenger load-only zone.

An usher stopped me cold at the door. I flashed my ID in her face, but she was adamant. It isn't often someone earning minimum wage gets to wield any kind of power. She was getting a real bang out of it.

Finally, alerted by the disturbance we were making at the entrance, the house manager showed up to shush the noise. He told her to let me in.

"I still haven't seen Dan," he said, once we were inside the lobby.

"I've got to talk to some of the other people backstage, then," I said.

He glanced at his watch. "Intermission is in about three minutes. Why don't you wait here until the lights come up?" He led me to a door that opened onto one of the aisles. When I stepped inside, the sudden darkness was disorienting. I stopped a step or two inside the door and waited.

The stage seemed far away from me. On it, bathed in a brilliant spotlight, Jasmine Day stood singing. She was wearing the blue dress, the white gloves, and the blue shoes.

As she sang, she threw her head back. One hand held the microphone, but the other arm was outstretched as if to embrace the audience. The mane of blonde hair shimmered and gleamed in the spotlight. I wondered how many people besides me knew that under that wig was a little girl named Mary Lou Gibbons whose hair was practically shaved off because of a sick kid she had known twenty years earlier in seventh grade. And I wondered, too, how many people besides Ed Waverly, Jasmine, and J. P. Beaumont knew that the tour would end with that night's performance.

I brought myself up sharply. I couldn't afford to have my concentration diluted. I was impatient, anxious for the song to be over, ready to get on with the task at hand. Somebody was trying to pin a double homicide on the lady onstage, somebody who was probably in the theater at that very moment. I had to lay hands on that sucker, find him and nail him.

Jasmine's song ended. The audience broke into tumultuous applause. A red velvet curtain rang down briefly and then sailed back up, allowing

Jasmine to take another bow. After a third curtain call, the house lights came up and I looked around.

The huge auditorium was nearly full. People had taken the newspaper critic's advice. They had come to the show, and they were enjoying it enormously. When the clapping ended, the audience was still energized, buzzing with enthusiastic anticipation for the second act.

As people began streaming up the aisle toward the lobby, I took a deep breath and started in the other direction. A lady stepped heavily on my toe, her foot reminding me of my last encounter with a foot—with Jasmine Day's foot. I wondered if she'd let me get close enough to talk with her.

It was the same old story. I had to fight my way past the same security guard to get backstage, only this time I didn't have Dan Osgood to help me. When I pitched a fit and brandished my ID under his nose, the guard finally relented and allowed me up the stairs and onto the stage.

I had just entered the dressing-room area when the door to Jasmine's room swung open and Ed Waverly came out. His face was grimly set. Without seeing me, he strode to the back of the stage, where Alan Dale and several others were shifting the band shell into position.

I stopped at the door with my hand poised to knock, but at the last minute I changed my mind. There was no sense in giving Jasmine a chance to refuse to let me in. So without knocking, I tried the knob, half expecting the door to be locked. It wasn't. The door swung open.

Jasmine stood with her back to the door, shrugging her way out of the blue gown and letting it fall carelessly to the floor. She was naked except for a brief, lacy bra. She swung around as the door opened. Her mouth tightened when she saw who I was; her face registered equal parts of disdain and disgust.

"It's you," she muttered.

She turned away from me as though I wasn't there and reached for her black satin jumpsuit. It wasn't done out of modesty. It was more like I was invisible, nonexistent, beneath contempt or notice, and she was busy with her costume change.

"I have to talk to you," I said.

"Get out."

"Jasmine, it's important," I insisted.

She jerked up the zipper on the jumpsuit and turned toward me; she moved toward me, her body wound tight, like a panther preparing to spring.

I crouched, ready to defend myself. "Don't try it," I warned her. "I know those moves too."

"You son of a bitch, I said get out!" She spat out the words, anger seething in every syllable.

"Jasmine, I've got to talk to you. Someone's trying to pin two murders on you."

"I'll give you two guesses who that might be, and he's standing right here in this room. You've got two murders now? You must have been busy today. You've added another one since I talked to you this afternoon."

"Listen to me, please."

"I won't listen to you. You've done enough already. You've wrecked the tour. No one will touch me now that Westcoast's been burned. I'm finished, washed up. Are you happy?"

"No, I'm not happy, Jasmine. Who's after you?"

"What do you mean, who's after me? Why should I care who they hire next?"

"I'm not talking about the tour. Who's got a grudge against you? Who would be out to get you?"

"No one."

"Somebody is. Think for a minute. Any old boyfriends hanging around, maybe somebody with a jealous wife?"

"I already told you. I don't know of anybody like that."

At least she was listening to me now, answering my questions. I had finally gotten her attention, even though she continued dressing. "Do you remember when one of your costumes was stolen, that first night here, while they were doing the load-in?"

She nodded. "What about it?"

"We found it tonight, in a dumpster at Dan Osgood's house."

"What does that mean? I don't understand."

"You remember Dan Osgood?" She nodded. "What do you know about him?" I continued.

Jasmine looked at me and made a face. "You

mean other than the fact that he set me up with you?" Her voice dripped with sarcasm.

"He's done a hell of a lot more than that," I told her. "From what we've been able to noodle out so far, he wore your costume later on that night when he met Richard Dathan Morris down by the market. Osgood probably killed Morris first, then he went to Morris's house and killed his room-mate."

Jasmine looked dazed, puzzled. "He murdered them while he was wearing my clothes?"

"That's right. So it would look like you did it."

"But isn't that the costume they said Morris stole? If he took it, why was somebody else wearing it?"

"I don't have an answer for that yet. Have you had any problems with anyone working on the show, Jasmine? Alan Dale, for example, or Ed Waverly?"

She shook her head. "No. None at all."

I went back to a question I had asked her before, hoping this time I'd get a better answer. "You're sure there aren't any extracurricular activities that might be causing difficulty, like with wives or girlfriends?"

"No."

"What about the guys with the comp tickets?"

Her mouth hardened when she answered, but I couldn't help the way my mind worked. "No," she said coldly.

"By the way, is anyone using that ticket tonight?"

"Someone's there, but I told Ed I was finished. If the tour's over, so's the public-relations campaign."

"Did you see Dan Osgood here at all today?"

"I tried calling him from the hotel, but they said he wasn't in yet. When I got here, I couldn't find him."

"What did you need him for?"

"I wanted to give him a piece of my mind." She shook her head. "I don't believe any of this. It doesn't make sense. What's going on?"

"Drugs," I answered. "Drugs are what's going on. I think Morris stumbled onto what is evidently a major cocaine network. They took him out before he could do anything about it."

She finished lacing the first boot and stared at me in disbelief. "What kind of network?"

"A distribution network, Jasmine. Sales. In a big way. And I think they've been using your tour as a front."

"My tour? Using me and my name to sell drugs?"

At my nod, her face went rigid. "And because of my past, you assumed . . ."

"It was more than just your past that suckered me in. They've gone to great lengths to make it look as if you were personally involved in the murders."

She stepped toward me with the limping gait of someone with one shoe off and one on. She stopped only inches from my face. "You said 'to make it look like.' Does that mean you no longer suspect me?"

"Of the murders? No, I don't."

"What about the drugs?"

"The jury's still out on that."

Her face went stony and she swung away from me. She snatched up the waiting boot and jerked it onto her foot.

There was a knock on the door. "Five minutes, Miss Day."

"Leave me alone," she said wearily. "Just go away and leave me alone. I've got a show to put on."

When she bent over to slip on the second boot, the neckline of the jumpsuit fell open, offering a brief glimpse of what lay underneath. A glimpse and a reminder.

"Jasmine, let me help you. Let's try to get to the bottom of this together."

Her fingers were busy lacing the boot. She didn't look up at me. "Fat chance," she said. "You've helped me enough already. Ed told me from the beginning that if there was any trouble, it would be my ass."

She finished with the boot and straightened up abruptly, but she didn't look in my direction as she stalked over to the dressing table and picked up a pot of makeup. With a practiced hand she began to touch up her face. When she finished, she set the makeup back on the counter, her eyes defiantly meeting and holding mine in the reflection in her mirror.

There was another knock on the door. "Curtain, Miss Day."

She stood up. "I'd better go," she said.

"I have a witness who says the killer let himself into the Morris-Thomas house with a key to the front door. I'm willing to bet the key to that house is here, either in your dressing room or your purse, or in your hotel room."

Without a word, Jasmine opened a wire drawer underneath the Formica top of the dressing table and pulled out a small, white, beaded clutch bag. She unsnapped the top and held the purse upside down above the table.

A collection of junk tumbled out of it onto the counter. There were several tubes of lipstick, some unidentified makeup containers, a nail file, a hodgepodge of loose change, an open checkbook with some paper money visible inside it, a few slightly used tissues, and a collection of credit-card receipts. There were also some keys, a single hotel room key along with two other separate key rings.

She looked down at the pile and frowned. "That's not mine," she said.

"What's not yours?"

She started to reach for one of the two key rings, a chain with a Greenpeace Save-the-Whales charm on it. I caught her hand in midair.

"Don't touch it," I commanded.

For a moment our eyes met. Then she nodded quietly and allowed her hand to drop to her side.

There was another urgent pounding on the door. "Jasmine, where the hell are you?" Alan Dale shouted. "It's time. You're on."

"I'm coming," she answered. She started for the door.

"Break a leg," I told her.

She stopped, her hand on the knob, and turned to look at me. All the anger and rage had drained from her face. She gave me a wan imitation of a smile.

"Are you going to come watch?" she asked. "Since it's my farewell performance, I plan to put on one hell of a show."

"I'd like to," I said. "If you don't mind."

She grinned, ruefully. "I don't mind."

Jasmine Day opened the door then. The members of the orchestra were fidgeting with their instruments, tuning them, checking them out, making noise to cover the fact that the second act was slow in starting.

I watched as she took a deep breath and squared those slender shoulders. She did a final check, her hands smoothing the material of her jumpsuit, patting the wig to be sure it was in place, straightening her collar.

She seemed to grow taller as she stood there, becoming somehow more imposing. Westcoast Starlight Productions might have canceled the tour, but there was no doubt in my mind that Jasmine Day was every inch a star. I watched her go, striding with feline grace toward the piano I knew waited for her on the other side of the stage.

Using my own keys as a lever, I turned the Greenpeace charm over. On the back of it was Richard Dathan Morris's name and phone number. I located an evidence bag in my inside jacket pocket and stuck the key chain in that. If there were any prints on the keys, I didn't want to risk ruining them by carrying the key chain around unprotected. I was just finishing shoving the contents of Jasmine's purse back where they had come from when Alan Dale bounded into the room.

"She said you were here. You've got more nerve than a bad tooth! There's a phone call for you, asshole. Take it and then get the fuck out of here before I clean your clock."

With that, he grabbed the purse out of my hand, tossed it onto the counter, then turned and stomped out of the dressing room. I followed him back to the side of the stage where, next to the curtain pulls, a wall-mounted phone showed a blinking line on hold. I picked up the receiver.

"Hello."

"Detective Beaumont?" a woman's voice asked. She sounded relieved.

"Yes."

"Just a minute. Let me put Ron on the phone."

There was a momentary shuffling and then I heard Peters say, "Thanks, Amy. Beau?"

"Yeah. I'm here."

"I've been calling all over town looking for you. Have you heard the news?"

"What news?"

"The DEA made a major drug bust in L.A. this afternoon."

"So?"

"At Westcoast Starlight Productions."

"No shit!"

"They arrested fourteen people at the corpo-
rate headquarters, and the news broadcast says
they have warrants out for at least sixteen more.
Evidently they have people scattered all over the
country. KIRO Radio did a news flash here about
half an hour ago. Somebody must have tumbled
to the fact that Jasmine Day's show is a Westcoast
production."

"I'm a son of a bitch," I said.

Onstage, the orchestra was beginning the
second-act overture. Alan Dale came up to me.
"Get off the phone," he said. "You can't talk here
when the show starts."

"I've gotta go, Peters," I said. "Intermission's
over. Thanks for the tip."

I put the phone down. Alan Dale was in the
process of herding me down the steps when we
both heard raised voices coming from the dressing-
room area behind the stage. The head carpenter's
concern for maintaining silence on the stage overcame his eagerness to run me off. He turned
toward the noise, and I followed him.

Big Bertha Harris, a fat pit bull of a woman, was
standing in front of the dressing room, barring
the way of two well-dressed men who towered
over her.

"No way are you going in there," she was saying. "I don't care who you are."

"Hey, you guys," Alan Dale called. "Knock off
the noise. The show's started."

They all three turned to look at us. I recognized one of the two men right away. He was Roger Glancy, agent of the day for the DEA.

"What are you doing here?" I asked.

Glancy looked surprised to see me. "I could ask you the same thing. We've come to arrest Jasmine Day."

"You what?" Alan Dale exploded. He moved toward Glancy and attempted to bring a haymaker up from the floor. I caught Dale's arm in midswing and pulled him back.

Glancy regarded the head carpenter warily. "Who's this?" he asked. "We've got warrants for Jasmine Day, Dan Osgood, and Ed Waverly."

Dale shook his arm loose from my hand. Without another word, he stalked away from us.

"His name's Alan Dale," I told Glancy. "He's the head carpenter."

"Let him alone, then," Glancy said. "He's not on the list."

Glancy turned his attention back to Big Bertha. "We've got a search warrant here. Now, either you get out of the way, or we'll move you out of the way."

Silently Bertha stepped to one side. She had heard enough. She wasn't fighting anymore. Glancy motioned the other man into the dressing rooms.

"You guys are a little late in making your move, aren't you?" I asked. "My partner just called. He says it's already been on TV."

Glancy nodded grimly. "Nobody's been able to

raise Wainwright on his pager. He may be up in his plane and out of range. We were supposed to be here by six, but it was after seven when L.A. finally reached me. It took time for me to get the local warrants signed."

"Goddamn it! There goes the son of a bitch again!" I heard Alan Dale's oath and looked in his direction. He was frantically motioning several stagehands to follow him onto the stage where the band shell was sitting. It had stopped halfway down the stage and halfway into its turn.

With the orchestra continuing to play, Alan Dale, Ray Holman, and the rest hurried onto the stage and muscled the heavy piece of equipment into position. From the wings I watched while Jasmine, already draped on the piano and bathed in the spotlight, waited silently for them to finish.

When the broken band shell was finally facing the audience, the conductor give a slight nod in the direction of the piano player and Jasmine Day. She nodded back in acknowledgment.

The first number was "Sophisticated Lady." I don't think I had ever heard the lyrics to that song before, but I did then. That night, every nuance of disillusionment and hurt was clear to me as Jasmine Day sang her heart out. She was that sophisticated lady, mourning for what was lost—not a man, but a dream.

As far as I knew, no one had told her that Roger Glancy was waiting in the wings with a warrant for her arrest. But she sang as if she knew he was there, as if it was all over and this was her last chance to take wing with an audience. She cast a spell with her music, one that held me enchanted, watching and listening.

Roger Glancy, however, was evidently immune to her magic. Halfway through the second number, he tugged at my sleeve and motioned me toward the dressing room. "Detective Beaumont," he whispered. "You'd better come take a look at this."

CHAPTER 21

IN JASMINE'S DRESSING ROOM A HUGE TRUNK STOOD empty, its contents spilled carelessly on the floor. I was sure it hadn't been there the night before when I was in the dressing room. It probably had been there while I was talking with Jasmine earlier, during the intermission, but I didn't remember it. My mind had been occupied with other issues.

Glancy urged me forward, and I walked over to the trunk and looked inside. A false bottom had been removed and stood leaning against the outside of the trunk. At first glance, the bottom surface seemed to be covered with clear plastic. Only a closer examination revealed that it was really plastic-covered white bricks that filled the entire bottom surface of the trunk. White bricks of cocaine, no doubt, packed in so tightly that a dime couldn't be shoved into the cracks between them.

"They're three deep," the other DEA agent was

saying to Roger Glancy. "I'd say there's at least a million dollars' worth right here."

The third man hurried into the room. "We've got Waverly," he announced. "We picked him up out in the lobby, but there's no sign of Osgood anywhere. I understand he never showed up for work today."

Glancy nodded. "Okay, keep Waverly under wraps in one of the dressing rooms."

"Seattle P.D. has already issued an APB on Osgood," I told them. "We want him too. We've checked the airport and his house, but so far there's no sign of him."

Glancy turned back to his men. "Leave two people with Waverly and have the others block every possible exit." He turned to the agent who had searched the dressing room. "Okay, Dick, you go to the other side of the stage and wait there. I'll be on this side. Let's just make damned sure she doesn't slip through our fingers."

"Right," Dick answered, melting through the door.

"Wait a minute," I said. Glancy paused and looked at me. He must have thought I was talking to him, but I was actually speaking to Big Bertha, who had followed us into the dressing room and stopped right inside the door.

"Where'd this trunk come from? It wasn't here last night."

Bertha struggled to find words. Her chest was heaving as though she couldn't quite catch her breath. I was afraid she was having a heart attack. "They usually put it in the dressing room during the final performance. That way we can start the load-out as soon as the show is over."

"And where was it when it wasn't in the dressing room?" I asked.

She pointed. "Out there in the common room."

"Locked?"

"Yes."

"Is this Jasmine's private trunk?"

"No one on this show has a private trunk," Bertha declared.

I turned to Glancy. "It isn't Jasmine's trunk," I said.

He glared at me. "So what does that prove? It's in her dressing room now, isn't it? Her name was on the door when we came in."

"Somebody's been trying to frame her," I said. "I'm convinced of it."

Glancy looked at me and shook his head. "You may be convinced of it, pal, but I'm not. And the judge who signed this warrant isn't either. She's in it up to her eyeballs."

"Yes, but . . ." I began.

"No buts, Detective Beaumont. We're arresting the little lady the moment she sets foot offstage."

With that, Glancy walked out of the room, leaving me alone with Big Bertha. "Who has a key to this dressing room?" I asked.

She looked at me doubtfully for a moment, as though afraid I was going to accuse her next. I tried to reassure her. "Look," I said. "Someone is trying to frame Jasmine Day. I've got to find out what's going on."

"I do," she said finally. "And Alan Dale and Ed Waverly both have keys. The same goes for the guy with the theater, that Dan Osgood. He has a master."

"When did you get here?"

"Just at six," she answered.

"And was the trunk already here?"

Bertha nodded. "It was. I thought it was kind of odd, but I never had a chance to talk to Alan about it. It didn't seem that important."

"Who usually brings it here?" I asked. "Did you see anyone?"

Bertha shook her head. "One of the stagehands does it," she answered. "But I don't have any idea which one."

"Someone who was smart enough to make sure it was in her dressing room when the DEA guys came through with their search warrant." I said it aloud, but more for my benefit than for Bertha's.

"And you think someone's trying to frame her?" Bertha asked.

"I'm sure of it," I answered. "And they're not missing a trick."

A burst of applause from outside told me another number was over. I hurried out of the dressing room. Alan Dale was standing alone off to one side of the stage. I went up to him, took him by the arm, and led him back to the dressing-room area so we could talk.

"Did you move the costume trunk into Jasmine's dressing room?" I asked.

"No."

"Do you know who did?"

"No. One of the stagehands, probably, right after intermission."

"What if I told you that tonight somebody did it before six o'clock, before Jasmine and Big Bertha got to the theater?"

"I'd say somebody had their act together."

"What if I told you there's a million dollars' worth of cocaine in the bottom of that trunk?"

"Bullshit!" he said.

"It's true. Want to look for yourself?"

He shook his head.

"And since they found it in Jasmine's dressing room, they're going to try to pin it on her unless we figure out who put it there."

Slowly, Alan Dale swung his face in my direction, a penetrating look in his eyes. "You mean you don't think she put it there?"

"No. It's a setup. I just don't know who's behind it."

"Wait here," Dale commanded.

I didn't do quite what I was ordered to do. I came out of the dressing-room area far enough to see Jasmine onstage and close enough to hear the music. I was dimly aware of Alan Dale moving silently among the members of the stage crew and whispering to them. And to one side, I could see Roger Glancy standing with one of his men, patiently waiting. But mostly I was aware of Jasmine, of Jasmine Day and her music.

During the next round of applause, she came over to the wings to pick up her wooden stool. Glancy made a move as if he planned to grab her then, but Alan Dale appeared out of nowhere and stopped him. After the applause died down, the spotlight found Jasmine and her stool in center stage.

The auditorium was breathlessly silent as she lifted the microphone to her lips. "First," she said, "I want to thank you for being such a wonderful audience tonight. I've loved being here with you, and I know you've enjoyed the show."

Applause started to trickle through the audience, but Jasmine raised her hand to quiet it. "During this tour, my comeback tour, I've taken some time out of each show to share with others what's happened to me in the course of the last few years. I've told people how I screwed myself up on drugs and how, with the help of Betty Ford's treatment center, Rancho Mirage, I finally got my life back on track again. But tonight there's something else that needs to be said.

"This afternoon my manager, Ed Waverly, got a message from his boss in California saying that the remainder of my tour has been canceled. We were supposed to be in Vancouver, B.C., tomorrow night. Instead, we'll be packing up and heading back to California."

An audible groan rumbled through the audience. Jasmine smiled. "Thanks," she said. "I needed that. But I want to tell you what caused the cancellation. The audience response, both here and in other cities, has been wonderful. The reason the tour was canceled is that the financial backers are scared, scared of me and my reputation. They weren't all that happy to take on someone who had the kind of history I do. They were afraid I was too risky. I was told from the beginning that if there was any hint of trouble, they'd drop me like a hot potato.

"Well, my friends, there's trouble, and I've been dropped. During the next few days, I'm sure you're going to hear lots of rumors about me. Evidently, someone connected with the show has been selling drugs, and the backers are convinced I'm part of it. I'm not, but I don't suppose I'll be able to change anyone's mind. As far as they're concerned, once a druggie, always a druggie.

"So tonight is my farewell performance. There are probably a lot of you who don't know that I started out singing solos in the First Baptist Church of Jasper, Texas. Back then, my name was Mary Lou Gibbons, and what I wanted more than anything was to get out of Jasper and stay out. Right now, Jasper is looking pretty good to me.

"During the next few days, when you all are hearing all those rumors and reading all those stories that they write to sell newspapers, I want you to remember what I'm tellin' you." A soft Texas drawl had somehow drifted into Jasmine's pattern of speech. It fit her like a warm glove.

"There's no sense in me tryin' to stop all those

rumors, because lies have a life of their own. But I want to tell you right now that I gave up drugs two years ago, and I haven't touched them since. And I'd die before I'd be a part of sellin' 'em and sendin' somebody else into the hellhole I've spent the last two years tryin' to climb out of. And no matter what they say about me, I'm not a part of any murder either.

"So tonight I'd like you all to help me say good-bye to Jasmine Day, whoever she is." She reached up then and tugged at the blonde wig, peeling it back from her head like a cabbage leaf and tossing it offstage, where Alan Dale caught it. She reached up and rubbed her head, scratched it, and laughed.

"There, that's not so bad, is it?"

A few bits of nervous laughter drifted through the audience, but mostly the huge room was silent.

"Jasmine Day started the concert tonight, but Mary Lou Gibbons is going to end it," she continued. She turned away from the audience and spoke briefly to the piano player, who nodded in understanding. Then she swung back around on her stool.

"The two songs I'm going to sing aren't on the program, and the orchestra may not know them, so we'll do them with just the piano. They're songs Mary Lou Gibbons used to do back home in Jasper."

The audience was now totally silent. No one coughed or moved or cleared a throat. The pianist hit a chord, and Jasmine's bell-like voice soared through the auditorium, filling it with an old gospel song, "It's Always Darkest Before the Dawn." When she finished, the place was still silent. People didn't know what to do, whether to applaud or cry.

I happened to glance at Alan Dale just then. He seemed to have gotten something in his eye. I was suffering from the same problem. I doubted there were many dry eyes on the other side of the curtain either.

Before the audience had time to recover its equanimity though, the piano player bounded off into another song. Jasmine picked up the wooden stool by one leg and tossed it offstage. They could have been rehearsing it for years. Alan Dale caught it one-handed.

"You all know this one," Jasmine was saying into the microphone. "And if you know it, help me with it: 'Put your hand in the hand of the man who stilled the waters . . . '"

The second time through, the orchestra picked up the tune, and by the third pass, the audience was on its feet, singing along and clapping. The sound must have rattled the huge crystal chandeliers hanging from the ceiling.

I've never had much luck with Billy Graham or Jerry Falwell, and I've lived my whole life without ever having attended an old-fashioned revival meeting. But that night, in the Fifth Avenue Theater, Jasmine Day took the place by storm. I felt I'd truly been revived. When the music finally stopped, the applause was thunderous.

The standing ovation wouldn't stop, so she went back out front and did one final chorus. Even then, there were three more curtain calls after that. As Jasmine came offstage for the last time, Alan Dale started out to meet her, but Roger Glancy cut him off at the pass.

He was waiting by the curtain with an open pair of handcuffs in his hand. "I'm Roger Glancy with the DEA, Miss Day," he said. "I have a warrant for your arrest on a charge of possession of cocaine with the intent to distribute."

She gave him an appraising look. "My name is Mary Lou Gibbons," she said. "You didn't say anything about the two murders. Did you forget those?"

"I wouldn't know anything about murder, ma'am," Roger Glancy said. "That's his department." He turned and nodded toward me. I shook my head and said nothing. There was nothing to say.

When the cuffs snapped shut around Jasmine's wrists, Alan Dale sprang into action. I saw him move, heading toward Glancy, and I cut him off before he could do any damage.

"Cool it," I ordered. "You can't help her that way."

"But they can't do this. It's a put-up deal. You said so yourself."

"They can do it. They are doing it."

Dale gave me a shove, trying to push me out of the way, but Jasmine put an end to it once and for all. "It's all right, Alan," she said. "I'll be okay."

He stood still then. Meanwhile, the other agent, the one named Dick, had come across the stage and taken hold of Jasmine's arm.

"Take her into her dressing room," Glancy ordered. "We'll wait there until the crowd breaks up. Waverly's in another. I don't want to try to take them out of the building until it quiets down outside. If we do it now, it'll cause a riot."

Dick led Jasmine back toward the dressing room. She walked quietly offering no protest.

Alan Dale started after them, but I held him back. "Who moved the trunk?"

"They all denied it."

"All of them?"

"Every last goddamned one of them. When I figure out who did it, I'm going to tear the son of a bitch limb from limb."

Those were my sentiments exactly.

CHAPTER 22

THERE WAS A FLURRY OF ACTIVITY AT THE TOP OF THE stage stairs and B. W. Wainwright, Agent-in-Charge Wainwright, strode into view. He marched directly into the main circle of activity. "What's going on here?" he demanded. "Where's Glancy?"

"In the back," someone told him. "In the dressing rooms. They've got two of the suspects back there, the woman and Ed Waverly."

Wainwright nodded. "Good work. Where's the other one? What's his name, Osburn?"

"Osgood," said the DEA agent who was supplying the information. "We don't know. He didn't show up here for work today, and this guy"—he motioned toward me—"he says Seattle P.D. has already issued an APB on him."

Wainwright glanced toward me. "Hello, Detective Beaumont. How's it going?"

"Who knows?"

Wainwright headed for the dressing-room area,

and I tagged along. As soon as he saw the agent in charge, Glancy looked enormously relieved. "I'm glad you're here, boss," he said. "L.A. called me when they couldn't raise you on the pager. We've got Jasmine Day in one dressing room and Waverly in the other."

The agent in charge glanced briefly at the two closed doors. "Someone's in there with each of them?"

Glancy nodded, watching Wainwright pace back and forth across the room. "I don't know what those assholes in L.A. are thinking," Wainwright stormed. "They've got their heads up their butts, pulling off an operation like this without giving us any advance notice.

"I was out flying," he added. "I got the message as soon as I landed and came straight here. It looks as though you've got everything under control. Good work, Glancy." Wainwright turned to me. "Any idea what became of Osgood, Detective Beaumont?" he asked.

I shook my head. "None. We've talked to his wife. She told us he had moved out. We're afraid he may have skipped town. We've got people staked out at the airport looking for him, and we've notified customs at Blaine in case he tries to get out that way."

"Good. That was smart."

Just then someone tapped me lightly on the shoulder. I twisted around to find Big Bertha Harris standing right behind me. "I have to talk to you," she whispered.

Obligingly, I followed her out of the room. "They're all like that," she said as soon as the door closed behind us.

"What are all like what?" I asked.

"The other trunks," she answered. "They all have false bottoms."

"Are they full or empty?" I asked.

"I don't know. I didn't check."

We looked at three more trunks. One was for costumes and two were for instruments. Bertha was right. They all had false bottoms, and they were all empty.

Alan Dale had followed along. He scratched his head. "Jesus Christ! How could I have been so stupid? This must have been going on the whole time and I never had an inkling." Angrily, he shoved his hands in his pockets and walked toward the edge of the stage. I went after him.

"What are you going to do?" I asked.

He shrugged. "I might just as well go ahead and start the load-out. I don't know where they're going to take the stuff or who's going to pay for it, but I've got to get it out of here, and I can't keep the stagehands on duty all night." He looked around. "Where the hell is Ray?" he asked.

"Ray Holman?" I asked. "Is he missing?"

Dale shook his head. "Probably didn't think we'd start this soon and snuck off to have a beer."

The head carpenter summoned his crew. "Okay, you guys, let's strike this sucker, starting with the band shell."

Ray Holman's being gone bothered me a whole lot more than it seemed to bother Alan Dale. I went back to the dressing room where B. W. Wainwright had taken charge. "You ought to send someone out to check the rest of the trunks," I told him. "It looks to me like they've all got false bottoms."

Glancy and Dick were dispatched to take care of that. I looked at the closed door to Jasmine's dressing room. I knew she was in there, and I wanted to go and talk to her, to reassure her and tell her not to worry, but I thought better of it. Moments later, Alan Dale came pounding on the door to the common area.

"Beaumont, can you come here for a minute?"

"What's going on?" I asked as we walked away from the dressing rooms.

"You'd better come take a look at this."

"What is it?"

"Just come look."

He led me to the back of the stage, where the pedestal used to support the band shell stuck up out of the decking like the empty stump of a tree. The band shell had been removed to one side and was being dismantled by several stagehands.

"You got a strong stomach?" Dale asked, handing me a flashlight.

"Strong enough," I replied. "Why? What's going on?"

"Crawl under there and take a look."

I got down on my hands and knees and crawled

along the worm-gear track. As soon as I put my head under the decking, I smelled the unmistakable odor of human feces and blood and death. The decking had somehow contained it, kept it bottled up. It wasn't necessary to go any farther to know there was a body under there. I shone the light along the track until I saw the outline of a man's shoe. Then I crawled back out from under the decking. Alan Dale was standing there waiting for me.

"Do you know who it is?" I asked.

He shook his head. "I turned around as soon as I saw the shoe."

"Me too," I said. "I've got to call the department. They'll have to get a team over here."

"Help yourself to the phone," Dale told me. "You know where it is."

I started for the phone with the head carpenter trailing behind me. "Looks to me like he got bound up in the worm-gear drive. That's about where it ran off the track. Shouldn't we try to get him out?" he asked.

"No. It's too late for that. He's dead; I'm sure of it. Doc Baker from the medical examiner's office and the crime-scene investigators from the crime lab have got to be here when we uncover him. Is it possible it's Ray Holman?" I asked.

"Maybe," Dale said.

I dialed Sergeant Lowell James's desk directly. There wasn't much point in going through 911.

"Hello, Sarge, this is Beau."

"It's about time you called in. We've had complaints from parking enforcement about your car. I understand it's still parked in front of the theater with its emergency lights flashing."

"That's what this is," I countered, "an emergency."

"For two hours?"

"Look, Sarge, do you want me to report this homicide, or are you going to climb my frame about parked cars?"

"What homicide?" James snapped.

"Beats the hell out of me. We've got an unidentified body under the decking on the stage of the Fifth Avenue Theater. And the DEA guys are here. They've already arrested two people on drug charges and are looking for a third."

"The DEA? How'd they get called into this, and why weren't we notified?"

"Would you do me a favor and just call Doc Baker's office? And contact the crime lab. We can handle all this paper-pushing bullshit later."

"Right," James said. "We'll handle it, all right."

Twenty minutes later, Sergeant James and I were waiting near the back of the Fifth Avenue's stage when Doc Baker came huffing up to us, his tie flapping loose around his neck, his white hair standing on end. The same young female photographer was trailing behind him.

"All right, all right. What's going on here?"

"There's a body under the decking," I told him. "We left it there until you got here."

Doc Baker walked to the back of the stage. He looked at the space between the decking and the floor; then he looked at his own wide girth. There was no way he would fit.

"Get somebody to take this thing apart," Baker ordered. "How long will it take to dismantle it?"

"The whole thing?" Alan Dale asked.

"No, just enough so we can see to work."

"About ten minutes or so," Dale told him, "if all you want me to do is open a lid over the track."

Dale started to summon the lounging stage-hands who were clumped in a subdued group on the far side of the stage. I'm sure he intended to put them to work on the decking, but Baker squelched that idea in a hurry.

"No. Just you," he said to Dale. "I don't want any unnecessary fingerprints."

"It'll take a lot longer," Dale said.

"That's all right," Baker returned. "It'll be worth it."

Alan Dale pulled a small battery-operated drill from his tool belt and slid under the decking. We heard the rat-a-tat-tat of the power drill as it loosened the bolts. Meanwhile, Doc Baker sauntered over to us.

"I don't know why you guys didn't have brains enough to take up that decking before I got here. Nobody could have gotten under there."

I managed, barely, to keep my mouth shut. None of the smart-ass remarks I could have laid on Doc Baker right then made it past my lips. Of course, he was right. It would have made a hell of a lot more sense for us to have gone ahead and had Dale raise the planking before Baker got there, but

I've worked with the medical examiner too many years not to know that that would have pissed him off too. Nobody pleases Doc Baker in the middle of the night. It was far better for him to have made the decision himself after he got there, even if everything was delayed a good forty-five minutes.

After several long minutes, Dale finally raised one corner of a section of decking. "Have somebody come take this, will you?"

Two of the stagehands came over, but they did so with considerable reluctance. By now, everyone who was still in the theater knew there was a body lurking under the decking, and no one was eager to be the one to uncover it.

Baker directed the stagehands to take the section of decking and lean it against the back wall. A few minutes later, another section came off. As the lid opened up, the stench became more pronounced. Only in the movies do people die with their eyes and mouths closed. Only there is death a sanitary, odorless, painless process.

When the last section of decking came off, Alan Dale erupted from the opening and made for the fresh air outside the alley door on the other side of the stage. For two cents, I would have joined him.

Impervious, Doc Baker hopped down from the decking into the opening and motioned for the photographer to follow. I saw the look of horror on her face, but she eased her way into the opening behind him. Soon intermittent flashes from the camera told us she was doing her job.

Sergeant James, Agent-in-Charge Wainwright, and I moved slowly to the edge of the opening. It was bad, as bad as anything I've ever seen. It was Dan Osgood. His face was recognizable, but that was about all.

The worm-gear drive, moving in its track like the spiral center piece in a meat grinder, had pushed the body ahead of it, even as the gear itself had torn into him. Eventually his body had been caught between two supporting struts that stood on either side of the track. The pressure of the body, stuck between the struts, had created enough countervailing stress to force the worm gear from its track.

It was a terrible way to die, a horrifying way to die. Doc Baker pulled himelf up out of the hole onto the decking, shaking his shaggy head.

"Why didn't he try to get away?" I asked.

"Hands and feet were both tied," Doc Baker answered. "Not only that, it looks as if he was probably out cold."

"Drugged?" I asked.

Baker nodded. "I imagine."

Now the photographer, too, was climbing out of the pit. In the stark light of the stage, her face was ashen, but there was no other visible sign of distress. "I'm done, Dr. Baker," she said, moving past us to the sidelines.

"I've been told we've got a positive ID," Baker said to Sergeant James. "Is that true?"

The sergeant looked at me. "What do you think, Beau?" he asked.

"It's Dan Osgood, all right," I answered. "Is his wife still down at the department?"

Sergeant James shook his head. "No. I sent her to her mother's in a cab a while ago."

"You working this case, then?" Doc Baker asked me.

Sergeant James answered for me. "No. Beau and Big Al already have their hands full." He turned to the DEA agent in charge. "Wainwright, are you going to want this to be a joint investigation?"

Wainwright nodded. "All right, then," James continued. "You'll be working with Detectives Andress and Cunningham here. I'll be the liaison between you and each pair of detectives working one of the related homicides. I think that's the best way to handle it."

"Makes sense to me," Wainwright agreed. "Is the crowd pretty much dispersed out there?"

"It's not bad. There are reporters hanging around, but that's about all."

It was agreed that Jasmine and Waverly should be taken down to the department to be booked and questioned. I stood to one side and watched as Roger Glancy led Jasmine out of the dressing room. To avoid the reporters, they took them out through the side door that led back into the Skinner Building, the same door Dan Osgood had used to take me into the theater for the first time the previous afternoon. It seemed like eons ago.

Jasmine Day walked out with her head held high. Waverly looked like a whipped dog. Once they were gone, I went looking for Alan Dale. He was sitting in the common area outside the dressing rooms. He didn't look any too healthy. He had his head in his hands and looked a picture of despair.

"Is she gone?" he asked.

I nodded. "Don't worry about her. We'll bail her out tomorrow."

"We?" he asked.

"That's right," I answered. "All they can charge her with is possession with intent."

"What about me?" he asked.

"What about you?"

"I'm the one who killed him. I was the one who pulled the switch on the worm gear."

"You didn't know he was under there, did you?"

Alan Dale shook his head. "No, but I remember smelling a funny odor during the second act. I didn't have time to check it out. I should have. Maybe he wasn't dead yet."

"Don't beat yourself up, Alan. He was already dead, believe me."

"You're sure it's Osgood?"

"I'm sure, all right. It ran through his gut, not his face."

"Do they have him out of there yet?" Dale asked.

"Not yet," I told him. "This stuff takes time."

"And you do this for a living?" he asked.

"Every day," I said.

I left Dale sitting there and went outside looking for Ray Holman. I didn't find him. Instead, I came across the photographer, sitting off by herself in the middle of the front row of seats. Like Dale, she looked sickened and worn.

"Thinking about getting into another line of work?" I asked.

"The thought had crossed my mind," she said.

"Mine too," I told her.

CHAPTER 23

I ENDED UP OFFERING THE PHOTOGRAPHER A RIDE home. For a change, my attempt to be suave and urbane didn't backfire. When we stepped outside the theater, my car was still there, the flashers were still flashing, and the engine turned over on the first try. Sometimes things do work out all right.

We took the departmental car back to the Public Safety Building. I talked to Sergeant James from the garage and told him I was beat, that I'd have to do the paperwork the next day. He let me off the hook. I bailed the Porsche out of the twenty-four-hour garage at the bottom of James Street, and we headed home.

The photographer's name was Nancy Gresham. I'd had nothing to eat for a long time, so long that even the dead breakfast Jasmine and I had left uneaten on my dining-room table was beginning to seem palatable.

Since Nancy lived in an apartment on the north side of Queen Anne Hill, it was natural for us to stop off at the Doghouse for something to eat. That's one of the advantages of being a devotee of twenty-four-hour dives. They're always open when you need them.

"I take it you come here a lot," Nancy observed when everyone in the place, including the cook and the busboy, greeted me by name.

"It beats cooking," I said.

When the waitress came to take our order, she smiled at Nancy Gresham's insistence on separate checks. So did I.

Although I thought I was hungry, when the food came I picked at it, pushing it around on my plate without eating any of it. There was a leaden weight in my gut, one I couldn't ditch or explain, one I couldn't manage to shove any food past. I guess I wasn't exactly a barrel of fun.

"Someone told me the guy back there in the theater was the suspect you were looking for in those other two murders, the one down by the railroad track and the other one up on Capitol Hill," she said over coffee. "So you've closed two cases tonight. It seems to me congratulations are in order."

"I don't feel much like celebrating," I told her dourly.

"Why not?"

"Because something's out of whack. Something's wrong and I can't tell what it is."

"Maybe you're feeling cheated."

"Cheated?" I repeated the word, puzzling over it. "How so?"

"You didn't get to take him in. Somebody robbed you of the arrest. Doesn't that bother you?"

She was on the money, but I didn't let on. "Not particularly," I said. "Should it?"

She smiled behind her cup. "That's not what I've heard."

"What exactly have you heard, and where?"

"You're something of a legend, you know. They say that you sleep and eat your job, and that you don't give up. Incidentally, you've got quite a reputation around the department, especially among the raw recruits. The story goes that J. P. Beaumont is only one small step below godliness."

That made me laugh. "Your over-the-hill legend seems to have feet of clay," I said. "You should have seen me this afternoon."

She cocked her head to one side and looked at me. "Why?"

"Because Jasmine Day could have kicked the shit out of me, if you'll pardon the expression, and I never even saw it coming."

"Don't do that," she said sharply.

"Do what?"

"Don't apologize for talking like a cop. I'm one too, remember?" She got up abruptly, taking her check with her. I caught up with her at the cash register.

"I didn't mean to offend you."

"Don't talk down to me," she said. "My ears won't fall off if I hear those words."

been a terrible mistake. He said he understood now how valuable the evidence was that my son had provided, and would I go with him right then to get it."

"Wainwright said that?" I asked incredulously.

"Yes, yes. He said we'd have to hurry to get to the bank before it closed. He said to be ready, that he'd pick me up and fly me to Bellingham so we could be there before the bank closed at six."

"And did you make it?"

"Yes. We were at the bank about twenty minutes before six. I got the stuff out of the safety deposit box and handed it over to him. There must have been twenty envelopes in all. It seemed like that many, but I don't know exactly. I didn't count them."

"What did Wainwright do with them? Did he show you what was inside?"

"No. He sent me home in a cab. We had taken a cab from the airport into town. He said he'd take charge of the evidence, see that it got into the proper hands."

Mrs. Grace Simms Morris paused to blow her nose. Over the phone, it wasn't exactly a ladylike sound. I'm sure she would have been embarrassed to know she sounded like a foghorn trumpeting in my ear.

"I still don't understand why you're so upset," I said.

"Just wait a minute. I'm coming to that. The cab dropped me off at my house. There was so much mail piled up that I didn't feel like looking at any of it right away. I went around the house and opened windows and unpacked and started a load of wash before I picked up the mail."

She had been rushing forward. Now she paused, as if to draw breath.

"Have you ever gotten a letter from someone after they're dead?" she asked. "I mean, a letter someone wrote before they died, and you didn't get it until after you knew they were gone?"

"I guess I have," I said. "At least once."

"It's a weird feeling, isn't it?"

"Yes," I agreed.

"Well, when I finally sat down to do the mail, there was an envelope from Richard, one that he had mailed on Wednesday afternoon. I knew it was from him because of the handwriting, and for a long time I couldn't bring myself to open it. I just sat there and held it. Finally, I had to open it, had to know what it said."

"What did it say?"

"There was no letter, just a note telling me to put this away along with the other stuff at the bank."

"This what? What was it?"

"A tape. A cassette tape."

"So what did you do?"

"I was a little angry at Mr. Wainwright," she confessed. "I mean, it would have been polite for him to at least show me what was in those envelopes after I had kept them for all that time. But he didn't bother. So I decided to listen to the tape. I wanted to know what it was that Richard was doing. I needed to know. Can you understand that?"

"Yes. So did you listen to it?"

"Yes." Her voice dropped. Her answer was almost a whisper. "It's him," she said. "Wainwright."

"Tell me," I commanded.

"I heard these two men talking. They said nobody had to worry about getting caught, since Wainwright was running the show. I'm scared, Detective Beaumont. What should I do with this tape? What if he comes back here looking for it?"

My mind was racing. "Does he know you have it? Did you call him?"

"No. I wanted to hear it first, and then, afterward . . ."

"You're sure they were talking about drugs?"

"Do you want me to play it for you?"

"We can try it." She tried, but I couldn't understand what was being said. There was too much interference. "Just repeat it for me in your own words," I told her. "Tell me what it says as best you can. Can you make out any names?"

"Yes, I think so. One seems to be named Dan, and the other is Ray. Yes, that's it."

"Shit!" I said.

"Pardon me?"

"Never mind," I said. "I just sneezed."

"I don't understand this, but first Dan asks if the setup is working, and Ray says yes. That she's gone out with all the dealers, and that when they pull the rug out, it's going to look as if she was doing it all on her own."

That has to be the comps, I thought. So it was a setup. The whole thing. Maybe even the whole tour.

"After that, that's when one of them says Wainwright's a genius. You know, I rode all the way home with that man in a plane. I almost got sick when I heard that."

"Me too," I echoed. "What else?"

"Then they talk about the money, lots of it, and then later, they say that with Wainwright running the show, nobody had to worry about what L.A. was doing. That's it."

I tried to keep my voice calm. "You're sure that's what they said: 'With Wainwright running the show'?"

"Yes, I'm sure. Are you calling me a liar, Detective Beaumont?"

"No, I just wanted to be sure. Mrs. Morris, do you understand how important this is?"

"I certainly do," she answered. "If the man from the DEA is selling drugs, who can be trusted?"

"He's not just a man from the DEA, Mrs. Morris. He's the guy running the DEA here in Seattle. He's scared and dangerous, like a cornered rattlesnake. Are you there by yourself?"

"I've locked all the doors," she said. "Closed all the windows."

"Listen to me. I'm going to call the Bellingham Police Department. I'm going to ask them to come get you and put you in protective custody—do you understand?"

"Yes," she said.

"Don't open the door to anyone but a uniformed police officer, and whatever you do, don't let that tape out of your possession, not even for a minute, is that clear?"

"Shh," she said.

"What?"

"I thought I heard a noise."

A wave of gooseflesh ran down my legs, and a torrent of helpless rage washed through my body.

"Turn off the lights," I ordered. "Hide the tape somewhere, and don't hang up the phone. I'm going to be off the line for a minute."

I pressed the switch hook and got a dial tone on my other line, thanking Ralph Ames for his insistence that I have two lines on my phone. My hand shook as I dialed the operator. "This is a matter of life or death," I said. "Get me the Bellingham Police Department."

The dispatcher sounded sleepy when he came on the phone. "It's an emergency," I said. "Send everything you've got to 1414 Utter Street. Hurry! There's an armed robbery in progress at that address."

"I'll have to get your name and address," the dispatcher said.

They always want to fill in all the forms. They always want the paperwork right. I wanted to rage at him, yank his ears through the telephone, but the only weapon I had at my disposal was to keep calm, to force him to get on track.

"My name is J. P. Beaumont. I'm a detective with the Seattle Police Department. I was talking long-distance with Grace Simms Morris when somebody started trying to break into her house."

"How do you know . . ."

I depressed the switch hook one more time, turning on the three-way calling. I heard shattering glass and a woman's scream. A moment later, the line to Grace Simms Morris went dead.

"Are you there?" I shouted at the dispatcher. "Did you hear that?" But he was off the line too.

I sat there, strangling the phone with hopeless impotence, remembering all my other failures, counting them up: Ann Corley and Ginger Watkins and, yes, Ron Peters too. Maybe that's my cross to bear in life, to always want to help, but to never quite measure up, never be there quite on time to do any good, always to miss the mark.

Suddenly the dispatcher was back on the line. "We have officers at the scene, Detective Beaumont. We had a patrol car that was only two minutes away."

"Is she all right? Is she still alive?"

"I don't know. Stay on the line. I'll let you know as soon as I find out."

He went away again, and I sat on hold, uttering an urgent prayer for Mrs. Grace Simms Morris and for J. P. Beaumont too, that for once in my life I might be the knight on the white horse who wouldn't be too late. The minutes loomed into what seemed like hours before he came back on the line again.

"We have a suspect in custody," the dispatcher said. "And an ambulance is en route."

"Is she okay?" I demanded. "Is she still alive?"

"Mrs. Morris is okay," the dispatcher said. "She threw a vase at him and broke a window. It cut him pretty good, but the medics say he'll make it."

I felt a war whoop rising in my throat. I wanted to dance and sing and throw a vase through my own window. But I stifled the impulse. Twenty-four stories is a long way for broken glass to fall. I managed to get control of myself.

"Who is it?" I asked. "Who's the suspect?"

"Just a minute," the dispatcher said. "I'll check." Once more he was off the phone. Soon he was back. "His ID says his name's Holman, Ray Holman. Does that mean anything to you?"

Jubilation died in my throat. "It sure as hell does. Is he alone?"

"They found a rental car. No one else was in it."

I took a deep breath. "Listen to me. This is vitally important. Holman isn't in this alone. He's got an accomplice named Wainwright who works for the DEA. Mrs. Morris has evidence, incriminating evidence, that they'll do anything to lay their hands on."

"The DEA, really?" the dispatcher said.

"You've got to get Mrs. Morris out of there," I said. "Put her in protective custody. Lock the tape in a safe, and don't let anybody near either one of them—you got that?"

"Yes, sir," the dispatcher said. "I'll get right on it."

I gave him my number. "Call me back here when you've got it done," I ordered. "Leave a message on my machine. I won't be here, but I'll be able to get my messages."

"Right," the dispatcher said. "Will do."

I opened the drawer in the table that held the answering machine and took out the remote that Ames had also given me. He had told me someday I'd thank him for being able to pick up my messages without having to be home.

That day had just come. Maybe I'd like Ralph better if he wasn't always right.

CHAPTER 24

NATURALLY, B. W. WAINWRIGHT WASN'T IN THE PHONE book. Neither was Roger Glancy. That was hardly surprising, however. Neither is J. P. Beaumont.

I called the department and asked for Sergeant James, only to be told he had left for home some fifteen minutes before. I hated calling his home and waking his family, even though he was probably still awake, but there was no choice.

Lynita James answered on the second ring. "Just a minute," she said sleepily. "He's brushing his teeth."

"It's Beau," I said when he came on the line.

"What the hell are you doing calling me at this hour?" he demanded.

"There wasn't any choice. Wainwright's the ringleader."

"He's what? Come on, Beau. Have you been drinking, or what?"

"Wainwright's the mastermind behind the

whole Westcoast operation and he's been running it from a catbird seat in the DEA. The whole thing just blew sky-high. Richard Dathan Morris sent a tape to his mother, naming names, and Ray Holman just showed up to try to get it back. He's in custody in Bellingham. Now all we've got to do is lay hands on that other son of a bitch."

James was convinced. "So what do you need, Beau?"

"Just tell me this. Does somebody have Roger Glancy's phone number?"

"Sure, I've got it. I've got all their numbers. I told you I was the liaison, remember?"

"Do you have it there?"

"It's in my briefcase, in the car. Just a minute." He put down the phone, and I could hear Lynita grumpily questioning him about what was going on. Being married to a cop is hell.

Sergeant James came back on the phone. "I've got it, but I was just thinking. What if Glancy's in on it?"

"I'm worried about that too, but it's a chance we'll have to take. Glancy's name wasn't mentioned anywhere on the tape."

"Are you going to call him, or do you want me to?" James asked.

"Let's call him together," I said. "Give me the number and I'll patch us in."

From the way he answered the phone, I knew we had awakened Roger Glancy out of a sound sleep. "This is Detective Beaumont with Seattle police, and Sergeant Lowell James."

"Who?" Glancy mumbled.

I repeated the names. "Oh, that's right. I remember now. What's happening?"

"Roger," I said slowly, "this may be hard to follow, but we need you to give us Wainwright's address. Better yet, we need you to take us there."

"What do you mean? How come?" Glancy was still struggling to wake up and not entirely succeeding. I figured I might as well douse him in the face with cold water.

"We have reason to believe he's working the other side," I said quietly. "We think he's the one who's been running the Westcoast operation."

"Oh, come on. You guys are shitting me."

Sergeant James stepped into the fray. "Look, Glancy, this isn't a joke, and we've got to move on it. Where does Wainwright live?"

"Windermere," Glancy answered. "He lives on Ivanhoe, a few blocks north of Children's Orthopedic Hospital."

"All right, meet us at the southwestern corner of University Village. You can lead us to the house. That'll be faster than having us all bumble around in a residential neighborhood at this hour of the night."

"Who all's coming?" Glancy asked.

"I'll be there," Sergeant James said. "Detective Beaumont and probably a couple of squad cars. But no lights and no sirens."

"Right," Glancy said. "I can make it in fifteen."

"Fifteen it is," James responded. "See you there, Beau," he added.

I splashed some cold water on my face. It was going to be another long night.

It was a good thing I looked at the gas gauge when I got back in the Porsche. It's a good car, but it doesn't run on fumes. I was close enough to the appointed meeting place that I was able to stop at a self-serve place on Denny, fill up, and still be at University Village on time.

As I drove north on I-5 my sense of outrage heated up and boiled over. I'm a cop who happens to work in Seattle, not L.A., not New York or Chicago. I know about what goes on in those other jurisdictions, about the graft and corruption that turn law-enforcement officers into monsters and worse. And I know what it's like to be a cop in a city where cops are looked on as something lower than the scum of the earth.

But Seattle's different. That's one of the reasons I like it. Crooked cops aren't tolerated here, and B. W. Wainwright was a crooked cop of the first water. My gut instinct said to treat him like the vermin he was, take him out, blot him off the face of the earth. I patted my .38 Smith & Wesson for luck, just to know it was available in case I got a chance to use it. And I fully intended to use it if I could.

Sergeant James and Roger Glancy were already in the parking lot when I got there. From the look of things, James had managed to convince Glancy that we weren't jacking him around, that Wainwright had been living two decidedly different lives.

Glancy seemed shaken, disoriented, almost. I would have felt the same way if someone had just told me that Sergeant Lowell James robbed banks on the weekend for fun and profit. When someone you've worked with and respected falls from grace, it's hard to know how to go on.

"Do you just want to show us the house and then back off?" James was asking Glancy. "This is hard enough as it is."

Roger Glancy shook his head. "If what you're saying is true, we've all been played for a bunch of fools. I want to get a little of my own back."

It made perfect sense to me.

Because we were afraid Wainwright might recognize Glancy's car, he rode with me in the Porsche. We led the way.

"Damn," I said as I started the car. "I'll bet nobody thought to get a search warrant."

Glancy patted the breast pocket of his coat. "Don't count on it," he said. "I've got a neighbor who's a judge. His kid died of an overdose at seventeen. He told me to come see him any time of the day or night and he'd sign one for me. He lives two houses away. It only took a minute."

I looked at Glancy with new respect. He wasn't along for the ride, and I'm willing to bet he was grappling with his own set of crooked-cop demons.

He directed me off Sand Point Way a few blocks north of Children's Orthopedic. I could see the wisdom of Sergeant James's strategy the moment we turned off the arterial. The short blocks didn't follow any particularly logical pattern. You simply had to know where you were going.

"Is Wainwright married or divorced?" I asked.

"Divorced," Glancy answered. "It happened just before he transferred in here three years ago. According to him, she wiped him out."

I glanced around at the imposing houses, gracious colonials and low-slung brick ramblers. "It looks like he landed on his feet," I said.

"I'll say," Glancy replied grimly.

We didn't say anything more. The house was a two-story job without a light or car showing. The three-car caravan parked and Glancy directed us around the place, arousing the ire of at least two neighborhood dogs. When we were sure all possible avenues of escape were cut off, Glancy and I approached the front door.

I stood to one side, and Glancy rang the bell. There was no answer. He waited only half a minute or so before he kicked the door in with a one-shot DEA technique that put this particular Seattle cop to shame.

With adrenaline pounding through our systems, we made a quick survey of the house, moving from room to room warily, covering one another. The place was empty. The clothes closet had been gutted. Underwear and sock drawers had been hastily emptied. B. W. Wainwright had left in a hurry, and wherever he was going he didn't plan to come back any time soon.

When we got back to the living room, Glancy

paused and sniffed the air. "Do you smell smoke?" he asked.

I followed suit. There was indeed the acrid smell of paper smoke lingering in the air. We both headed for the fireplace. I felt the bricks under the mantel. They were still warm to the touch.

"He hasn't been gone long," I said.

Glancy got down on all fours and moved the fireplace screen out of the way. There was a stack of curled ashes, the remains of individual papers. Wainwright had been in too much of a hurry to be thorough. One envelope was only partially burned. In the upper left-hand corner, still plainly visible, were the initials RDM.

"Don't touch them," I told him. "The crime lab may be able to pull something usable from this."

Sergeant James came in the front door. "Nothing?" he asked. I nodded.

Glancy rocked back on his heels. "So where the hell is he?"

"He has a private plane, isn't that true?" James asked.

"It's usually parked at Boeing Field," Glancy said.

"I'll bet it isn't tonight," James commented thoughtfully.

Both Glancy and I looked at him. "What makes you say that?" I asked.

"Think about it; if you had come back from Bellingham, knowing that your life was about to blow up in your face, would you park your plane where you usually park it?"

"By God, he's right," Glancy said. "That's why he had someone call a cab for him when he left the Public Safety Building."

"When was that? He left before we did. Maybe a little before midnight."

"Does he have one car or two?" I asked.

"One, as far as I know. A BMW. Why?"

"Because if he caught a cab home, he probably took another cab when he left here to go back to the plane."

"That doesn't do us a whole hell of a lot of good, does it?" Glancy sounded discouraged.

"Don't give up. We've got one more card."

By this time, I had memorized the Far West Cab Company number. I went to the phone and dialed. Larry was still there. "It's Beaumont again," I said. "Can we do this one last time?"

"You bet. The other guys are getting a real charge out of this. We feel like we're playing cops and robbers."

"You are," I told him. I gave him B. W. Wainwright's address.

When he came back on the line, Larry was laughing. "You're closing in on him. He's in a Yellow even as we speak."

"A Yellow Cab? Where?"

"They picked him up from the address you gave me and took him down to Boeing Field. While he was there, the driver called his dispatcher to say he was heading from Boeing to the Skyport Airfield in Issaquah, so he was quitting for the night. Skyport's evidently only a mile or two from where the cabbie lives."

"How far ahead of us are they?"

"The dispatcher says they left Boeing Field about ten minutes ago, is all."

"Larry, thanks. I owe you."

I dropped the phone and raced for the door. "Come on, you guys. There isn't a minute to lose."

"Why not? Where are they?"

"In a Yellow Cab somewhere between Boeing Field and the Issaquah Skyport."

"How'd you do that?" Glancy asked wonderingly as we climbed into the Porsche.

"It pays to know people in high places," I told him. "And taxi dispatchers are pretty close to the top of the list."

CHAPTER 25

WE CAME FLYING THROUGH THE MONTLAKE UNDER-
pass that leads from Interstate 5 to Highway 520
and the Evergreen Point Bridge. It was two o'clock
in the morning, and it should have been clear
sailing.

It wasn't.

As soon as we topped the rise, I saw the traffic
backup and hit the brakes. The problem was there
was no alternative, no other way to get across the
great water. Interstate 90 was closed for the weekend because of work being done on the Mercer
Island Bridge. Now we were stuck in a massive
backup because a couple of drunk teenagers leaving a rock concert had kamikazied into the rail-
ing on the eastern high-rise part of the Evergreen
Point Bridge.

I glanced in the rearview mirror to see Sergeant James waving at me frantically, gesturing
for me to pull over. I did, and he swung around

me. I saw him place his emergency flashers on the roof of his car as he went past. He then motioned to me to fall into line behind him.

And that's how we crossed the bridge, in a tight little line following James's lead, working our way along the emergency-vehicle shoulder, with my red Porsche sandwiched between James's unmarked but flashing sedan and the two squad cars. I'm sure the police escort accompanying my Porsche raised a few hackles in the process.

"What kind of a shot is he?" I asked Glancy as we eased our way along the shoulder.

"Crack," Glancy responded.

I winced. That wasn't the answer I wanted to hear. It's one thing to go up against creeps and bullies, cowardly scumbags who don't know their ass from a hole in the ground. This was different, and everyone in the caravan knew it. Wainwright was a trained police officer, a *cornered* trained police officer. A renegade. It wasn't a confrontation any of us was looking forward to. The best we could hope for was to surprise him, to overwhelm him with sheer numbers.

"What kind of plane?" I asked.

"A Piper Tomahawk," Glancy answered. "At least I think that's what he bought. He's only had it for six months or so. He went down to Wichita, Kansas, and picked it up from the factory."

"Any idea what he'll do?"

Glancy shook his head. "It's funny. If you had asked me that question yesterday, I would have answered it in a minute. We've worked together for three years now. I thought I knew him like a book, but it turns out I don't know him at all. I wouldn't dare hazard a guess about what he'll do."

We didn't make fast work of crossing the bridge, but it was far better than it would have been if James hadn't pulled rank and dragged us through the traffic jam. The state patrol officer directing the one open lane of traffic glared at us as we went past the wreck, but he let us through.

Once we cleared the last of the emergency vehicles, we made good time. We roared down Interstate 405 and onto I-90, where we headed east. As we passed Eastgate, Sergeant James turned off his emergency lights. The squad cars did the same.

James pulled off the freeway at the Newport Way exit. We all swung into line behind him and parked in a row in the parking lot at the trail head of a hiking trail. We were a group of grownups playing a deadly version of Follow the Leader.

The sergeant came up to the window. "If we all come off the freeway together, he's sure to catch on. I'll cross the freeway here and come up on the access road on the other side."

James motioned the uniformed officers into the conference. "You guys go beyond the Lake Sammamish exit and come down on the other side. Beau, yours looks the least like a cop car. You try driving directly onto the field. If you see him, do what you can to stop him, but don't do anything stupid."

"In other words, no stunts. No hanging on the wings, right?" I said.

"Right," James replied.

He sent the squad cars on ahead, giving them a minute or so lead time before he motioned us forward too. The idea was for us all to converge on the airport at pretty much the same time.

For years I've prided myself on being ignorant of events that happen on the east side of Lake Washington. That kind of prejudice is part and parcel of Seattle's downtown-living mystique. So I confess I was surprised that the Issaquah Skyport still existed. Nestled in prime real-estate development space along the freeway, it's been on borrowed time for years. I had assumed that the local haven for skydivers had long since succumbed to progress, but I was wrong.

Not only did the Skyport still exist, it had regressed a little. There were no landing lights on the short, seven-hundred-foot grass runway, and the scatter of buildings, open only on weekends except during skydiving season, were dark and deserted. It may have been skydiving season at the time, but it was also two o'clock in the morning, and all the skydiving enthusiasts had gone night-night.

I pulled off the access road into the Issaquah Holiday Inn parking lot, hoping that, if Wainwright saw our headlights, he would assume we were nothing but late-night arrivals stopping off at the motel.

"Can you see him?" I asked Glancy.

"I see something moving," he replied. "Hot damn! It's the cab! He's just now pulling away. I never thought we'd catch him, but we're going to make it. Try to get closer, can you?"

"Will do," I said under my breath.

I saw a break in the grass, a place where there seemed to be a vehicle track leading from the motel parking lot onto the grass field next to the runway. I took it and was rewarded with a gut-wrenching bounce where thick grass, heavy with early-morning dew, had concealed a drainage ditch.

My Porsche is a finely tuned, lean, mean machine. On pavement, wet or dry, it's impossible to stop, but an all-terrain vehicle it's not. And for negotiating that lumpy open field of dew-slick grass, it was practically worthless. It was a wonder we didn't high-center on that very first hole. We bumped along, slipping and sliding, with the rear end scraping ominously over every high spot.

The tension in the car was almost palpable. Glancy was like a bird dog on point, sitting forward in his seat, eyes straining to see through the early-morning gloom.

"Why the hell isn't this place better lit?" he demanded irritably. "And can't you go any faster?"

"No, I can't go any faster, goddamn it! Don't you think Wainwright picked it because of the lack of lights? He chose this field because he knew it would be deserted, because he knew there'd be no landing lights."

There was no question about it. If Wainwright had landed the plane after he got back from Bellingham and before he came to the theater, it must have been almost dark when he set down. It doesn't take a Philadelphia lawyer to figure out that it's a hell of a lot easier for a plane to take off in the dark than it is to land without lights.

Glancy lapsed into gloomy silence. The only sound in the car was the grinding thumps and bumps as I eased my newly clumsy Porsche over the rough uneven terrain.

Suddenly I felt Glancy's hand on my sleeve. "Look, over there." He pointed off to the side of the runway, where a shadowy line of small planes sat outlined against a slightly lighter sky. "Is that him?"

I turned the car to the left, letting the headlights illuminate the row of planes. For a fraction of a second, the glare of the headlights caught the frozen figure of a man. His face was turned to us, his eyes squinting, blinded by the sudden light.

It was Wainwright, all right. He was in the act of lifting a heavy suitcase, ready to load it into the plane's passenger seat. He paused for only an instant before he heaved the suitcase into the plane and ducked down to kick the restraining wooden chocks away from the plane's wheels.

"He's gonna make a break for it," Glancy said. "Let me out."

I stopped. Taking his gun from his pocket, Glancy flung open his door. The light came on in the car. I saw Glancy fall to the ground and roll into the tall, wet grass that lined the edge of the runway.

Feeling vulnerable and exposed, I ducked down

and leaned across the car seat to pull the door shut behind him and turn off the damnable light. That action probably saved my life. If not my life, at least my eyes.

I was facedown on the seat when the splatter of bullets sliced through the windshield and thumped into the leather seats behind me. The overhead light went out when a bullet smashed into it.

"Jesus Christ! He's got a semi-automatic!" I yelped, feeling sudden trickles of blood where flying glass had bitten into the side of my face and the tops of my hands.

B. W. Wainwright was playing for keeps, and he planned to kill anyone who got in his way.

"Are you all right?" Glancy was calling to me.

"I think so. Just cut up, that's all."

The plane's engine turned over and it lurched out of line onto the runway. Behind us there were more headlights as Sergeant James pulled onto the field. And off to the east we could hear the wail of sirens as the patrol cars, alerted by James, let out all the stops, bringing reinforcements.

I sat up. Outside the car I caught sight of Glancy slithering forward on his belly, holding his gun, taking aim. He fired off one shot and then another, but they made no difference. The Tomahawk kept moving. It was on the runway now, taxiing away from us. Glancy got to his feet and started after it on foot, but there was no way he could close the distance.

Shoving the Porsche into gear, peering blindly through the shattered windshield and broken headlights, I started after them both, the moving plane and Roger Glancy. The Tomahawk bounded over the bumpy field like a fleet-footed deer while I struggled to catch up. It was a losing proposition.

Down the runway, I saw Sergeant James's sedan make an attempt to cut Wainwright off, but that didn't work either. In seconds the plane was airborne, wobbling slightly as it cleared the end of the field.

I bounded out of my car and stood watching in helpless frustration as the plane gained altitude. Glancy came puffing up to me.

"Damn," he said over and over. "Damn, damn, damn!"

Sergeant James pulled up beside us. He was holding his radio's microphone to his mouth, issuing orders, asking for help. It was the only thing to do.

"Where do you think he's headed?" I asked.

Glancy shrugged, squinting to watch the plane's blinking lights as they disappeared. "California, maybe. That's where he's from."

James got out of his car and came over to me. "I've called for a state patrol plane," he said. "And we're trying to get a fix on him from the air-traffic controllers at the airport." He paused. "Beau, you're hurt. You're bleeding."

"It's nothing," I said. "Just some glass cuts, that's all."

He took me by the shoulders and turned me so I was facing into the headlights of one of the arriving patrol cars.

"Holy shit!" Glancy shouted, grabbing me by the arm and shaking me. "Take a look at that!"

I turned and looked in the direction he was pointing, the direction Wainwright's plane had gone. A brilliant explosion was lighting up the top of Cougar Mountain like a giant candle.

"He must have hit something!" James exclaimed. "Let's go. Leave your car here!"

I turned off the idling engine of the crippled Porsche and hustled into James's Dodge. Glancy was already crammed into the backseat. James turned a credible wheelie and bounced us across the field to the road with the two patrol cars right behind us.

All three cars went screaming down the freeway, sirens blaring and lights flashing. As we came to the Eastgate exit, we could see emergency vehicles making their way up the mountain toward the fire. By now the whole neighborhood was illuminated as if by a giant torch. I could see the outlines of houses and roofs on The Summit.

Jonathan Thomas's parents were losing their good night's sleep.

"Does anybody know how to get up there?" Sergeant James demanded.

"I know a back way," I answered. "Go straight up 150th. Left at the flashing light."

We left the cars on the street and jogged on up the hill. As soon as we topped the rise, we could see what had happened.

The Summit's developer had left only two trees

standing on the top of the mountain when he clear-cut it. B. W. Wainwright had missed the radio antennas with their flashing warning lights, but he hadn't missed the trees. They had no lights. He had smashed into one of those, setting it afire, while the plane plowed nose-down into the ground.

Firefighters were attempting to spray water on the inferno, but there seemed to be some difficulty with the fire hydrant. They could only get a tiny trickle of water.

Stunned residents, most wearing nightclothes, gathered around to watch. I caught sight of Dorothy and William Thomas standing there on the edge of the crowd, but I didn't bother to talk to them. If they wanted information, they could read it in the papers.

Sergeant James had made his way to the fire truck. Now he came back to us.

"He didn't make it out," James told us.

The announcement was hardly necessary. No one could have survived that scorching fireball.

"Good," Glancy said with satisfaction as the reflection of leaping flames glowed off his face. "He just saved the state a hell of a lot of time, trouble, and money."

CHAPTER 26

WE WENT STRAIGHT TO HARBORVIEW. I DIDN'T WANT to, but Sergeant James insisted. There, in the emergency room, they cleaned the glass out of my face and hands. It was a time-consuming process. When they finally let me loose, Amy Fitzgerald, Ron Peters's physical therapist, was waiting for me.

"What are you doing here?" I asked.

"Ron asked me to come see how you were. If you're okay, he'd like you to stop by his room for a few minutes before you go home."

"Sure," I said. As she led me to the elevator, I added, "I really appreciate your helping Peters find me last night."

Amy smiled. "I was glad to help."

When we reached the rehabilitation floor, she led the way into Peters's room. She walked straight up to the bed where Peters was lying, bent down, and kissed him. Then she reached down and placed her hand in his.

I stopped at the door, not sure what to do. "What is this, a new form of physical therapy? Or is it the new improved version of a bedside manner?"

Peters grinned at me, the kind of open-faced grin that I had given up hope of ever seeing from him again. "The best," he said. "How are you, Beau?"

"I'm fine. Just a few cuts from flying glass, that's all."

"You look like hell," Peters said.

"That makes us even," I told him. We all three laughed at that.

Just then, Sergeant James hustled into the room behind me. "Goddamn it, Beau, I turned my back on you for one minute to take a phone call, and you disappeared!"

"It's my fault," Peters said. "I wanted to see him for a minute before he left the hospital."

"Well, the party's over," James said. "We've got a mountain of paperwork to do."

"Paperwork!" I echoed. "Come on, Sarge, have a heart. Do we have to do the reports now?"

Sergeant James looked at me and grinned. "You'd better believe it. You're doing your paperwork so I can do mine. The only guy in this investigation who doesn't have to write up a report is Detective Peters. He's got an excuse. You don't. Besides, they won't release Jasmine Day until we get it done."

James left the room, and I had no choice but to trail along behind.

"Hey, Beau," Peters called after me. "Are you still going to the airport to pick up the girls?"

I stopped in the doorway. "The girls?"

"They come home today, remember? Their plane is due in about ten-thirty this morning. I told Mrs. Edwards you'd probably be there to meet them, but if you're not, they should catch a cab."

"I'll be there," I said, beating myself for forgetting their arrival and remembering guiltily that I still hadn't given Peters the postcards his daughters had sent him from California.

"Come on," Sergeant James urged. "Hurry it up." I hurried.

James led the way into the elevator. "That phone call was from the chief of police in Bellingham," the sergeant continued. "According to him, Holman spilled his guts. He's made a complete confession, including the fact that Osgood planted the cocaine in Jonathan Thomas's pillow to hide the fact that they were looking for something else."

"The tape?"

James nodded grimly.

"It worked," I said. "We're just lucky Mrs. Morris called us."

"Ain't that the truth," Sergeant James agreed.

When we got down to the Public Safety Building, Alan Dale was asleep on one of the couches in the fifth-floor lobby. I woke him up. His eyes were hollow as he rubbed the sleep out of them.

"What are you doing here?" I asked.

"You said you'd help me bail her out, remember? I called here and they told me you'd be back eventually, so I came down to wait. I've got the name and number of a bail bondsman. How much is it going to cost?"

I shook my head. "Not a dime," I told him. "It's going to take some time, but it's not going to cost you anything."

Alan Dale followed me into my cubicle while I told him what had happened since we left him at the Fifth Avenue.

"So she wasn't in on it?" he asked when I had finished.

"She never was," I replied. "The whole thing was a setup from beginning to end."

"Those sons of bitches," Alan Dale muttered. "Those no good sons of bitches!" He pounded a clenched fist into the open palm of his other hand. It was probably a good thing for Ed Waverly that he was locked up and out of harm's way about then, because I think the head carpenter would have hammered him if he'd gotten the chance.

It all made sense to me then, although I hadn't seen it before. It was written all over Alan Dale's haggard face. He was like a faithful old hound dog, hanging around outside his owner's door, waiting for a table scrap or maybe, if he got really lucky, a pat on the head. I wondered if Jasmine Day had ever noticed. If not, maybe Mary Lou Gibbons would be smart enough to figure it out.

"Come on," I said. "Let's see what we can do."

They released Jasmine Day at five o'clock in the morning. I was waiting in the lobby when they brought her out. Alan Dale held his arms open for her, and she fell into them as if she belonged there. She was crying; I'm not sure why. Dale held her so tight I was afraid she'd break, but she didn't.

"Are you still staying at the Mayflower?" I asked finally.

He shook his head. "I checked us both out. I'm unemployed, remember? I can't afford it on my own nickel."

"Come home with me, then," I said. "I've got lots of room."

Sergeant James dropped us off at Belltown Terrace.

Nobody can say I'm a sore loser. Without any discussion, I let Alan Dale and Jasmine take my room. With the guest room not yet furnished, I ended up on the couch in the living room. As I stretched out full length, I was grateful that Jim Hunt, my decorator, had insisted I buy an eight-foot sofa. By then, it was already getting light.

I slept the sleep of the dead. I woke up when somebody landed on my chest hard enough to knock the wind out of me. The alarm clock next to my head was still chirping, but I hadn't heard it.

Tiny arms wrapped themselves around my neck, and a warm face buried itself under my chin.

"Who are those two guys in your bed, Unca Beau?" Heather Peters demanded. "And how come you weren't at the airport to meet us?"

It took a minute to clear the fog out of my head and figure out who and where I was. "Those people are friends of mine," I told her. "One of those guys is a lady, Heather. She's just got a short hair-cut."

"Can I have my hair cut that way? Please, can I? Then the boys couldn't pull it anymore. I hate it when Mrs. Edwards braids my hair."

"We'll have to ask your father about that," I told her. "I don't think he'd approve."

CHAPTER 27

WHEN ED DONALDSON OF THE LOS ANGELES OFFICE OF the DEA showed up late that night, the rest of the pieces began to fall into place.

According to him, Richard Dathan Morris really had been working undercover for the DEA, but out of the Los Angeles office, not out of Seattle. Westcoast Starlight Productions had been under suspicion for some time, but Donaldson had also become aware of something amiss in the Seattle office.

Richard Dathan Morris, after he'd been turned down in Seattle, had tried the L.A. office. The opportunity had been too good to miss all the way around. Donaldson had hired Morris on the spot and put him to work undercover, but he had done it outside all usual channels so no hint of it could possibly leak back to the Seattle DEA. Morris hadn't had any trouble making contact with Osgood, who, unknown to his wife, hung out on the gay side of town when she wasn't looking.

No one in L.A. had known of Morris's death until Friday morning, and Donaldson had ordered the Westcoast arrests in L.A. without notifying Seattle until it was absolutely necessary. Unfortunately, once Morris had obtained the tape naming Wainwright, he had never gotten a chance to contact Donaldson. Unable to reach Donaldson by phone, he had at least had the presence of mind to mail the tape to his mother in Bellingham.

On Sunday, Donaldson went to Bellingham and took charge of Ray Holman. Ray, of course, blamed it all on B. W. Wainwright, who wasn't there to defend himself. And maybe that was true.

Wainwright had evidently had some hint that things were beginning to come unraveled. According to Holman, he had come up with the idea of Jasmine Day's tour with the sole purpose of framing her. Ed Waverly, in too deep to prevent it, had helped ensnare Jasmine. No one had ever intended that the show would be a hit. That had been a surprise side benefit.

Tom Riley, Jonathan's nurse, wasn't the only one who thought Richard Dathan Morris was a scuz. He had played the part well. It was only when he was caught in the costume trunk that he came to Waverly's and Wainwright's attention. They had assumed initially that he was only trying to cash in on the coke concealed in the bottom of the trunks. But then Holman discovered the tape recorder. The incriminating tape was gone, but Holman and Osgood knew what had been said, and Richard Dathan Morris was on his way out.

Since Osgood had been the one who had brought Morris into the group, Wainwright assigned him the task of getting rid of him and finding the missing tape. They had him use Jasmine's costume, hoping we'd discover it. After all, it fit right in with the rest of the scenario.

Osgood managed to murder Morris, but he bungled the job of finding the tape. When Jonathan Thomas woke up and found him in the bedroom, Osgood was forced to get rid of Jonathan too.

The problem with Osgood was that he really was only a pusher. He didn't do murder the way some people don't do windows. It must have bothered him. When we started to get too close, he tried to bail out, attempting to bargain with Wainwright for either some money or some cocaine to help him relocate and start over.

Osgood had met Ray at the Fifth Avenue between five-thirty and six. By then, Wainwright and Holman knew things were falling apart. Ray was there packing up the coke. When Osgood showed up, Ray took care of him. Holman had rented a car in downtown Seattle. He took the coke down to Boeing Field and loaded it into Wainwright's car. They had planned to leave town as soon as Wainwright got back from Bellingham with the damning evidence.

But by the time Wainwright got back to town, he knew the tape wasn't in the collection of evidence he had picked up from Mrs. Grace Simms Morris. So Wainwright made one more futile attempt at damage control.

He sent Ray to Bellingham to try one more time to get the tape while he himself put in an alibiing appearance at the Fifth Avenue Theater. And Ray muffed it. He seriously underestimated Grace Simms Morris. She chucked him over the head with that vase, and he's on his way to the electric chair. Of course, it'll be years before he exhausts all his avenues of appeal, but with any kind of luck he'll pay, eventually.

The National Air Transportation Safety Board investigated Wainwright's crashed Tomahawk. They finally determined that, in attempting to keep from hitting the radio towers, Wainwright lost control of the plane and hit the tree. They said the load in the passenger seat probably shifted. Too bad.

Donaldson, Sergeant James, Watty Watkins, and I spent all Sunday afternoon on the phone. At two-thirty on Monday, three hundred and fifty law-enforcement officers from all over the state of Washington showed up at Bellingham's First Lutheran Church for Richard Dathan Morris's funeral. It was everything Mrs. Grace Simms Morris had wanted for her son.

Six agents from the DEA, all of them—including Roger Glancy—wearing black armbands, served as pallbearers. Richard Dathan Morris wasn't what you could call a cop's cop, but we all had to salute him for what he had done. Working under almost impossible conditions, without any help or backup, he had single-handedly put B. W. Wainwright and his friends out of business. There wasn't one police officer at that funeral who wasn't grateful.

When Donaldson took the folded American flag from the coffin and handed it to Mrs. Morris, she turned to me and dissolved into tears. I held her and let her cry on my shoulder. It was the least I could do. At last Mrs. Morris looked up at me and said, "Richard would have just loved you."

Knowing what I did about Richard Dathan Morris's sexual preference, I didn't quite know how to take that remark, but I finally decided to accept it in the manner in which it was intended, as a sincere compliment.

Maxwell Cole tackled me after the funeral and demanded to know why I had lied to him about Jasmine Day. I told him I hadn't. Then he wanted to know why, if I hadn't lied, was the lady in question staying in my apartment. I told him that was none of his business.

It was several days later before I got back up to Harborview to see Peters. Mrs. Edwards and the girls had just left, and Amy Fitzgerald was sitting close to the head of Peters's bed. She wasn't wearing her uniform.

"How's it going?" I asked.

"Better," he said. "Lots better."

Feeling like I was intruding on a private conversation, I walked over to the washbasin. The mirror was plastered with Peters's entire collection of gaudy postcards. The girls had given up on me and delivered them to him in person.

"Thanks for sending the girls to California, Beau," Peters said. "I know they had a terrific time. It's hard for me to think of other people having fun when I'm lying flat on my back."

"And feeling sorry for yourself," Amy Fitzgerald added.

"That too," Peters said.

I looked first at her and then back at Peters. "She doesn't exactly pull any punches," I said.

"I noticed," Peters replied, but he didn't sound as though he minded.

Amy glanced at her watch and stood up. "I'd better get going. It'll be late by the time I get home." She leaned over and kissed Peters's cheek. "See you in the morning," she said.

Amy paused briefly in the doorway to wave and then disappeared down the hall.

"She's something else, don't you think?" Peters asked.

I nodded.

"You remember the other day, when I hung up on you?" Peters continued. "When you were telling me about that nurse, the one who worked with the AIDS patient for free?"

"I remember. What about it?"

"I was afraid that that was what was going on with her. I'd been watching Amy for weeks, but I was afraid she just felt sorry for me."

"That didn't look like a very sorry lady to me."

For a time, Peters was quiet. Finally he said,

"Captain Powell came by to see me this afternoon."

"Oh?" I deliberately kept my tone noncommittal. Before, Peters had been downright crabby about departmental visitors. "What did he have to say?"

"Did you know Arlo Hamilton is thinking about retiring?"

"No."

"Larry wanted to know if I'd be interested in working in the Media Relations Department."

I thought about the newspapers Peters devoured daily, about his photographic memory and his phenomenal ability to put names with faces. Whoever had come up with that job possibility was a real genius. I wanted to turn handstands all around the hospital bed, but I didn't. I played my cards close to my chest for a change.

"So are you interested?" I asked distantly.

"It's a job I could do in a chair if I had to," he answered. "Or on crutches."

When I left Peters's room a few minutes later, it was all I could do to keep from dancing a jig in the hall. I was surprised to find Amy Fitzgerald standing next to the elevator.

"I thought you left," I said.

"I was waiting for you. Did he tell you?"

"Did he tell me what?"

"About the public-information job."

I nodded.

"Do you think he'll take it?" she asked.

"That depends."

"On what?"

"On you."

She looked up at me, her eyes serious under long thick lashes. "No," she said firmly, shaking her head. "It depends on him. He's got to want it for himself."

The elevator came then, and I rode down to the lobby with her, worrying about what she meant by that answer. My brotherly protective instincts rose straight to the surface. I didn't want Peters hurt any more than he had already been. Maybe his first instinct was right and she was leading him on, hoping to get him back on his feet physically so she could drop him like a hot potato.

"What about you?" I asked. "Are your intentions honorable?"

She regarded me silently for a moment before she answered. "I don't know."

"Why?" I asked, blundering on with questions I had no business asking. "Because he's broken? Because he's hurt?"

She frowned. "Of course not, Detective Beaumont," she answered archly. "I've never dated someone with children before. I'm not sure I'm ready for instant motherhood."

With that she turned and walked away. I don't think I'll ever figure women out. Maybe I should just give up and stop trying.

Within days of the Westcoast closing, Jasmine Day and Alan Dale headed back to Jasper, Texas. On their way out the door, they asked if I would come to Texas and be best man at their wedding.

I told them I wouldn't miss it for the world, but they must have changed their minds. A few weeks later they sent me a note saying they had tied the knot in Vegas.

That's all right. All either one of them ever wanted was each other, and that's exactly what they got.

Turn the page to join Beaumont in his new adventure as he encounters something from his past, and this one's personal . . .

SINS OF THE FATHERS

PROLOGUE

MY NAME IS J. P. BEAUMONT. RECENTLY I'VE LEARNED that sometimes when life hands you the unexpected, you just have to run with it. For instance, I never expected to retire from police work. Far too many of my fellow cops tend to die while still in harness but not necessarily in the line of duty—unless stress-related illnesses like too much booze, early-onset heart ailments, and suicides end up in that category.

I spent most of my career working Homicide at Seattle P.D. and was happy to do so until all of a sudden I wasn't. Why? Because the brass upstairs decided to promote a brownnosing pile of crap named Paul Kramer, my least favorite partner ever, to be my boss. That was it. I was done. I pulled the plug and walked.

But what is it they say about one door closing and another opening? About the time I quit the

Seattle P.D., Ross Alan Connors, who was the Washington State Attorney General at the time, came calling and asked me to go to work for him on his Special Homicide Investigation Team, fondly referred to by those of us who worked there as "the SHIT squad." There was something wonderfully ironic about being able to tell people with a perfectly straight face that "I work for SHIT." What made it even better was that my direct supervisor on that job was a cantankerous SOB named Harry Ignatius Ball, who prefers to be addressed by his full name, as in Harry I. Ball. Try telling someone that you work for SHIT and your supervisor's name is Harry I. Ball. See how far that gets you!

But the thing is, working for Special Homicide was a good deal for me. I got to keep working. I met and married a wonderful lady named Melissa Soames (Mel, for short), and I gave my pension a healthy boot in the right direction. Then one winter's day it all came to a crashing halt—literally. Ross Connors died and Harry was gravely injured in a car wreck at the base of the Space Needle while they were on their way to a Christmas party. (Ross, as cantankerous as Harry, refused to call it a holiday party. It was a Christmas party, like it or lump it!)

As soon as Ross's successor came on board, SHIT was shuttered and we were all given our walking papers. Mel landed on her feet with a gig as the new chief of police in Bellingham, Washington, ninety miles north of Seattle. As for me?

Suddenly I found myself in the odd position of being an unhappily unemployed house husband, a position for which I am totally unsuited.

I'm a lousy cook. So is Mel for that matter. Our answer to the question of what's for dinner is generally carry-out. Mel's office is in downtown Bellingham. Our home is on Bayside in an area called Edgemoor in Bellingham's Fairhaven neighborhood. When possible, I join her for lunch downtown so we often have our main meal of the day both out and together. On this particular Tuesday early in March, lunch together was off the menu due to Mel's being the guest speaker at a local Rotary Club.

Months earlier I had been involved in solving the homicide of a longtime acquaintance, former *Seattle Post-Intelligencer* reporter Maxwell Cole. In the aftermath of that case, Mel had encouraged me to fill out the paperwork to become a licensed private investigator. That process was complete. I had my license, but I hadn't exactly been out beating the sidewalks looking for cases to work. I had done a couple of background checks and had been involved in research on a couple of cold cases for a volunteer organization called The Last Chance, but nothing about any of those had really grabbed me. For one thing, I was enjoying spending time with the new love of my life, a ninety-pound coal black Irish wolfhound named Lucy.

Lucy had come to Mel and me under what had been proposed as a fostering arrangement after a domestic violence incident. A local shelter had taken in the victims—a woman and her two kids—but that particular shelter had no room at the inn for dogs. Having never had a dog in my life, I wasn't the one who volunteered to bring the dog, Rambo as she was known at the time, to our place. Mel did that all on her own. In case I haven't mentioned it before, she's a strong-minded woman—and strong willed, too. When she showed up with a dog in tow, I did what any reasonable, right-thinking husband would do in that situation—I overcame my unspoken misgivings and opened the door.

After opening the door, I wasn't necessarily prepared to open my heart. That changed, however, when the domestic violence perpetrator came gunning for Mel, and Lucy literally took a bullet for my wife. From that moment on, I'm proud to confess aloud to one and all that "I love Lucy!"

There was, however, and continues to be a period of adjustment. For one thing, when we brought Lucy home after her emergency surgery at a veterinary hospital in Seattle, she was still one very sick puppy and required round-the-clock nursing attention provided by none other than yours truly. When it comes to dealing with the sick or injured, I've never been very good at it.

I was still in college when my mother died of breast cancer. There was none of this "early detection" stuff going on back then. By the time the tumor was discovered, it was already too late. The doctors did what they could, and so did I, but there wasn't much anyone could do but look on helplessly from the sidelines. When my first wife, Karen, died of the same ailment a number of years ago, her second husband, Dave Livingston, was the one who performed that incredibly tough, day-to-day, sickbed duty. Come to think of it, that's probably one of the things the two of us have in common—walking through that cancer partner hell. When it comes to sharing holidays and birthdays with kids and grandkids, Dave and I are on the same page. We probably won't ever be the best of pals, but we know how quickly everything can be snatched from your grasp, and we're both determined to savor every moment.

But I digress. Caring for Lucy when she first came home was my first real hands-on nursing effort. She was unable to walk on her own. In order to get her to do her business, she had to be half carried with a kind of sling. (By the way, if any of the rest of you are faced with an ill or aging dog, one of those firewood carrying slings will fill the bill nicely.) But with a ninety-pound dog, it wasn't easy for either Lucy or for me. The first time she was able to go in and out by herself was a huge relief for both of us.

The vet said that her injuries were serious enough that it might take months, if ever, for her to fully recover. We were advised that she needed to take it very easy. In other words, I was supposed to keep her from overexerting herself—no running, no jumping, no becoming overly excited. Good luck with that.

My first wife, Karen, wasn't someone who minced her words. When it came to disciplining the kids, she said I was as useless as . . . well . . . as certain items of female anatomy applied to a male boar. (I sometimes resent the way political correctness has robbed us of some of the English language's most colorful expressions. But then again, I digress. I'm seventy-three years old, so I'm entitled to digress. I'm also entitled to tell the same stories over and over if I choose to do so. If that offends you, bite me.)

The real upshot is this: if I was useless when it came to disciplining the kids, you can bet I'm not much better when it comes to disciplining dogs. Our half-acre lot is on a bluff overlooking Bellingham Bay. The house is located at the front of the lot with a long stretch of grassy lawn leading down to the property line. Out of concern for the grandkids' safety, that whole stretch of property (regularly mowed by someone who isn't me) is surrounded by a six-foot-tall wooden fence. Because of the difference in elevation, the fence doesn't interfere with our view of the bay from either the house or the deck, but it does keep unwary little kids from tumbling down the bluff. It's also tall enough to keep Lucy inside.

For a while during her recuperation, Lucy was content to walk sedately on a leash at my side, both inside the yard and out. But a month into her recovery, on the day I let her out into the yard and removed the leash, she took off like a shot—racing down that long stretch of grass and back up to me as though I had just given her the best present ever. She seemed to suffer no ill effects from her outing, but I didn't exactly come straight out and mention it to Mel. It became Lucy's and my little secret.

Mel is a cop. She's up, dressed, and out of the house early in the morning. Sometimes I'm up in time to have coffee with her, but more often than not, she's long gone before I poke my head out of the bedroom. So Lucy and I have the mornings to ourselves. I make coffee, feed the dog, and then settle in by the gas-log fireplace to work my collection of online crossword puzzles, something that is evidently not an Irish wolfhound approved activity. Each morning, at the stroke of ten o'clock, Lucy lets herself out through the doggy door. She finds her wet frisbee wherever it might have been left out in the yard, brings it inside, and drops it on my bare toe. Subtle she's not. It's time to go play.

And so we do. Her DNA hails from Ireland. That means she's totally oblivious to wind or rain. I bundle up in sweaters and jackets, sometimes topped off by a hooded slicker. All Lucy requires is for me to stand on the deck and fling the frisbee as far as I can so she can go speeding down the hill, catch it in mid-air, gallop back up the hill, and drop it at my feet. She would be happy doing this for hours on end. I have a somewhat more limited attention span, but that's what we were doing that morning when Lucy abruptly dropped the frisbee and hurried over to the side gate, standing on her hind legs at full alert, and peering over the fence at someone who had just driven down our driveway.

The house is one of those view homes where visitors have no real access to the front door without being let in through the side gate which—because of Lucy—we keep latched and locked. That means guests are let in through the back door where they can be ushered into the great room via a short hallway.

It's been my experience that most arriving guests don't want to come face to face with a soaking wet humongous dog, so even before I heard a car door open and close, I ordered Lucy into the house and put her on a "stay on your rug" command at the far end of the living room. By the time the doorbell rang, I was already on my way to answer it.

I spent years as a cop. Mel is a cop. We've both made enemies here and there along the way— the kind of enemies that aren't especially good at forgetting or forgiving. Security peepholes are fine as far as they go, I guess, but if someone shows up on your doorstep intent on plugging you full of holes, the last place you want to be is standing in front of a door with your eye plastered against a peephole. Our system is different. There's a camera mounted over the outside door with a feed to a monitor located on a wall in the kitchen. That way we know who's at the door without being anywhere near it.

I checked the monitor as I went and could see a man as he stepped up onto the porch. He wasn't anyone I recognized right off. He appeared to be in his sixties maybe, balding, and rail thin. I was pretty sure he wasn't a Jehovah's Witness because, instead of carrying a fistful of religious tracts, he was holding an infant-carrier in his right hand and had what looked like a diaper bag strapped over his left shoulder.

When the doorbell rang, Lucy made her presence known with a low-throated woof from her spot in the living room, but a quick check over my shoulder told me she hadn't strayed from her rug.

I opened the door. "Yes," I said. "May I help you?"

"Detective Beaumont?" the man asked uncertainly.

He had dark circles under his eyes, as though he was suffering from a lack of sleep.

"I used to be Detective Beaumont, but I haven't been that for a very long time," I told him. "Sorry, but are you someone I should know?"

"You probably don't remember me. My name's Alan Dale. I used to be the head carpenter with a bus and truck show, back in the day—with Jasmine Day's bus and truck show. This is my granddaughter, Athena. May we come in?"

Thirty years flashed by in an instant. Jasmine Day had been a former rock band singer who seemed destined for real stardom until her career had been derailed by drug and alcohol abuse, not unlike what happened to Janis Joplin. The difference between the two is that Janis Joplin died very young while Jasmine went through treatment and got well. Once out of rehab, she had reinvented herself as a jazz singer. She had been in Seattle playing a two-night gig at the Fifth Avenue Theater when the investigation into the death of a local stagehand had placed her directly in my path and blown her comeback tour to smithereens. For the last two songs of her final set, she had ditched the glam by peeling off her long blonde wig. Standing alone onstage, she had reverted to the old gospel songs she had sung in church as a child back home in Jasper, Texas. Gospel singing had been there at the start of her career, and that night at the Fifth Avenue she had returned to her roots in a career-ending performance that had garnered thunderous applause.

The last I had seen of Jasmine Day, she and Alan, the touring company's former head carpenter, were headed back home to Texas together. On their way out of town they had asked if I'd consent to be their best man a few months down the road at their wedding. I had agreed, of course, but my participation never came to pass. Later that year they sent me a Christmas card saying that they'd ended up doing a spur-of-the-moment wedding in Vegas. That long-ago card was pretty much the last I'd heard of either of them—until now.

"Alan Dale, well, I'll be damned!" I said, reaching out to shake his hand. "Long time no see. How the hell are you?"

"Not well," he said. "I'm afraid I need your help. I'm looking for a private eye, and somebody at Seattle P.D. told me that's what you're doing these days."

I hate it when Mel is right. That was exactly how she had goaded me into shaping up and getting my private investigator license—by saying that there would be people out there who desperately needed my help, and that I'd be better able to help them with a license than I would be without. And now here was Alan Dale, standing on my doorstep big as life and requesting my assistance.

"It is what I'm doing now," I acknowledged, "so come on in and get out of the cold. Let's talk about it. Can I get you some coffee?"

"Please."

"Cream and sugar?"

"Black," Alan replied. "Black and strong. I need all the help I can get." That's when he caught sight of Lucy, lying flat on her rug, studying him intently from across the room with her coal black eyes.

"What about the dog?" Alan asked warily, lifting the baby-carrier chest high, although if Lucy'd had a mind to go after the baby, that wouldn't have been nearly high enough to get Athena out of reach.

"Have a seat, and don't worry about the dog," I assured him, turning the bean setting on my

DeLonghi Magnifica to full strength and pushing the brew button. "Lucy may look fierce, but she loves kids. Not only that, I told her to stay on her rug, and she will."

"You're sure?"

"Count on it."

As I stood in the kitchen, watching the brewing coffee dribble out through the spouts into the cup below, I couldn't help wondering what was coming, but there was one thing that seemed pretty certain. Whatever it was wouldn't be good, but I was also pretty sure that I was going to run with it all the same, just like Lucy and her damned frisbee!

But I was also about to discover something important about Alan Dale's proposed case, and that's this: No matter how fast you run, you can't outrun your past.

CHAPTER 1

BY THE TIME I BROUGHT THE COFFEE INTO THE LIVING room, Alan had removed Athena's outer layer of pink blankets. I took a look inside the carrier as I set the cup down on a side table. At that moment, I didn't remember much about babies. I'm sure I'll know a lot more three months from now when my new grandson is expected to arrive on the scene. In the meantime, it occurred to me that the baby in my living room appeared to be a very new baby—a very young baby. So what was Alan Dale doing driving up and down I-5 with a newborn infant in tow?

"How old is she?" I asked as I sat down.

"Six weeks old," he answered, "six weeks tomorrow. She just got out of Children's Hospital yesterday."

The natural follow-up question would have been, "Where's her mommy?" but something— some newfound restraint that never used to be part of my conversational makeup—kept me from going there.

"How's Jasmine these days?" I asked instead.

He shook his head miserably, looking as distraught as anyone I've ever seen. "I lost her," he said.

The word "lost" taken in that context generally means one of two things. Either Jasmine had done Alan wrong and had taken off on him, or else she had died. The utter defeat and desolation in his demeanor hinted that it was the latter.

"What happened?" I asked.

"Hep C," he said bleakly.

And those two words said it all. Hepatitis C, an often fatal liver infection, can be contracted any number of ways, including reusing dirty needles, but it can also come about due to serious drinking. I've been sober for years now, but there was plenty of serious drinking in my past. When they started advertising that new Hep C treatment on TV a couple of years ago, I went to see my doc and got tested—"an ounce of prevention," as Mel had called it. When I came up clear, we both felt as though we had dodged a bullet. I knew that Jasmine Day had been deep into drugs back in the late seventies, a time when things like HIV and Hep C weren't even a blip on the radar for most people. I suspected that since she'd been an IV drug user back then, that Hep C had been lying in wait, ready to spring on her, years and years after she quit using.

"When?" I asked.

"Six years ago," he said.

"There are medications for that now," I offered.

He nodded. "I know. They were coming then, too, but by the time Jasmine tried to get into one of the human trials, it was already too late for her. She was sick for a long time, in and out of the hospital. No insurance, of course, so I ended up losing pretty much everything, including the house. If it hadn't been for my mother-in-law, I would have been up shit creek."

"I'm so sorry to hear this," I said. "But what's the deal here? Why do you need my help?"

"It's about my daughter," he told me, "Jasmine's and my daughter. Her name is Naomi—Naomi Louise Dale."

Knowing that Hep C can be transmitted from mother to child, I hated asking the next question, but I did it anyway. "What about Naomi?" I asked. "Does she have Hep C, too?"

Alan shrugged and slumped in his chair. "Maybe," he said darkly, then, after a pause, he added, "Make that probably. She might have inherited it from her mother, but she's also been into drugs big-time, so she could very well have contracted it on her own. At the time Jasmine was diagnosed, we tried to encourage Naomi to get tested, but by then she wasn't listening to a word we said. I doubt she took our advice."

"I take it Naomi is Athena's mother?"

Alan nodded and his reply made me wonder if that was the case, why was baby Athena driving all over hell and gone with Alan rather than being with her mother? And if Naomi had come down with Hepatitis C . . .

"If Naomi has Hep C," I asked, "what about Athena?"

"I worried about that, too," Alan admitted. "Given the family history, I asked Athena's doc at Children's to test her. He says she's clear."

"Thank God for that," I murmured. "So what's the story, then, Alan? Why exactly did you come looking for me?"

"Naomi's gone missing," he answered. "I'm hoping you can find her."

"She went missing somewhere around here?"

"Yes," he said. "She disappeared in Seattle."

"Tell me what happened."

"When Naomi was admitted to Harborview Hospital to have the baby, she listed her grandmother, Helen Gibbons, as her next of kin."

"Helen is Jasmine's mother?"

Alan nodded. "After Naomi disappeared, the hospital called Helen, and she called me."

"You're saying she disappeared from the hospital?"

"Yes, she got dressed and walked out before anyone realized she was gone."

"And left Athena behind?"

"Abandoned her at the hospital," Alan corrected. "At the time Naomi took off, Athena was locked up in Harborview Hospital's neonatal unit because she was both premature and underweight. She was also addicted to methadone. The hospital called Helen, and she called me. I quit my job—I was working a bus and truck show in Cincinnati at the time—and caught the next plane out. By the time I got here, Harborview had already transferred Athena over to Children's. I've been with her ever since."

"On your own?"

"Yes, on my own," he said with a hopeless shrug. "Who else is there? Helen has health issues that make it no longer feasible for her to fly. I've had a room at the Silver Cloud in Seattle's university district for over a month now, but I haven't spent much time there. It's expensive as all hell, and I wouldn't be able to cover it if Helen wasn't willing to help. But it's close to the hospital. While Athena was an inpatient, I generally stopped by the hotel just long enough to grab a shower and eat some breakfast. Most nights I spent in the nursery at the hospital—holding her, rocking her. She was hooked on methadone at birth and had to go through withdrawal." He shuddered, remembering. "It was horrible," he managed at last, choking on the words as he spoke. "How a mother could do that to her own baby—feed her that kind of poison—is more than I can understand!"

He broke off then. I sat there in the silence trying to figure out where I fit into this unfolding family drama. Was Alan searching for his missing daughter in hopes of affecting some kind of reconciliation with her, or was he concerned that Naomi had landed in some kind of hot water, and he was here hoping to bail her out of it?

"Methadone is what they use to help get addicts off drugs," I said at last. "Maybe Naomi was trying to get clean."

"I doubt it," he said. "The thing is, now that Athena has been released from the hospital, I'll have to locate someplace less expensive for us to stay until we get things sorted out."

"What kind of things?" I asked.

"If I hadn't shown up, Athena would have gone straight from the hospital into foster care," Alan explained. "I'm petitioning to be appointed her legal guardian, but that takes time. I can't even leave town with her until all of the guardianship issues are settled, and that's why I have to find Naomi now. I need her to sign off on her parental rights so I can take Athena home to Jasper with me."

Legal guardianship? Whoa! Here was a widowed guy in his sixties signing up to take full responsibility for a newborn? That takes guts—lots of them. My respect for Mr. Alan Dale shot up about ten thousandfold.

The baby stirred in her carrier and made a tiny bleat. Alan immediately dug in the diaper bag and produced one of those foil covered containers that are advertised for keeping hot things hot and cold things cold. After removing a baby bottle, Alan leaned over and plucked Athena out of the carrier. That's when I noticed that while we were talking, Lucy had silently oozed her way across the hardwood floor until she was resting less than two feet away from the baby-carrier.

She had somehow managed to drag the rug along with her and was still touching it. In other words, she hadn't officially broken my stay-on-the-rug command, but she was pushing the boundaries.

"Lucy," I said reprovingly, "what do you think you're doing?"

Without raising her head, she thumped her long tail at me in acknowledgment, but her black eyes remained focused totally on the baby.

Alan settled Athena in the crook of his arm and offered her the bottle. As she began to pull on the nipple, Alan sent a wary look in Lucy's direction.

"What the hell kind of plug ugly looking dog is that anyway?" he asked.

Since it seemed like a change of subject was in order, I told him the Rambo/Lucy story, about how the dog had been brought into the picture and trained precisely to help protect a woman and her two small children from a guy who loved to rule the roost with his fists. On the day when push really did come to shove, for his own protection, he'd made sure that the dog was locked in the bathroom before he'd launched an attack on his wife.

"My understanding is that Lucy almost tore the bathroom to pieces trying to get out and take him on."

"But she didn't hurt the kids?"

"Nope."

"So if she started out being named Rambo," Alan asked, "how did she turn into Lucy?"

"The asshole wife-beater was the one who named her Rambo. Later, when I met her trainer, I discovered that the dog's original name was Lucy, and that's what Mel and I call her—Lucy. The DV incident happened here in Bellingham, where my wife, Mel, happens to be chief of police. After the attack, she was able to place the woman and her kids in a shelter situation, but they couldn't take the dog along with them. That's how she ended up here with us. Originally we were supposed to foster the dog until her family got into some kind of permanent housing. About that time, though, the bad guy was cut loose from the slammer and came gunning for Mel. When he showed up, Lucy got in the middle of it and ended up being shot, thus saving Mel's life. It cost a bundle in vet bills to patch her up, but it was worth every penny. And when her family ultimately decided against taking her back, there was no way I was willing to part with her."

Athena had evidently drunk her fill. After putting the bottle away, Alan threw a cloth pad of some kind over his shoulder. He placed the baby on that and then patted her on the back until she burped.

"She's probably ready for a diaper change," he said. "Where should I do that?"

I directed him to the guest bedroom. While he took care of business, I made both of us another cup of coffee. I was back in my chair in the living room by the time they returned.

"I left the diaper in the trash in the bathroom," he said. "I hope that's okay."

"Don't worry," I said. "I'll take care of it." Cleaning up after Lucy has made me a whole lot tougher in those regards than I ever used to be.

After being fed and changed, Athena seemed perfectly content to go back into her carrier. While Alan was carefully tending to that, I studied his appearance. I couldn't imagine being his age and staying up night after night with the daunting task of tending to a newborn baby 24/7, especially a drug-addicted newborn baby. No wonder the poor guy had dark circles under his eyes. He was probably completely exhausted.

Alan didn't notice the new cup of coffee until after he had resettled himself in the chair. "Thanks for the refill," he said. "I appreciate it."

I glanced at my watch and realized it was already half-past noon and well into lunchtime. "What about some food?" I offered. "Have you had anything to eat?"

"Breakfast back at the hotel is all," he answered.

In my experience, those "breakfast included" breakfasts don't amount to much.

"I'm not exactly a gourmet cook," I told him, "but I'm capable of making a killer ham sandwich when called upon to do so. How about one of those?"

"Sure," Alan agreed. "That would be great."

I left him there and went to the kitchen. When I returned a few minutes later carrying two ham sandwiches on separate plates, I found him sound asleep in the chair. I didn't wake him. Lucy, having abandoned all pretense of staying on the rug, had curled into a surprisingly small tight ball and positioned herself between Alan's feet and the baby-carrier. I let her be, too. She had yet to decide if Alan posed a threat to the little one, and she obviously wanted to place herself between the baby and him. Given her unfortunate history, I didn't blame her a bit.

Without disturbing any of the three, I placed Alan's sandwich on the table next to his cup before retreating to my own chair and my own thoughts which, given the circumstances, turned out to be more than slightly problematic. Naturally, my mind wandered back to Jasmine Day's stirring but final performance at the Fifth Avenue Theater. I couldn't come up with an exact date for it, but I estimated it must have been somewhere in the late eighties—1988 or so. And there's a good reason my thought process about those times and places is somewhat fuzzy.

Let's just say that the eighties weren't especially good for me. For one thing, I was still drinking at the time—drinking a lot. When Karen divorced me, I did what every drunk in the world always does—I blamed her for everything. The fact that our marriage had ended was all her fault. It had nothing whatsoever to do with me or with any of my actions. And trust me, my actions back then were pretty far out there.

People don't just happen to drop in on their local neighborhood AA meeting for no reason at all, without having done some pretty scuzzy things that finally bring them to the conclusion that they're in deep trouble. At the time I was an unmarried, over-sexed, and underfed heterosexual male, and I was out on the prowl and looking for action way more often than was good for me or anybody else. Thank God it was decades before the #metoo movement arrived on the scene, or I would have been run out of town on a rail.

By the eighties, the sexual revolution was a couple of decades old. The pill was readily available, and hookups and one-night stands were pretty much the order of the day. Unfortunately, one of my one-night stands happened to have been with Jasmine Day. It had been a put-up deal. I had been called to the theater to investigate that murdered stagehand. Eventually it turned out that the traveling show company had been using the tour as a cover for transporting illicit drugs back and forth across the country. When I turned up at the theater asking awkward questions, the stage manager had been anxious to keep a lid on the investigation, at least until after Jasmine's two-night gig was over. With that in mind, he had comped me a front-row ticket. What I didn't realize at the time but what Jasmine understood full well was that whoever ended up in that comped seat also got to have Jasmine Day for dessert. It was a standard arrangement, one of those cases of pay to play. Jasmine had wanted a comeback tour and playing escort to the producer's honored guests was the price of admission.

After a dinner with way too much booze under our belts and not nearly enough food, Jasmine's and my trip to the bedroom and everything that had happened there had been consensual on both sides. I seem to remember that she had ended up driving us back to my place, something I seldom let happen. But our "affair," if you will, was what it was—a one-night stand with no strings attached. The next night, when the whole drug transportation conspiracy had blown up into two more homicides, Jasmine had immediately sought solace in Alan's waiting arms.

As soon as I saw the two of them together, I knew their relationship was the real deal, and I backed off completely. I don't know if Alan had any knowledge about the reality of Jasmine's comped seat arrangement. He may have known or then again, he may not. He sure as hell didn't know that the bus and truck company was really nothing more than camouflage for a drug smuggling outfit, and neither did Jasmine. The investigation into that concluded weeks later without either one of them ever being charged with a crime.

And now, here Alan was, all these years later, asking for my help. Obviously Jasmine had never told him about what had happened between the two of us. If she had, it seemed unlikely that he would have come to me looking for help concerning his errant daughter. And if Jasmine had never let on about what had happened between her and me, I sure as hell wasn't going to be the one to tell him.

Alan let out a soft snore that startled him awake. "Sorry," he said, sitting up straight. "I didn't mean to drop off like that."

"Not to worry," I told him. "I suspect you needed that nap way more than you need either food or coffee."

"Probably," he agreed, picking up his sandwich. "So where were we?"

"I believe you were about to tell me about Naomi," I said. "How about if we start there?"